THE BRIDES OF ROLLROCK ISLAND

Also by MARGO LANAGAN

Tender Morsels

Red Spikes

Black Juice

White Time

MARGO LANAGAN

THE BRIDES *of* ROLLROCK ISLAND

Alfred A. Knopf New York

THIS IS A BORZOI BOOK PUBLISHED BY ALFRED A. KNOPF

Visit us on the Web! randomhouse.com/teens

Educators and librarians, for a variety of teaching tools, visit us at
RHTeachersLibrarians.com

Library of Congress Cataloging-in-Publication Data
Lanagan, Margo.
The brides of Rollrock Island / Margo Lanagan.
p. cm.
Summary: On remote Rollrock Island, men go to sea to make their livings—and to catch their wives. The witch Misskaella knows the way of drawing a girl from the heart of a seal, of luring the beauty out of the beast. And for a price a man may buy himself a lovely sea-wife. He may have and hold and keep her. And he will tell himself that he is her master. But from his first look into those wide, questioning, liquid eyes, he will be just as transformed as she. He will be equally ensnared. And the witch will have her true payment.
ISBN 978-0-375-86919-8 (trade) — ISBN 978-0-375-96919-5 (lib. bdg.) —
ISBN 978-0-375-98930-8 (ebook)
[1. Witches—Fiction. 2. Selkies—Fiction. 3. Magic—Fiction. 4. Islands—Fiction.] I. Title.
PZ7.L21Br 2012
[Fic]—dc23
2011047466

The text of this book is set in 11-point Goudy.

Printed in the United States of America
September 2012
10 9 8 7 6 5 4 3
First American Edition

THE BRIDES OF ROLLROCK ISLAND

CONTENTS

Daniel Mallett

"The old witch is there," said Raditch, peering over the top to Six-Mile Beach. "Well settled with her knitting."

"It's all right. We're plenty," said Grinny.

"We're plenty and we have business," James said with some bluster—he was as scared of her as anyone. He shook his empty sack. "We have been sent by our mams. We're to provide for our families."

"Yes, we've come all this way," said Oswald Cawdron.

"We have."

And down the cliff we went. It was a poisonous day. Every now and again the wind would take a rest from pressing us to the wall, and try to pull us off it instead. We would grab together and sit then, making a bigger person's weight that it could not remove. The sea was gray with white dabs of temper all over it; the sky hung full of ragged strips of cloud.

We spilled out onto the sand. You can fetch sea-hearts two

ways. You can go up the tide wrack; you will find more there, but they will be harder, drier for lying there, and many of them dead. You can still eat them, but they will take more cooking and, unless your mam boils them through the night, more chewing. They are altogether more difficult.

Those of us whose mams had sighed or dads had smacked their heads for bringing that sort went down toward the water. Grinny ran ahead and picked up the first heart, but nobody raced him; hearts lay all along the sea-shined sand there, plenty for all our families. They do not keep, once collected. They can lie drying in the tide wrack for days and still be tolerable eating, but put them in a house and they'll do any number of awful things: collapse in a smell, sprout white fur, explode themselves across your pantry shelf. So there is no point grabbing up more than your mam can use.

Along we went, in a bunch because of the witch. She sat some way along the distance we needed to go, and exactly halfway between tide line and water, as if she meant to catch the lot of us. She had a grand pile of weed that she was knitting up beside her, and another pile of blanket she had already made, and the end of her bone knitting hook jittered and danced at her shoulder as she made more, and the rest of her looked as immovable as rocks, except her swiveling head, which watched us, watched the sea, swung to face us again.

"Oh," breathed James. "Maybe we can come back later."

"Come now, look at this catch," I said. "We will gather them all up and run home and it will be done. Think how pleased your mam will be! Look at this!" I lifted one; it was a doubler, one seaheart clammed upon another like hedgehogs in the spring.

"She spelled Duster Kimes potty," he whimpered.

"Kimeses are all potty," I said. How like my dad I sounded, so sensible, knowing everything. "Duster is just more frightenable than the rest. Come, look." And I thrust a good big heart into his hands, sharp with barnacles to wake him up.

The ones that still float are the best, the most tender, though the ones that have landed, leaning in the wet with sea-spit bubbled around them, are fine, and even those that have sat only a little, up there along the drying foam, are still good. The other boys were dancing along the wrack up there, gathering too much, especially Kit Cawdron. He was only little and he had no sense; why didn't Raditch stop him? We would have to tip most of that sack out, or half the town would stink up with the waste.

"They'll not need to go as far as us," said Grinny at my elbow.

I dropped a nice heavy-wet heart in my sack. "We could get them back down here, to walk along with us, maybe."

No sooner had I said it than Grinny was off up the beach fetching them. He must have been scareder than he looked.

I busied myself catching floating hearts without sogging my pants hems. Some folk ate the best hearts raw, particularly mams; they drank up the liquor inside, and if there was more than one mam there they would exclaim how delicious it was, and if not they would go quiet and stare away from everyone. If it was only dads there, they would say to each other, "I cannot see the attraction myself," and smack their lips and toss the heart skin in the pot for boiling with the rest. If you boiled the heart up whole, that clear liquor went to an orange curd; we were all brought up on that, spooned and spooned into us, and some lads never lost the taste. I quite liked it myself, but only when I was ailing. It was bab food, and a growing lad needed bread and meat, mostly.

Anyway, the wrack hunters came down and made a big crowd with us. Harper picked up a wet heart and weighed and turned it, and emptied his sack of dry ones to start again. Kit Cawdron watched him, in great doubt now.

"Why don't you take a few of these, Kit," I said, "instead of those jawbreakers? Your mam will think you a champion."

He stared at the heart glistening by his foot, and then came alive and upended his sack. Oh, he had some rubbish in there; they bounced down the shore dry as pompons.

His brother Oswald was dancing in and out of the water-edge, not caring what Kit gathered. I picked up a few good hearts, if small. "See how the shells are closed on it? And the thready weed still has some juice in it, see? Those are the signs, if you want to make mams happy."

"Do they want small or big?" Kit said, taking one.

"Depends on her taste. Does she want small and quicker to cook, or fat and full of juice? My mam likes both, so I take a variety."

And now we were quite close to the witch, in the back of the bunch, which was closer, quieter, and not half so lively as before, oh no. And she was fixed on us, the face of our night horrors, white and creased and greedy.

"Move along past," I muttered. "Plenty on further."

"Oh, *plenty*!" said Misskaella, making me jump and stiffen. "But no one wants to pause by old Misska and be knitted up, eh? No one wants to become piglets in a blanket!" Her eyes bulged in their cavities like glistening rock-pool creatures; I'd have wet myself, if I'd had anything in me to wet with.

"We're only collecting sea-hearts, Misskaella," said Grinny politely, and I was grateful to him for dragging her sights off me.

"Only!" she said, and her voice would tear tin plate. "*Only* collecting!"

"That's right, for our mams' dinners."

She snorted, and matter flew out one of her nostrils and into the blanket. She knitted on savagely. The bone's rustling in the weed sent my boy-sacks up inside me like startled mice to their hole. "That's right. Keep 'em sweet, keep 'em sweet, those pretty mams."

There was a pause, she sounded so nasty, but Grinny took his life in his hands and went on. "That's what we aim to do, ma'am."

"Don't 'ma'am' me, sprogget!"

We all jumped.

"Move along, all of you, and stop your gawking," spat the witch. "What's to see? You think I'm ugly? Well, so are your dads, and some of you yourselves. Look at you, boy-of-Baker, with your face like a balled fist. So I'm out alone? What of it? You think all women are maundering mere-maids like your mams, going about in a clump? Staring there like folk at a hanging—get out of my sight, before I emblanket you and tangle you up to drown!"

Well, we didn't need her to say it twice.

"You can never tell which way she'll go," murmured Grinny as we scuttled on.

"You did grand, Grin," said Raditch. "I don't know how you found a voice." And Kit, I saw, was making sure to keep big Batton Baker between himself and the old crow.

"Sometimes she's all sly and coaxy? And sometimes she loses her temper like now."

"Sometimes all she does is sit and cry and not say a word or be frightening at all," said Raditch. "Granted, that's when she's had a pot or two."

We collected most efficiently after that, and when we were done we described a wide circle around behind Misskaella on our way back to the foot of the path. "From behind she's not nearly so bad," I said, for she was only a dark lump down there like a third mound of weed, her hook end bobbing beyond her shoulder.

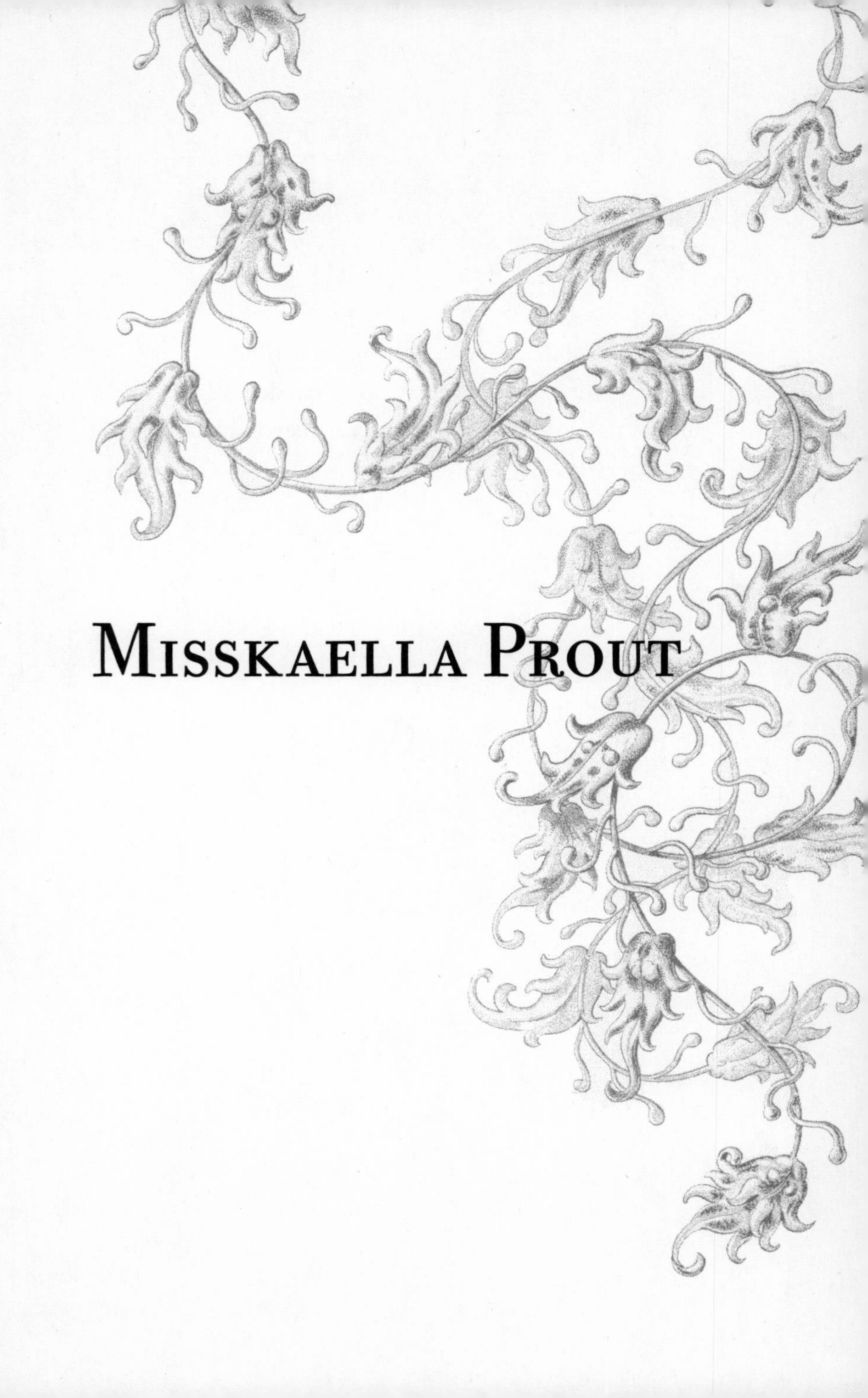

Misskaella Prout

Yes, Misskaella, seals. *See? She loves them!*

The seals gleamed in the sunshine. I tried to crawl to them, but Bee held firm to my ankle, and I could not go. Pink flowers on long stems nodded about my ears. I did not even have enough of a mind to know that the cliff dropped away there; I thought that the seals lay on the ground right in front of me, that they were seething worms or caterpillars, sleek and soft-looking. I thought I could catch up a handful of them, and understand them as I understood everything, by putting them in my mouth.

Ann Jelly carried me down the cliff path, back and forth in a tipped-steep world. As we went, I saw the seals more truly. They were grown-up-people-sized; they were bigger even than that. Still I reached for them. I leaned out from Ann Jelly's shoulder, and when she turned I leaned across her face.

Look, she's not at all afraid, she said.

They would roll on you and crush you, Missk, *for all their big friendly eyes*.

How they smell!

Oh, the king of them down there, fighting off those ones, isn't he the ugliest thing you ever laid eyes on?

I did not even see the king, for all the mothers so close to me, for all the seal babies that roamed and moaned over them. I did not find their smell foul; it was all one with their fascination. The mothers looked warm; I wanted to crawl over their hills, so much softer than those rocks and sharp periwinkles I had explored before, so much freer than being clasped tightly to Ann Jelly's side and not carried where I wanted. Why did we hang back so? Why did she not put me down, so that I could crawl to them and climb among them? Why did Bee turn us back, when we had only strolled once and distantly along the edge of the herd? Why must we climb away to the seal-less parts of the world? We might touch them! They might like to be patted, as dogs and cats did. Their babies might approach and speak to us! I pushed myself high against Ann Jelly's shoulder and watched the seals sink away. I would have cried at the loss of them, if I'd not been so busy being surprised by them, a flap of life here, a surge there, a head lifting to regard us.

We went home, and tea and bread happened as always, its clatter and talk held in by the kitchen walls, so different from the flying world outside, the wind and sun. I was tucked in between Tatty and Grassy Ella, behind my towering teacup.

And you should have seen Missk with the seals, Mam, down at Crescent! Lorel said across the table. I raised my face hopefully from my bread. Sometimes when they talked of me, Mam lost her sharp look. She even smiled on me now and then.

I should? Mam poured and put down the pot. She looked at me, and Lorel's words went in and pinched her face tighter. I watched her around my cup with one eye and then with the other.

She couldn't keep her eyes off them! said Bee, out of sight of me. *She wanted to crawl in among them. Of course we did not let her.* She sounded nervous now. She must have caught sight of Mam.

It's true, she was very interested, Ann Jelly apologized. *I have never seen her so fixed on anything—*

Strange, Mam said. *Was anyone else about, at Crescent Corner?*

There was a pause full of worry at Mam's loud voice, then, *'Twas just us six,* Bee's voice came timidly.

Just us six, and a thousand seals, said Grassy, poking over her bread all unawares.

Good, said Mam. *Watch her near those things.* She watched me hard herself. *And don't tell anyone else of this, that she loves them. No one needs to know that. Do you understand?*

We were all quiet. Grassy looked down at me. My face tried a squashed-feeling smile at her, but she did not smile back.

Yes, Mam, said Bee.

Nanny Prout's house smelt of the ages, and was gloomy from all those years holding only Nanny. She had never wanted company, said Dad, but had shut herself away from everyone, even us her family. She would still have been shut away if she'd had her choice, but because she was so ill Aunt Baxter and Aunt Roe could busy their ways in and interfere. It was they who had told us to come; this was the last time Nanny would be fit to see us, they'd said.

Aunt Roe had put us in the chilly parlor. The dead fireplace was hidden behind a screen; a dark dresser loomed against the wall. Mam and Dad sat on the edge of the strange sideways couch. The pin in Mam's shawl sucked all the light from the room, so that the rest of us must sit in dusk. Her hair, freshly tidied, left her face out in the cold, unsoftened. I wore a dress newly handed down from Tatty, and I felt blowsy and floaty in it, not held together properly; cold air crept in under the skirt. I clambered up between Mam and Dad, and drew some warmth off them.

Nobody spoke; that was alarming. No girl whispered, so Billy had nothing to snipe at. We all listened to the sickroom, the clinks and footfalls there, the murmuring aunts, the silence from the bed. We hardly knew Nanny Prout, any of us children. Ann Jelly remembered her outside Fisher's, windblown, shouting (*She didn't even seem to know I was a relative!*). Billy and Bee and Lorel had seen her in an armchair—perhaps *that* armchair, with the brown flowers on. I had no idea who she was, what she looked like, whether I should like her or be afraid. But her dying must be tremendously important; look at us waiting about so warily. The whole house, with the whole day and town beyond it, leaned in over her bed, preparing itself. What would it be like? Was a near-dead nanny awful to look upon? I feared so, from Mam and Dad's silence and stillness either side of me.

With a rustle of her brown dress, into the doorway stepped Aunt Roe, her face white and pointed. She waved us out of the parlor as if she were vexed with us. "She's very tired," she said, her own voice weary as if to demonstrate. "You mustn't stay long."

She led us into the sickroom, and stood aside from the door. "It's Froman, Mam," she said accusingly, "and Gussy and all their children." She turned and flapped her hand at us again, as if we must step forward for a beating.

Mam pushed us children into the room. Ann Jelly led the line of us alongside the bed—which held a tiny person, not much more than a doll. Tatty nudged me forward; the others passed me along; Ann Jelly held me by the shoulders. Nanny Prout's hand on the coverlet, pale yellow, held not the slightest tremble of life.

"Froman," said Nanny. Oh, the relief that she could utter a word! Her face frightened me, so collapsed and fissured that I worried it would crumple quite away. The bonnet frill around it tried vainly to distract from the fearsomeness.

"Mam." Dad gave a little bow. Anywhere else, the bigger girls would have laughed at him, but here in the room with Nanny and her approaching death, none of them even snickered.

"And Augusta?" Nanny managed. It did seem cruel of Mam, to have so many syllables in her name that the old lady must labor through.

"Nanny," said Mam, as if that name, though not as hard to utter, were just as distasteful.

"And all the little ones." Nanny looked along the taller row of us. "Don't tell me their names again. There are too many, and what is the point now of my remembering them?"

"Mam, what a thing to say!" Aunt Baxter fluted. She laughed, and twitched the quilt at Nanny's far elbow.

Nanny's colorless eyes worked their way back along the lower three of us. Her gaze met mine and stopped. She had been pretending interest, but she ceased it now. Her lips poked out, pulling her wrinkles after them like the mouth of a drawstring purse.

"This one here, though, at the end, the littlest." Her voice was dry and partial. "I don't like the look of her. She's a bit slanted, a bit mixed."

"That's our Misskaella," said Dad in his comfortable voice. "There's nothing wrong with Missk." But Mam pulled away and frowned at me, as if she had never noticed me before.

"She harks back, I tell you," said Nanny. "It is in her mouth and nose, and just in the general set of her. There's no denying it. She'll be hard to marry—that's if any men are left on Rollrock, after this rash of daughters has gone through. Look at them all! Only the one boy—and him bad-tempered, by the look."

"That's Billy," said Dad a bit more testily. "William, after your grandfather. He's a little afraid of you, Nanny, is all that face says."

"Hmph."

She *was* frightening, that Nanny-doll. I had thought a dying person might be weak and gentle, and distressed to be departing. But she was all opinions, and no manners to keep them inside her. She could say what she liked; being so old and dying gave her the right. I realized that my mouth was hanging open as I waited on her next judgment, and I snapped it shut—and thus drew Nanny's gaze back to myself.

"Yes," she said with dislike, "you can see it clearly, looking from the others to this one. She is much later than the rest?"

"There are four years," said Mam, "between her and Tatty, the next youngest."

"There is your problem, then," said Nanny. "Prout men should never breed late. Nor Prout women. They turn, you know, in their autumns, and then you get miscast faces like this, and who knows what behind them?"

"Oh, Mam." Aunt Baxter laughed even higher than before. "Here is Froman, come to see you before you go to your rest, and all you can do is fix on his children and criticize!" But her face was all dismay, looking at me. My hand came up to touch my nose and mouth, but they were only the same nose and mouth I had always had; there was nothing new or monstrous about them.

Only Dad was allowed to kiss Nanny goodbye—not that any of us minded one ounce not putting our lips to that crinkled cheek. It would be cold, I thought. It would smell of tallow wax, maybe, or mushrooms.

Then we were dismissed. Dad was quiet walking along the lanes, but the rest of us were glad to be out in the moving air. Billy lifted his head and looked about, for a change, and the girls danced from step to step.

Tatty eyed me where I walked at Mam's hand. "She had a set against our Missk, didn't she!"

"Hush, Tat," said Mam, and Dad clicked his tongue. But already Grassy and Lorel were caroling, "Ye-es! Missk and her funny looks!"

"'Miscast,' she said." Ann Jelly too examined me. "What could she mean?"

"I've always thought Miss *did* look differently." Tatty galloped sideways ahead of us. "Not quite part of the same family." And now they all stared. I screwed up and stretched my face so that they should not see my difference clearly.

"That's *enough*," said Mam. "Take the word of a dying woman, would you, one who's always hated me and mine? Of course she's going to find fault with us! And who safer to insult than the very littlest of all!"

"Gussy," said Dad.

"Tell me it isn't true, then," said Mam. "She won't miss us and I won't grieve after her."

He shrugged and looked away, and the matter seemed done with. But Mam did not look down at me, and her grip was tight and wrenching of my shoulder, as if I ought to be punished rather than consoled.

"You see?" said Bee.

"I don't," said Tatty. "Which stone is it, even?"

Neither could I see. I stood away from the garth wall. The stones, in the lumpiest part above the gate, looked even more higgledy-piggledy in this slant of light.

"The seal head is fallen away *that* side of the maiden." Lorel waved to the left and then to the right. "See the skin of it, along and across, those three lines coming to the point, then to the little tail?"

"The tail is almost worn right away," said Bee.

"Oh, *that* is the tail, is it?" said Tatty doubtfully.

"And so the maiden is *rising out* of the skin, you see? And her beautiful hair? That is all those whirls—though Nanny Paul used to say *her* nanny told her that all their hairs were flat as boards, not a kink or curl among them."

"She has a big head," I said. "And hardly any body at all."

"See, Tat? Even *Missk* can see her," said Grassy.

"A head and a bosom." Billy chewed a grass stalk, slumped against the opposite wall. Lorel laughed dirtily. The circles of the stone bosoms popped out at me, the peck marks of the nipples. My face went hot. Imagine carving such a thing, for all to see!

"She doesn't look a very happy maiden," said Tatty, "to be come to live among us."

"Oh, they were right miseries, everyone says," said Grassy.

"Everyone?" said Bee. "Who have you heard say? I cannot get anyone to talk for long about it. Mam closes up like a trap, and Dad will find something he must be busy with. And Nanny Paul, sometimes she would rattle on as long as you liked, but most often she would only put up her eyebrows, insulted."

"Maybe it's *boring* for them," groaned Billy. "Seeing as it never happens anymore."

"There's nothing keeping you here, Billy," said Bee crisply. "Go and kick footer if you're so bored of us."

"Plenty say it never happened at all, girls coming out of seals," said Lorel.

"Well, how could it?" said Tatty. "It would be like a cat birthing a dog, or a horse throwing a goat."

"There's no birthing of it at all," said Ann Jelly. "It is the same creature. Only its skin comes off and the girl is within."

"Oh, pfft," said Tatty. "Whoever heard of such a thing?"

"I've heard of it," said Grassy. "What's wrong with *your* ears?"

"And you *hide* that skin," said Bee darkly. "For if she finds it, she snatches it up and is gone, no matter how nicely you've treated her, no matter how many children she's had on the land."

"She will abandon her *children*?" said Ann Jelly, and I was shocked too. I knew Mam didn't like us, but I couldn't imagine her leaving us. We eyed the bosomy woman high on the wall. She stared out unashamed.

"As if they never were," said Bee. "And never come back to visit them either."

"What dreadful creatures," said Lorel. "What would a man ever want with one of those?"

Ann Jelly and I sat with Gert along Strangleholds' step, in the sunshine.

"Slide aside," said Gert's mam. "I must go down to May's and get those eggs. Stay about till I'm back, Gert. I'll not be blamed for letting Prouts' little one wander off."

We let her through and watched her hurry along the lane. She paused to greet Ardle Staines's mam, then continued on around the corner.

"I'll show you something." Gert scrambled up.

Ann Jelly made eyebrows at me and jumped up too.

After the sunshine, all I could see in the house was the window through the back. Gert's parents' bedroom was quite black, the two girls hissing and giggling in there. I stepped in and waited, and their shapes emerged, shadows bent over a chest with its lid open against the wall.

"Don't move anything," said Gert. "It's right at the back here. Hold the clothes and blankets away so it doesn't catch on them."

The back of the chest seemed to come away in her hands. She pulled it up. Then she tipped it, and I saw the wire by which it had once hung on a wall, and the glass front reflecting the curtain edge with its bit of trapped light.

They bent over the picture.

"It's a person," said Ann Jelly.

"A lady," said Gert.

"I can't see anything," I said.

Gert pulled the curtains a little apart. I edged in next to Ann Jelly. The lady's eyes were large in her face, and dark. She looked as if she had suffered a great shock and was staring from it, not seeing us, waiting for an explanation.

"Who is she?" said Ann Jelly.

"She's an ancestor."

"But she looks like no one! None of you have those eyes, or that hair either."

"It fades out quick, says Mam, that look. The red takes back over—thank heaven, she says."

I had seen that mouth before. I had fingered it in front of the mirror; I had pressed the lips tightly closed as I was doing now, so they would not show so much. But if I had had *that* face around my lips, they would have been beautiful; they would have fitted with the other features, and been nothing to be ashamed of at all.

"Why don't you have her on the wall?" I reached out and rattled the wire. "She is all ready for hanging."

"She's a secret, Mam says. She is our greatest shame. She must stay hidden away."

"What's her name?" said Ann Jelly.

"No one remembers, she's so long ago in our family. Isn't she beautiful?"

"She looks like a Spanish queen," said Ann Jelly thoughtfully. "Out of Mister Wexford's storybook, up at school."

"Yes!" Gert sounded pleased. "Perhaps she was royal there, under the sea."

They pulled the curtains wider, examined the woman more closely. "Her delicate hands," said Ann Jelly.

"See, they have made her smile here, just a little?" Gert waved a finger over the lips in the painting, and I bit my own away again. "But her eyes are still sad." She covered the curvy mouth; the eyes gazed out mournfully over the edge of her hand.

"We must put her away. Mam mustn't know I showed you. And you mustn't tell— Misskaella won't tell, will she?"

"Not if I tell her not to." Ann Jelly widened her eyes at me.

"I won't say a word." But she didn't need to caution me. I had not the words or the worldliness to describe the Spanish-queen lady, and how new she was to me, yet how familiar.

They slid the picture back down behind the blankets, and closed the lid; I pretended to help, although I was really too small to be of much use. I only wanted the chance to touch the wood, so old, so ornamented—the perfect container for a secret. My plump little hand looked so impertinent among the carved flowers! I snatched it away.

We went out and sat as we'd sat before, along the step. We hardly spoke until Gert's mam came back, and called us monkeys in a row, and freed us to run off and play. Gladly we sprang away from our naughtiness and solemnity, and from the stare of the lady in the picture.

Some months after my ninth birthday, I woke one day to find everything stretched and reaching, as if the world were a pot on the boil and someone had taken its lid off and let the steam pour up wildly. I must be ill, I thought, but I felt no pain, no turmoil of my stomach, and I could get up and move about much as I always did. No one else seemed to notice how high or heightened everything had gone, how the essence of things rushed and flapped in my heart. My sisters chattered among themselves as usual, cried at me to hurry along.

When it came my turn to cross the threshold to go to school, I was as fearful as a field mouse about to dash from under a rock, the huge sky over me threatening hawks. Nobody seemed to suspect the act of will it took me to move from hallway to step. Once out, for a moment I felt myself to be a queen stepping stately from my palace, my subjects cheering that I glorified their world by walking upon it; then I was only wretched Misskaella again, and walls and chimneys twitched and flickered when they should stay still.

I hung back from the others, their bent backs as they climbed, their turning aside to speak; now they laughed, faces pale against the slope of damp cobbles. How lucky they were, not to have gone raw like their sister!

"Do stop dawdling, Missk!" cried Tatty.

Time and again I must force myself to see that no actual wind frayed or bent the air. I feared that at any moment I would be caught up bodily and thrown high away, or dissolved grain by grain up into this invisible wind. Surely my mind would break soon from seeing this, from seeing through the skin of things to the flesh and the bone, to the breath gusting through and the blood pouring about? I would die of it, or fall into some kind of terrible fit. For the first time I was seeing life truly, and the truth would overwhelm me; a person couldn't bear this sight for long—a girl of nine should not be *expected* to bear it. Look at the power all but bursting from every cobblestone and grain of grit between! See how it was loosed in dribs and drabs so measuredly, moss crawling there in a corner, a schoolboy here running along his lane to join us, his greetings peeping within the roar-that-was-not-a-roar. Oh, the sky! I was glad of the clouds, the glowering light, for they seemed to my timid eyes to contain this ongoing event, though another, fresh-born, braver Misskaella behind those eyes knew that cloud or clearness was nothing to the purposeful flaring. It would leap regardless, pushed on outward by the forces from below.

The schoolhouse stood as solidly dreadful as ever, in a sea of children whirling excitedly, throwing off almost visible whoops and cries. The bell rang, and its chimes sent a ripple through the air, which crossed and combined with the energy fountaining from below, and flew off as bright curling streamers into the gray.

Inside, all day, my mind's flames kept burning up the world, never consuming it; its winds howled and yet moved nothing and took nothing away. Each action and object in this tiny schoolroom seemed a marvel to me—Mister Wexford so certain of himself, the rows of us so willingly chanting this, imagining that, writing the other thing upon our slates. At moments everything's solidity quite gave way, and the schoolhouse seemed constructed of dream matter, plastered with illusion, the heavy desks as liable as all the rest to be snatched up and scattered into the sky. When would I fall in the fit or faint that would end this?

That afternoon I waded through the spangled air and handled all the dazzling objects necessary to completing my chores. When they all were done, "I am going down the town," I told Bee, "to walk on the mole, if Mam asks."

"Very well," said Bee from inside her book on her bed. I had chosen to tell her because she was the most distracted sister, and the least likely to find another chore for me, or to insist on coming too.

I let myself out of the flickering house. Outside, cobbles and houses shuddered, rain spat and the clouds glared; the air was bitter, empty of spring promise. I descended the town all eyes and ears and goosefleshed skin. I stayed composed, though I felt like running, leaping with the leaping stuff, calling out, encouraging it and being encouraged.

So as to have told the truth to Bee, I did walk upon the mole, right out to the end and back again. My eyes lied to me: the town sat as it always did, they said, above the waterfront. But my mind insisted that the houses were in a continual slow scramble on its slope, and that colorless matter sheeted up between myself and that effortful movement, between myself and the tiny glinting windows, the town's many eyes. Behind and around me the horizon shook in the upflying wind, as if the sea were on the point of bursting from its bowl, taking flight entirely.

I strode away north along the main beach so that no one

looking out from Potshead should know what I intended. When I was out of sight of the town I took the dune path up past Thrippence's bothy, through and through the slipping sand. Across McComber's fields I went diagonally; not a soul walked the road or hill there, only McComber's cows stared, chewing their cud. Up and over the stile at the top I climbed, and then I was on the straight road. I ran; I had hardly run at all since people began to laugh at the spectacle, but now—oh, the joy of being alone and unjudged!—I all but flew along, not feeling in the least clumsy or ridiculous. The rain spat cold and gleefully in my face; the road ahead seemed as cheered to be empty as I was to see it so. To either side, high on the hilltop, far out to sea, the shaken-out cloth of creation took flashing fire here and there, and the flame rushed upward and away, and was renewed from below.

I slowed toward the cliff top, then peered over it. There the seals lay like bobbins in a drawer, grays and silvers, fawns and browns, some mottled, others smoothly one-colored tip to tip. The babies, very brown, were all movement and enterprise among the lounging mothers. I remembered crawling forth as a bab myself; I felt the same urge now as I had then, to run from the top of the cliff and fall in among the seals below. Surely I would be buoyed up by this fountaining air, like a coracle in the top of a wave?

Instead, I hurried, sister-free, alone in the land- and seascape, around the rim of the cove. I began down the path, and it was as if I stepped into a pool of quite a different temperature, or put myself in the way of a different angle of the wind. I touched my hair, but it was only fluttered a little by the natural wind, not streaming starkly upright as it ought to in this other flow.

Halfway down I paused, because the nursery had begun to boil below me. The bull and the bachelors, out beyond the main crowd, had stopped dueling in the shallows, and now they sat up, alert to my approach. More and more heads rose among the mothers and the mothers-to-be. Slower I went now, down the path. The closer I came to them, the clearer I saw—distributed through the pearly-coated blubber-bulk of each seal's body, and even along the delicate flippers and tails, like blooms across a spring field—the stars, the seeds, the grains that could be brought together. If time, tide and circumstance were right, I could persuade them to combine, at the center of the seal-being, into a manlike or a womanlike form. I saw that the creature on the garth wall, the woman rising from the skin of a seal, was no fancy, that the crumbs of story Potshead people dropped all fitted together, much as these grains did, and made a history—a history that might be repeated if such as I happened along. I had known it and never known it. I was astonished, even as so many questions were laid to rest.

I stood in the welter of power and shadow at the bottom of the cove. I gritted my teeth and stepped from path to rock; I lifted my gaze to meet the seals'.

The king, down in the shallows, yawped and snarled and swung his face in the sky. In front of him the restless mothers tipped and raised themselves and eyed me, one or two giving cry; from among them, struggling through their soft shivering hills and dales and tumbling forth onto the damp purplish rock, the young and the darker brown babies came, and when they had found flipper-footing they began to gallop toward me, as sheep hurry over their snowy field to a fresh-dropped hay bale, or pigs cross a sty at the clank of the slop bucket.

Some of the mothers lumbered to follow, hoisting themselves

up and rippling across the rock. What would they do when they reached me? Those babies' eagerness alarmed me, and their clumsiness, and the mothers were so big! Did they aim to catch and crush me? Did they love or hate me? I could not tell from their black shiny eyes, from their rippling hides, from their pink mouths gaping and their gruff vague calls.

I stepped back up onto the path. On they came, the mothers enlarging toward me, the babies so fast! Their edges wavered and glowed, left trails on the air; I could not tell how much was the magic of the day and how much was the weather, working up toward a storm—or indeed how much was mistakes of my own eyes, born of this new illness.

Up the cliff path I scrambled. Halfway, puffing, I paused to look down; the pups boiled at the bottom, and one had managed to climb the path's first step. I felt not the least desire to launch myself in among them now. How much wilder they were than people! And even if they had been tame, their weight and numbers would have terrified me.

I fled, rushing for home, pushing the seals out of my memory, trying to ignore the fraught flying air about me, to only see real objects within their flaring. I threw myself down on our front step, and sat there panting, hoping to settle everything around me by settling my own body and its thundering fear. The cottages opposite towered in the grimy clouds. Bowes's dog, watching me openmouthed, seemed one moment shrunken and hairy, the next the size of a donkey there, dream-large against the houses, its hip bone jutting beside the eaves. I looked away.

Bee and Lorel and Ann Jelly came up around the corner. My

gaze cleaved to their familiar faces—look how easy and comfortable they were in this nightmare street! Oh, to be one of them, never enduring such visions and sensations as I did! I ached to be as ordinary as I'd been only yesterday, as dull and frustrated and quietly beaten down. That smaller world, which I'd known only too well and found so disagreeable—would I ever be lucky enough to return to it?

"What are you up to, Missk?" said Lorel. "What have you run from, that you're so blown and bothered?"

"I've not run from anything." I shook away the picture of the galloping seal babs, the floundering mams. "I've only been running for running's sake, out along the tops of McComber's fields."

"Running for nothing? Oh, you young things," said Ann Jelly with a laugh. "So much energy, and nothing to use it up on. Come inside and scrub floors and make yourself useful."

I followed them in; I hid myself in the Prout house and Prout life all afternoon and evening, determinedly ignoring the sick fear I bore about. Not once, even as I put myself to sleep that night, did I open my memory and let the seals flap and fall out of it, crying up the path after me.

Leading us out to school next morning, Bee screamed, slammed the door and pressed wide-eyed against it.

"What on earth?" Mam came to the kitchen doorway.

The rest of us stared at staring Bee. "Seals!" she cried. "Like great *slugs*! One right outside, and all along the lane."

"Let me see, let me see!" Tatty clawed her aside. Mam came too, and the pair of them stuck their heads out the door and looked up and down. People were calling to one another out there, laughing, astonished. Fear welled up hard in my throat. I wished I could crawl under my bed and hide there.

"They look so much bigger, don't they, here than at Crescent Corner?" said Tat.

The others elbowed forward to see. Among them I caught sight of a seal's rump, and it was near waist-high to me even lying on the cobbles beyond our step.

"What have they come into town for?" Bee clasped her hands at her chin.

"What do seals always come to land for?" said Mam.

"To squash Bees flat as pancakes," said Billy, his head out the door.

Mam flicked the back of his head with her dish towel. "For a rest from the sea, a touch of the sun, or to raise their pups—which I hope they *don't* choose, all up and down our streets. They've mistaken themselves, that's all, and misread where Crescent is. There's room to pass them. Slip by this one and keep to the far side of the others. They cannot move fast, look at them, and they've not come to *eat* you. Go on, Missk, go on, Tatty—little ones must lead if big girls are too frightened."

We teetered on the step a moment, and then we ran, my sisters screaming between the seals and hiccuping past them, me silent, my stomach turning. Each seal lurched and swung its head as I went by. I would not meet their eyes; I would not show that I was linked with them, that I knew them. The main street was scattered with their pillows, all the way down; they must have swum around, rather than toiled up the cliff path and along the road. I ran uphill; there were no seals to trouble us that way. They had struggled as far as the Prout house and no farther.

When we were let out midmorning, the seals were thick in the main way, halfway up the hill. By the end of the school day, they had reached the gate, and one silvery lump had lolloped right in and lay huge there, and Mister Wexford must stand between us and it as we skittered and squeaked past, to keep the fainter-hearted girls and the tinier boys from refusing to leave altogether.

When we reached home, Mam told us of the bull, who had come ashore and been flinging himself about on the seafront, terrorizing people and breaking one of Fisher's little carts. Until then, I had had a plan to amble down to the sea and perhaps attract them out of the town, but this now became too terrifying to enact. I fell to bed, curling to the wall and covering my face, exhausted from being engulfed and poured-through by this invisible brightness. I refused to go to my chores or even to take my hands from my face. Sisters came and went, discussing me, feeling my forehead, scolding me for my laziness, but they could not shame or persuade me up. I slept, and that was some relief; I woke and lay with my eyelids tight shut against the flickering, listening to the seals gather in the lane outside, shifting and sliding on the cobbles, and every now and then one giving its horrible cry. Through the roaring of a wind that everyone else was deaf to, I heard my sisters and mother at the door, people outside conversing, a group of men come down from Wholeman's and trying to herd the animals away with cries and switches. Would this never stop, this flaming and the shivering around me?

I lay there in my shame and fear all the rest of the day, except for some moments spent at the front door in terror at how thickly the seals lay now. People stood around them, maneuvered among them, calling out to each other and laughing at this great joke.

"What about all their babies?" I said to Bee. "Back there at Crescent in the nursery. Do they not care that their babs will starve without them?"

She laughed and waved out over the crowded lane. "Clearly, they're worried half to death!"

I went back and hid in my bed again. Mam made the girls brew me up her tonic tea. They made it exceptionally strong and bitter, and I drank it down without protest; it seemed only a fair punishment for what I'd brought on the town. Then I turned away again, and covered my face.

"Come, Missk, you have no fever," Tatty said, feeling the back of my neck, seeing as my forehead was pressed against the wall.

"Everything's jumping about," I said. "My head is full of it, and it's worse when I look around."

There was talk of doctors then, and brain fever, and never had I wished so hard to be ill of something like that, some ordinary earthly illness. But as I did not rave or vomit or burn, Mam did not think my illness worth the bother of doctoring yet, and she and the sisters only came and went, regarding me suspiciously and making their suggestions. "She is certainly distressed," I heard Mam mutter in the hallway. "Is someone at school tormenting her?" And Tatty said back, more loudly, "She is just a lazy lump and needs a whipping."

I hardly cared what they said or thought, as long as they let me lie eyes-covered, out of sight of the seals, away from any light that would smear and flutter at the edges.

In the morning seals carpeted our lane. I got up, for if I stayed abed and the seals lay around me rather than struggling up to the school, it would be clear whom they were fixed on. So I suffered through another flaring day, grimly watched the fearful laughing and daring of the other children toward the seals. And I took to my bed again that afternoon. My sisters left me to my miseries, which bored them now.

Toward evening, through my half-sleep I heard a knock at the front door. Then the door to the bedroom was rattled and opened, and lamplight shone on the wall above me.

"Missk, Missk?" said Dad.

I turned to the blaze of the lamp, feeling all creased and unwilling. Mam stood there too, with a boy, quite a big boy. Ambler Cartney, it was, I realized as Dad carried the lamp in. Ambler was the kind of strong, handsome boy I had learned to steer well clear of if I wanted peace.

"Ambler here has a bit of something for you," said Dad.

I drew awkwardly up in the bed, feeling like nothing so much as a seal hauling herself into a corner of rock. I squinted at them, blocking the lamplight's glare with one hand. "A bit of *what?*"

"It's toffees," said Ambler watchfully. "They're from Cordlin. They are quite old." He held out a package to me, wrapped in bright patterned paper, a faded gold ribbon around.

"Toffees." I took them, and regarded them in my lap.

"What do you say?" Mam said sharply.

I held the smooth parcel, fingered the worn ribbon. "I say, what are toffees for, at this time?" Ambler stood between Mam and Dad quite straightly, leaning back and examining me as if he'd never quite seen me before—which perhaps he hadn't, at that. "And from you, who's never so much as spoken to me?"

"Oh, they're not from me," said Ambler cheerfully.

"They're from his great-grandmother," said Dad.

"Of all people," murmured Mam.

"Who's too infirm herself to bring them," finished Dad. "Being such a great age."

"She says to tell you," said Ambler, "that you should go about crossed."

"Crossed?"

"To protect you from seal-love, she says. Theirs of you, and you of them."

"What do you mean, crossed?"

"Crossed is with crosses tied on you, front and back." He drew a big *X* on his chest, and sketched one on his back with a thumb.

"Tied of what?"

He shrugged. "Bands, she says, crossed bands. Whatever bands are made of. Anyway, that's what she said; I'm just telling you. She's as old as Rollrock, Gran-Nan, and she knows an awful lot."

"I seem to have heard of this." Dad nodded. "This crossing. I'm sure I remember some old ones, men and women, who wore those crossings over their clothes."

"I'm sure I've never heard anything of the like," said Mam, her face made frightening by a shaft of lamplight. "What has Misskaella's illness to do with these seals? And is everyone out there gossiping about my daughter?" she said to Ambler. "And having opinions?"

"Oh no," he said. "It's only Gran-Nan has this bee in her bonnet. Dad and Mam have sent me up so's she will stop her nagging at them, bless her. She's worked herself right up, I tell you, full of fear and nonsense."

I looked at his calm bright face. How different other families were, the shape of them, the things they presumed, the children that grew up in them.

"Well, I thank you," finally I said. "Go about crossed. I will remember that." I held on to the toffee box, and like everything else in the room, and beyond it the house, and beyond *that* the town, it seemed to be part of a very odd dream. I was grateful for its hardness and heaviness, its decorative surface; I held to these in the uproaring inaudible storm.

"Grand," said Ambler. "I've done what I was told, then."

The parcel's shine and detail disappeared as the lamp withdrew, Dad thanking Ambler all the way out and sending respectful good wishes to his grandmam.

Mam stayed, a stiff-standing shadow above me. "Did you *really* do all this?" she said low and venomously.

In among all the noise, I clawed in vain for her meaning. "All what?"

She threw out a hand and I flinched away, but she only meant to point toward the front lane. "Bring these . . . *creatures*. Have you that power?" Yellow light slanted and swung on the hallway wall; Dad must be holding the lamp high to show Ambler his way among the seals. "And bring us the *attention*," she went on, even more incensed, "of Doris Cartney and such old blitherers? Sending up her grandson? For everyone to see?" She puffed with rage next to me.

"I did not *mean* to," I said humbly. "I did not *intend*—"

"But you did." I twitched again as Mam swept away to the door. "You did anyway, whether you meant it or not."

Then she was gone, and Dad was back in the doorway. I lifted the toffees into the lamplight, showed them to him. We looked helplessly at each other.

Then Mam returned; she showed him something. "From that gash Billy had," she said, "down his leg, mucking about in the mole-rocks that time." She threw it across to my bed, and the bandage unrolled, and would have gone off the side if I had not caught it. "Tie it up like he told you," she said shrilly, "crossed front and back. And wear it day and night. I'll not be shamed like this again. Leave her the lamp," she said to Dad, her voice low again, as if it came from a different person. She snatched the lamp from him and put it just inside the door as if she were too afraid or disgusted to come farther into the room. With a last glare at me she pulled the door closed, and I heard them go away to the kitchen, and my sisters' breathless questions begin.

"Toffees," I whispered, the word as weighty and rich in my mouth as the box felt in my hands. I put it aside and picked up the roll of bandage. I remembered Billy's cut shin. He had not cried or dramatized over it, but only admired the length and depth of the injury, the gleam of bone at a couple of places in the sponged wound. He had hissed through his teeth as Mam had bound him up, bound the sides of the wound together to heal. He had been such a *boy* about it, dry-eyed, set-jawed, smudged with blood.

I shook out the length of bandage, found the middle point and put it upon one shoulder. Aslant down to my waist, front and back, I took it, crossed the bands and brought them about my middle, slanted them up the other way.

The instant they met at my ear, quiet fell inside me, and the lightless flaring went out of all things. My heart continued pounding hard for a time, but as the stillness went on, that too eased. I held the ties together, and I wept a little at the terrors I had undergone these past two days, at the relief from them, at the simplicity of the remedy, and with gratitude toward Ambler's Gran-Nan Cartney, who had been kind and bullheaded enough to have it brought to me. Through the wall to the kitchen came the murmurings of my sisters aghast and agog, the rumble of Dad reassuring them, quiet snaps now and then from Mam. I rose and undressed in the reawakened roaring, wound the bandage again and this time tied it, pulled on my nightgown over it in the wondrous peace, folded away my clothes and hid the toffee box among them. I laid myself to bed in the lamplight and the quiet and the blessed solitude, and before long was properly asleep.

A high-summer morning. Tatty was first at the door.

"Oh, but look!" She let the door swing wider and bobbed down out of sight beyond the others. "What's this? A delicious *thing*. Oh, there's a note. Oh!" The note must have dived off in the breeze, for she leaped out the door.

We crowded onto the step and watched her chase it along the street, and stamp it stopped. She carried it back, in her other hand a glazed bun with jewels of rock sugar scattered over the top.

She scowled at the paper, straightening it with the littler fingers of her bun hand. "It doesn't make sense— Oh, I have it upside down, is why. So: 'For the . . . For the . . .'" She stopped to scowl some more.

"Let me see." Ann Jelly tipped herself off the step.

But Tatty held bun and note away from her. "'Little,' is what it says! 'For the little one.' The little one?"

"That has to be Misskaella," said Lorel.

They all drew away from me, looked down on me.

"I'm not little."

"Not widthways, it's true," said Billy. "But height-wise you're the littlest in this household, not counting the odd mouse."

"There, then," said Tatty jealously. She pushed the bun and note at me and dusted off her hands. "Let's get on."

"She can't just *take* it," said Ann Jelly. "She can't just *eat* it."

"Why not?" Billy hovered, unable to take his eyes off the bun.

"What's on out there? Not seals again, is it?" And Dad was there in the doorway.

"Here, Dad, whose writing is this?" Bee snatched the note from Tatty and held it up.

"'For the little one.'" He lowered the note, eyed me and the sparkling bun, took up the note again. "Someone very old, from that curling writing. And the shakiness. Someone very old and frail."

"So someone very old and frail is soft for our Missk?" said Billy in tones of hilarity, and the others prepared to laugh along.

"Or wants to *poison* her," said Tatty.

"Give me that," said Dad.

I handed him the bun, and licked my fingers of the sticky sweetness they'd picked up from it. He broke the bun apart—

silence fell around me at the sight of its soft yellow insides. He sniffed both pieces.

"I will eat it, to test," said Billy. "If you want."

Tatty pushed him off the step. "As if he'd rather risk his only *son*, when he has all these *daughters* spare."

"Here, eat it, Misskaella." Dad handed the bun back.

"Now?" cried Billy.

"She's full to the brim of porridge!" said Ann Jelly.

"Where I can see you," said Dad. "And all the rest of you. Otherwise you'll have nagged and badgered it out of her before you reach the end of the street. And it is for her." He flapped the note at them. Billy turned away and kicked a cobble.

"Shouldn't she be made to share?" said Lorel longingly.

"I don't see why," said Dad. "Is there anything in the note about sharing?" He pretended to read it again. "Why, I don't believe there is."

"He doesn't mind losing *you*, Missk," said Tatty. "As long as the rest of us aren't poisoned."

It was a waste to cram the bun, so light and sweet, into my mouth so fast, to gulp it down under all those envious gazes without properly enjoying it. Dad shooed us off as soon as I'd secured the last mouthful. We went silently, me still chewing.

"Who can it be," murmured Billy at my elbow, "so old and frail and in love? For the *little* one," he added sentimentally. "For the *little* one, that I would bounce upon my knee. For the *little* one, who I'd like to put my hand up the skirts of—"

"Stop it, Billy," said Ann Jelly. "It is not Misskaella's fault some old grandpa's taken to her."

"Or a grand*mam*," I said indistinctly, poking stuck bun scraps from my teeth with a finger. "A grandmam could have *made* that bun."

"Never," said Billy. "That's a mainland bun, that sort. That's a Cordlin-baker bun, that Fisher gets in sometimes."

I tried to enjoy the last tastes of exotic Cordlin. *Was* it some old man acting fond? Was that better than the bun's being something to do with the seals, and my attraction for them?

When we came home that afternoon I went straight in to Mam. "Can I see that paper," I said, "that came with the bun this morning? Did Dad show you?"

"Whatever do you want that for?" Mam looked up from scrubbing the table.

"To examine the writing. I never saw it properly. Only Dad and Tat got to see it."

"Too late; I have burnt it in the stove. You will have to wait until he favors you again, whoever it was." And she went back to scrubbing, hard.

On my birthday, a pair of thin socks, shop-bought socks with roses embroidered on the cuffs, was left on the little snowdrift at the door.

"Your lover man has left you a present, Missk!" Billy carried the socks in high over his head, and deposited them by my porridge bowl, from where Tatty immediately snatched them up.

"Oh, stop, Billy," said Ann Jelly. "It's Ambler's granny has put them there."

"She would have had Ambler bring them," said Grassy, "as she did before."

"Besides, she is dying," said Bee. I looked up, shocked. "Or so I heard," she said. "Didn't you?"

"Praps she is hoping Missk will come and cure her?" Billy went noisily to his porridge.

"She would have *said,* then," said Grassy. "She would have sent Ambler to ask. How are we to know that, from a pair of socklets with no name on them?"

"Well, someone wants *something* from our Missk. Who else would these fit? Look at them!"

"It's true," said Lorel. "For all the rest of her roundness, she does come down to tiny feet."

"Like a seal." Tatty was so taken up in her nastiness, she did not see Mam start toward her from the stove. "The way they—Ow! I was only *saying*!" Her spoon dropped and spilled porridge on the table, and she held the back of her head, and glared in outrage at Mam, who ignored her, taking up the pot ladle. "They have those tiny tails, I was going to say, to push their great fat selves along!" And for *great fat selves* she turned her glare to me, as if *I* had hit her.

"Ask Fisher who bought the socks," said Bee to me across the table, "and we will know who is your admirer."

I would not, and so that afternoon Bee and Lorel went down with the socks to Fisher's store themselves. They came back disappointed. "He says they were not bought from him," said Bee. "He has never carried that style, he says; perhaps they were bought in Cordlin."

"They look quite fresh," said Mam, taking the socks from Lorel and examining them. She put them to her face and sniffed. "Lavender. And camphor. They have lain for years in some old lady's camphor chest."

"See?" said Ann Jelly at Billy, all smug. "Ambler's granny. A last gift before she passed on."

Finally the socks arrived back at me, everyone having had their fondle and wonder over them. I smoothed them on my knee, imagining them lying on the sunlit snowdrift awaiting me, trying to see the shape of the person who had come along, perhaps before dawn so that no one else would spy them, and left them there and hurried away.

Fisher's great-grandfather was a little wizened man who sat blanketed by the fire in the store. I idled nearby. It was hard to get him alone, for everyone who came in made chat with him—but if I had chosen a quieter time, people would have remarked on my visit.

He farewelled Granger's dad. His gaze fell to me, but skimmed straight past, for I was of no account to him, some staring girl-child.

There was a good disguising noise of Missus Fisher making hearty talk with Blair Gower at the counter, and for the moment no one else was in the shop. "I was wondering," I said, standing forward.

The old man set his jaw, his face showing none of the cheerful creases he had presented Mister Granger with. "You were wondering? Yes, these are all my own teeth. That is what most children wonder, whose old ones keep their teeths in a jar, or manage without."

"I wondered if you knew anything about seals and seal-people."

Only now, when he went still, did I realize how much all of him had been tinily, busily moving. He ceased blinking; I looked into his staring gray eyes and thought he must have blinked most of the blue from them. In them I saw a Fisher I'd never suspected was there, from the time before he knew everything, when he could still be surprised or frightened. Just for a moment I saw that Fisher, before the granddad-Fisher covered him up, blinking several times to make up for the pause before.

"I am not *that* old," he said.

"I didn't mean you were," I said. "Only, things you may have heard, from *your* old folk."

"Oh no," he said quickly. "I was never privy." He pulled his blanket higher on his lap. "Missus Fisher!" he cried out, and I stepped back from him, startled.

"Yes, Pa?" came from the counter, and Missus Fisher and Gower glanced across, patience in both their faces.

"Some tea, if you'd please, when you have the time."

When Gower had gone out the door and Missus Fisher to the back room, old Fisher shafted me a look and said in a low voice, "I know nothing, girl, about any of that, nothing."

I did not believe him; nobody so old could know *nothing*. I waited in case he should say more, but he ignored me, and then I must stand aside to let Missus Fisher through with the rattling cup and saucer. There was an amount of fussing to do, to set the tea where the old man wanted it, and warn him of its hotness, and be told not to think him a fool, and during this I lost heart, and eased myself away along the rows of sacks and barrels.

Bustling back to her counter, "Girl!" called Missus Fisher. "Here."

She unlocked the money drawer and took out a coin; it shone silver. "He says you're to have a shilling."

"A shilling?" I was so astonished that I all but forgot what a shilling was. The word's sounds flew out of my mouth; the thing shone in the air. I felt a crashing shame. How would I hide the coin from Billy and my sisters, from Mam and Dad? And now Missus Fisher knew too. She might not know why her great-grandfather-in-law was being so generous, but she would know that he did not give shillings out to every child who came by. I had marked myself; she knew there was something odd about me—and how many other people would she tell?

I shook my head.

"He's quite insistent, my darling," she said unfriendlily. "Come, take it." She shook it. She neither smiled nor frowned, but her eyes worked on me. If I refused or ran away, she would think me even more peculiar. "It won't bite you. There." And the thing, all cold except where Missus Fisher's fingers had held it so long, was in my hand. "Now run along and put it somewhere safe."

Slowly, numbly, I walked up the town through the fine gray rain. What had I done, what had I brought on myself? Back home, I slid the shilling into the toe of one of the Cordlin socks; it was as if I had stolen it, the uncomfortable feelings that clustered around it. I was confused by its very shillingness; farthings and ha'pennies were all I had ever bargained with. Such a quantity of sweets was available to me now, I could hardly do the sums of it, and when I attempted them, I knew that I could never hide so much, or eat it all myself. And if I shared, everyone would ask me how I came by such a feast, and hear about Mister Fisher's favor, and wonder aloud what kind of nuisance I had been, that he had paid me so handsomely to keep away from him.

I had not been down to Crescent Corner in a while. After Ambler's visit and the Cordlin bun and the socks and the shilling, I was too conscious of the town's eyes on me.

But I did miss seeing the seals, however embarrassed I had been by their pursuing me into town. Whenever I took off the bands to wash myself, in among the earth's up-pouring and the sea's I felt the knowledge that the herd was there, an itch upon my mind; this faded in the autumn as they left on their great migration, but the following spring it returned when they assembled at the Crescent again.

When the sisters suggested walking down to the seal nursery, I thought I might risk going too. I dawdled along behind them on the field road, careful not to seem too eager. I stood along the cliff top with them, and closed my lips on the suggestion that we go down to see the seal babs closer. Grassy uttered it, though, and down we went.

At the bottom Ann Jelly and Tatty danced out across the

rocks. The others stood at the foot of the path, Bee calling out warnings and Grassy and Lorel encouragement—"Go up and touch one! Pick up a bab, and we'll take it home!"

I sat where the path ended in a wide step, and watched the silver-blue sweep of the ocean. When all the sisters had their backs to me, I loosened the tied bands on my shoulder, and took a long, deep look at the seals, and let them see me. Up they reared, ready to surge at me. My nearer sisters screamed at the sudden motion, the sudden attention, which they thought was directed at them, me being behind them. Tatty and Ann Jelly screamed too, and leaped back toward us, dodging the woken seals.

I tied the ties again as they squealed and laughed. I had seen what I wanted to see. Throughout each seal, what I had thought randomly scattered lights, each as bright as the other and all doing the same thing, were in fact different parts, in bud, of the human system. Solider, brighter buds lodged in the seal's joints. Smaller, paler ones, perhaps for the fine skin and hairs, floated closer to the surface, out to the tips of the tail and flippers, and some even out along the seal whiskers. Middling ones swam about between, and among them ghosted all-but-invisible lights, which must be compressed forms of mind, maybe, of spirit or feelings. With a little more looking—but the herd's movements would have given me away if I'd watched much longer—I would have seen how they all came together, the paths they must be drawn along if they were to assemble rightly into human form. For now, I only saw that there *was* a system to them—and that it was a complete system, that to make a woman within a seal, every last one of those buds or stars, those flickers or ghosts, must be gathered to the center. I saw the size of the operation, how complicated it would be.

But it could be done. And the very looking had done something to me, calling out some budding thing inside me too, the lights and lines of a braver and steadier Misskaella who floated all potential inside my thickset, unpromising shape. Contemplating the seals and, eventually, bestirring myself to bring those seal-lights together would form that new Misskaella just as surely as it would form the shapes of women from the blubberous matter of seals.

"Look at Missk!" called Tatty from among the sisters. "She is under the spell of these seals."

"Oh, do you wish you were a seal, Missk?" crooned Bee.

"She's about the right shape for one," said Grassy Ella.

"So unkind!" But Lorel was laughing as she pushed Grassy off the rock.

Grassy splashed into a shallow pool and occupied them all with her complaining, which I was glad of, for it took their eyes from me. They did not see, then, the sting of Grassy's insult, or the worse shame of the truth in Tatty's words, and the flush both sent across my face. The crossed bands might protect me from seal-enchantment, but they left me as vulnerable to my sisters' barbs as I had ever been.

For a time, when I went each morning for my visit to the privy I hurried up the side of the house, bending to scuttle unseen below the window. I checked our step for gifts, and most days it was blessedly empty. But I once snatched up a lace-edged handkerchief, the letters *MP* embroidered into its corner with a great deal of effort and grime. Another time a shining pointed tooth, of a whale by the size of it, stood there as if grown from the step, with a picture scratched into its side and black rubbed in to show it, a rendition of the garth-wall woman coming out of the sealskin.

I hid the handkerchief in my pocket, but the whale tooth was so heavy I must weasel my way back through the house and hide it with the socks and the shilling, up the back of my drawer. When I found a moment to take it out again, in private, I saw that a second woman was carved into the side of the whale tooth, a hooded figure, her face all wrinkles, her hands reaching around the curve of the tooth, clawing toward the seal-woman. A line was incised around the whole tooth, making the horizon. In the sky a full moon hung, and that was the best-carved part of all the picture, the pitted face of it; whoever had scratched it had sat under the moon itself, and by its light had matched it mark for mark.

Some time elapsed then, with no further gifts arriving. I told myself hopefully that the tooth's magnificence and mystery meant the end of the gift-giving, because nothing could be more exotic or expensive. And I ceased my morning ritual.

But in late spring a bunch of cornflowers was left, tied with a blue ribbon.

"Ooh, ooh!" said the girls as Bee turned with the flowers from the morning door. "Misskaella's sweetheart has been by again!"

"Take them, take them, Miss! They're for you! See? They have an M on them, for *Misskaella*."

But I clasped my hands together behind my back when Bee thrust the flowers at me. The shaky curls of the old-fashioned M, penciled on a paper scrap tucked under the ribbon, looked like a thread of my own fear unraveling; the flowers bristled at me. "I don't want them."

"Take them!" Tatty said louder. "We must get on!"

"And do what with them!"

"I don't care—trample them underfoot if you want!" And she strode out past me and glared back from the lane outside.

The noise brought Mam, and she snatched the bothersome bunch from where Bee was using it to press me to the wall and enjoy my discomfort. "She won't take them!" Bee whined.

"And neither she ought. Presents from strangers." She frowned at the initial, examined the back of the paper, the M showing like the curled legs of a dead spider between her fingers.

"It's *not* from a stranger, though," said Bee. "It's some old man we know; we just don't know which."

"I think *I* know which," said Tatty archly. "Creepy Arthur Baitman that snuffles about up at Wholeman's." As the others crowed and fell about, she nodded to me. "I think he thinks he has a chance with you, Missk."

"I hate the way you smutch and smirch everything!" I shouted. "It's only flowers. It might be from anyone's mad old granny, taking pity on me for having to live with *you*, you nasty nest of *snakes*!"

They all fell back from my noise, it was so unusual.

But Tatty looked on my passion coldly. "Oh, it's not that they *like* you, Missk—don't flatter yourself. They're only *afraid* of you, that you'll bring the seals again."

Mam shouted then, at Tatty and at me, but I could not hear her for the clanging of Tatty's words in my head. Whatever power I possessed, Tatty's face—all their faces—told me that it would never win me friends. My family would pretend it was nothing, or but a nuisance; the rest of the town would only ever shy from it or make the sign against it, and a few of the older folk leave these gifts—and secretly, so that I should never know who tried to appease me, and never bring any of my magics upon the town, out of consideration for those unknown givers.

"I'm going to *school*!" I turned away from shouting Mam and pushed through my sisters. Billy tried to stand and stop me, but I booted him hard in the shin. He howled and stepped aside; because Mam was there, he could not boot me back. I flung myself out the door. I knew I was ridiculous, my fat bottom flouncing away from them up the street. But I was always ridiculous, wasn't I? That was my place among the Prouts, to be always the smallest and most foolish, to have their attention only as far as they could milk me for laughter, and otherwise to count for nothing at all.

I sat sorting shells on the edge of the seafront road; several other girls, and a littler boy or two, still staggered about down on the beach, collecting. It was a clear summer evening except in the west, where the sun, in a festive fit before it went to bed, sprayed pinks and reds about among a few streaks of cloud.

A clutch of men walked by, gathered from the seafront houses to go up to Wholeman's together. From being entirely busy with my shells, I looked up to find all their eyes on me.

"Clear enough where that one's great-pa dipped his wick." Whoever had said it, deep in the group, lowered his head so that his cap brim hid his face.

"Prouts," said another, to my face. He would never have spoken or looked so confidently on his own, but with five men behind him, he could say what he liked to any girl.

"Yes." Another took courage. "Prouts were at it, bad as Cawdrons and Strangl'olds." They were all blush-colored head to toe with the sunset, and their eyes glittered. "Not that *my* great-folk stayed about to watch."

"Nor mine."

"Nor mine, neither."

I bit my lips in, turned to the sunset. I wished I were the sun up there, bloodying up the sky, with such small matters as men's ill will and a girl's embarrassment never approaching my vast-burning mind. *Prouts*. The disgust in that voice. *Prouts were at it*. I remembered, too, Gert's awed tone: *Our greatest shame*. That was the key, wasn't it, to the shadings of meaning of things said around me down the years at the school, in the town, glances passed and laughs stifled, hundreds of instances that I had not understood before? *Prouts were at it, Cawdrons, Strangleholds*. It was clear to me, suddenly, coldly, why Mam was always angry. All of Potshead was divided up like this; there were those who had had doings with the seal-women, and those who had not, and Mam had been born among the latter, and had married into the former. Perhaps she had not cared at the time, but she cared now, oh yes. It was written in every word she bit out, every impatient movement she made.

I turned from the sunset, which was fading from its greatest glory. The men were legging each other up to the higher path so that they could cut up Totting Lane. They were quite a way from me, clambering shadows, laughing; they had forgotten me.

Prouts. The shells I had collected were faded dry on the paving stones before me. Why had I brought them all up? Why had I thought them so wonderful that I must collect and sort them and take them home? I waited until I could no longer hear the men's voices over the slap and swish of wavelets down on the gravelly shore, and slowly I scraped all the shells chink-chiming together, and pushed the dull-colored herd to the edge and then over; they tinkled to the stones and shells below, and instantly vanished among the others.

There came a long dark winter, and Rollrock lost many of its older folk. Among them went whichever men or women had been leaving the gifts for me, or arranging for them to be left. Which was it? Nothing came for me through those dark short days, so it could have been any of seven old men or women. Some of those had been kindly to me as they were to all children, and some's faces had changed to watchfulness when they saw me, and others had been shut away as Nanny Prout had shut herself away, so that I hardly knew what they looked like.

Whoever it was, they had abandoned me, and I felt it sorely, for now I began to grow, up out of childhood and into a time of life when all the town, all of Rollrock, took a greater interest, not just in me, but in all the other rising young women about me, and they set us against each other as you set chickens at a market, comparing their feathers' gloss and the brightness of their eye, their temperament and general breeding. The boys they watched too, for signs of fecklessness, but boys' bodies and looks mattered less than did girls', however much my sisters compared them one to another. The girls' company had long had dull moments this way, but it was only as I grew toward marriageable age myself that I realized that if I did not join that marriage conversation, there was nothing else left for me to do. I could not go out on the boats like the men, or run away to Cordlin and find a living there—what skill did I have to sell? But I hardly dared turn my mind to the kind of marriage I might make, for from the one time my sisters had shrieked to each other about my possible prospects, and from Mam and Dad's uncomfortable silence on the matter—let alone the looks and jests that actual boys and men felt free to loose at me, out on the public street—I knew that I had little enough to offer. "Perhaps if you looked more cheerful," Mam would say hopelessly after a space of glumly regarding me. But I had seen my sisters going about smiling at nothing and tossing their hair. It was grotesque; I would have none of it. I was an unhappy pudding and I would not pretend otherwise. Why should I try to win the favor of one of those boys? If they had not grown up tormenting me, they had never stepped forward to prevent those who did. Even Bee's anxiously listing the men who might be expected to take an interest in me—defective in brain or looks or manners, or aged beyond caring whether a wife had a fine face and figure—could not move me to attempt to improve myself, try different ways with my hair or affect an interest in the lives about me.

I could have done with a gift being left for me now and then, to single me out as favored when all the world seemed intent on pointing out what I lacked. I looked forward sometimes to loosening the band upon my shoulder at night, just to remind myself of what I could see that others could not—but what consolation was that, to watch the essence of things in its dance-and-streaming, when I must always return to the flatter life and the silenter, where I was an object not of reverence or wonder but of scorn?

As I sat uncooperative, my brother and sisters turned from me and one by one took wing into *their* opportunities. Our Billy, first chance he got, upped and offed Rollrock. He sent us a gaudy card, of two flirtatious "Spanish flamenco dancers," but the card was post-stamped from a port in France, not Spain. Out of that port, he said, he was working some "proper ships." What kind of work he did not say, but it clearly was not fishing boats he talked of; he surely thought himself too fine for that work.

Mam was even angrier now—she could not look on those flamenco dancers without distaste, and so that they would not smirk at us she propped the card on the dresser shelf with Billy's scrawled message outward. Dad you could not mention Billy to; he would bluster away from you, full of unspeakable rage. I never saw him weep a tear of it, but his eyes would redden and blotch should other men's sons achieve things and please them. His mouth would pinch up and he would seek beyond the speaker's shoulder for something unrelated to talk of.

I was glad to see Billy gone. He had changed from rambunctious, sneering boy to hulking, sulking young man; add a little drink and he would be spoiling for a fight, and if he could find no one to have it with he would bring himself home to snipe and ridicule us. And Mam at his side would take his part if any of us saw fit to answer him back. It was almost as if she had taken pleasure in his nastiness, as if he dealt out for her all the pain and insult she had not the courage to loose on us herself.

My sisters went on and on about the great tragedy and loss of our brother, among themselves and with Mam, seeming to enjoy making her weep and then exhibiting their own kindness consoling her. They knew nothing to support their imaginings of what Billy might be up to, not a thing—none of us except Dad had ever been off the island, or knew anything about the bigger world. But that did not stop them having opinions and proclaiming them, or hissing along every bit of gossip they collected.

I thought our family would stay this way forever, my sisters ignoring me except to tell me to straighten my posture and close my mouth and *smile*, for goodness' sake!, Mam lining up with them against me and Dad striding among us with his eyes high and his chin stuck out, and Billy gone.

But a man came, a *lawyer*—or a beginning lawyer, some kind of under-lawyer yet. He day-tripped out to Rollrock from Cordlin, and he spotted Ann Jelly of all of them, and the moment his eye fell on her, she became something more than our sister, to our astonishment. She burst open, like a green bud into color and petal ruffle, and she smiled and laughed as she never had particularly before. She charmed us all, not just Skinny-Face Hurtle with his laboring syllables and his stiff collar propping up his head.

He wooed her mostly by letter, but he did cross to the island once or twice, and he joined us for an awkward dinner one Sunday.

"Sit *still*, Misskaella!" said Mam, though I was no more unsettled than any around that table, barring Ann Jelly herself, serene in her blossomed state with her lawyer-to-be by her side.

"Misskaella, there's an unusual name," said Skinny-Face. "What does it mean?"

Everyone looked at me surprised.

Ann Jelly said in charming puzzlement, "She of the execrable posture?" and everyone laughed.

"The sour-faced one," said Bee, and all had their mirth at that too.

Mam looked about at the swaying girls, at Dad, who was going about his food, and at Mister Hurtle, who looked upon me kindly as my face hotted up. "It's a girl's name for Michael," she said clearly, in her voice-for-visitors. "She is named for the archangel."

"I see," said Mister Hurtle, and nodded approvingly.

"Aye, she *looks* like a Michael," said Lorel, still laughing.

"Lorelei," said Mam, as if to point up the girlishness of Lorel's name, while I sat there slab-faced and mannish under my clunking mannish name, and the girls made a show of stifling their laughter around me.

When Ann Jelly and Mister Hurtle married, the wedding—*which must be modest,* said Dad, *for I don't want all the others expecting extravagance*—was on Rollrock. And wasn't Bee vexed that it was not her own! And wasn't Ann Jelly delighted! Triumphant, she was, in the spring wind at the church door, and the apple-blossom petals blowing around them like snow, and Skinny-Face's smile creaking on his face. His parents, fat on Cordlin butter and cakes, beamed and mouthed "quaint" and "charming" and "countrified" and "fresh air," and held themselves just a little apart from us, a little above us, under the trees in the garth during the wedding feast.

Then Ann Jelly was gone from us over the Strait, and Bee and

Grassy and Lorel went worse than ever at each other, without her there to intervene between them.

But Bee was snatched up too, in time, by Thomas Bolt in his brief moment of half-handsomeness and hers of nearly-beauty, and she went up the hill and started turning out babs as fast as a granny turns out thud-cakes. And Grassy went to poor John Tinker and the same, bab after bab, and Lorel to the curate Breachley, who gave her no children, which was no surprise to anyone. And Tatty Anna married Joseph Coil and had one son and then the girl that killed her, so Lorel and Breachley took on those two and had children after all, whom Lorel never treated as anything other than a very great burden on her.

There was no reason to think I would do any better than Tatty or Grassy, and certainly no lawyer-in-the-making would whisk me away to the mainland. One by one all the marriageable boys claimed or were claimed by the girls who flirted or *looked cheerful*, or were only slender and unobjectionable, while I remained like one of the Skittles rocks, a crag in the midst of the moving sea, marking the points on which no sensible man, no man with any prospects, would compromise.

What men were left, my age and older, were either one-legged or mad, or they made the sign against me if I crossed their path, or they did not even see me. I wanted no husband if marriage meant one of these. In the secretest of my moods and the darkest of my nights, I thought of traveling to the mainland, and finding myself a husband there. But if no Rollrock man could look on me without scornful laughter or fear, surely all Cordlin could offer me was a larger pool of such tormentors?

And after Dad fell ill I was well and truly tied to home. It was more accident than illness; he was man one day and he woke up back to bab the next, and he never found word or step, or grasp, or control of his bodily functions again. Mam's rages grew closer to the surface; where she had tutted and sighed and banged pots about, now she complained, and loudly—against Dad, against Billy, against her fate to live such a hard, dull life. She would unleash herself on me: "How fat you are getting! You are surely fatter than last summer. Are you eating your father's food when I don't look?" She seemed unable to stop sometimes, about my untamable hair, my eyes almost swallowed up by my cheeks, my sour expression. She never remarked upon my harking back to that shameful ancestress, but it hovered there between us; I waited for her to use it to harangue me, but she never quite did. She only lamented at how I was to be a burden on her forever, I was so unmarriageable. Dad was the only bab I should ever care for, she said. Perhaps I was glad of his illness, was I? Perhaps I felt he gave me an excuse for being so useless to anyone else?

"Useless, am I?" I would say, if she pushed this too far. I would put aside Dad's bowl and whip off my apron and go from the house with a slam. I would take a turn about the town, greeted by some and spat beside or skittered from by others. Or I would climb by field and fence to Whistle Top, and fill my teeth and hair with wind, my eyes with sea around three sides of me, rinsing the house's cramped darkness and sickroom smells out of my head. I would feel the rage and shame of being a Prout—and of being *this* Prout particularly, the unmarried one, the odd one, the one who *harked back*.

Or I would visit the seals, dangling my legs from the cliff path and soothing myself on the sight of creatures who had no opinion of me. They soaked up the sun, or they lay in the wind and snow unbothered; they birthed their young in shameless messes and the birds cleaned up after them. The bull, carelessly ugly, fought off his rivals, returning to mate with one of these sacks of well-being, it hardly seemed to matter which.

I would watch them a long time. My irritations would fly off and I would find a patient alertness within me. I was not tempted at all to loosen my crossed bands and disturb them. I had seen deeply into them once; once was enough to know what sparkled inside them, what I might bring out from them when I grew big enough and brave enough. My time would come, I felt sure, and then Mam and the girls would be sorry.

When I returned, Dad would be inexpertly fed, and Mam would be silent but for a clash of pan, a crash of firewood. And I would have some days' peace before she forgot again how much work I saved her, and recommenced complaining.

I hardly had leisure to think of what I held off from myself with the bands. I was too occupied keeping Mam and Dad's house, and helping when Grassy or Bee lay in, or were ill, or their children were ill or their men. For a long time I seemed to be everyone's but my own; I was like a broom or dishrag that anyone might pick up and use, and put aside without a thought when they were done with me.

During this time I saw many girls wed. I stood in the crowd outside the church waiting for bride and groom to emerge victorious, and I followed with everyone else as they proceeded to the feast.

There was no reason why Tricky Makepeace's wedding should set off my impatience; she was no relation of mine, and no particular enemy or friend. Neither was Jodrell Fence such an enviable catch, or the dress Tricky wore much finer a confection than most.

But that was the night I took flint and steel and went out, tiptoe through the town so as not to wake anyone, then out along the field road. The moon shone brightly—perhaps that had called me out? The air was as still as a held breath.

Down to the Crescent I went, to the seals, who were all the one silver under the moon, except for the bull, the king, who lay among his wives like spilled ink, and the babies, like dark droplets thrown off him throughout the herd.

I gathered driftwood and made a fire, and took off my clothes in the warmth of it, and stripped the crossed bands from myself, and down I went and called the king out from among the mothers.

His waking roar echoed around the Crescent rocks. He rose from the ruck and pitched himself through the bewildered mams toward me, right over some of them. His eyes rolled white in the moon, and his mouth was a paler splash within his dark head.

There with pups moiling and mewing around my ankles, and mams a-fret and a-waggle either side, I set my sights on the man-makings inside him. Like a swarm of bright insects they were, which I must waft and persuade toward his center, even as he lurched and shivered and made his monstrous sound and blasted me with his fish-rot breath. This I did; this I learned to do in the doing of it, searching every corner of him, gathering every seed and spark. The full moon conjured and encouraged the light, and I threw and threw myself as one throws a net, and I drew each speck toward and into the man-shape at his center. A head-blur parted from the body-blur; some limbs came good, splitting from the main shine. Then suddenly the man's outline sharpened within the seal. Arms lifted from his sides, reached up, and hands pushed out through the mouth hole and split the seal's head-end apart.

The coat collapsed to the rock, and the shining man stepped out. The moon lit his lifted face, and I laughed as I fell in love with it, in simple accordance with the terms of the old charm. Then he lowered his gaze to me, and likewise I dazzled him—it was none of my doing, only a matter of proximity and timing and our two natures—and we were locked together.

He glanced about at the sea, at the cliffs, at the fire. "That is your home, up there?" he said.

"That is my fire." I admired his long lean legs, his man-parts and his narrow hips, the smooth-dented front of him, his broad chest and fine shoulders, and above all his face, so full of strength and loveliness and, most marvelous of all, so fixed on me, with not an ounce of ill will or amusement in his eyes, not the merest smudge of guile in his expression, not a hint of curl in his lip.

Then he bent, and I heard my own little shriek, the most *girlish* sound I had ever made, as he lifted me. He started out among the mothers and pups, commanding them aside in their own tongue. I clung to his smooth neck, breathing in the heady, salty warmth of his skin. A soundless wind poured up through the air around us. It should muffle everything, as crashing surf muffles voices on a beach, as surf fume veils a headland. But instead every wave-plash and seal-snuffle was clearer, every rock bulked out brighter-edged, and every touch was sharper or more tender than it ought to be.

He lowered me to stand by the fire. He put his arms—long, strong and lean—about me. I stood to my toes and he bent from his heights and we met in the middle very sweetly, I thought, very neatly. And then I thought the kiss had finished, but still he pressed me there, and when my mouth softened wondering at the surprise of that, oh! In he slipped his tongue a little way! I exclaimed against it. I tested and tasted him; I put up my own arms and held him down to me, and up his hot neck and into his slithering hair my fingers found their way, and in among his teeth my own tongue darted, and up and down our bodies we were fast together.

He let me go as gently as he'd taken me up, soft smaller kisses finishing off the larger. He pushed back the curls on my forehead that would never submit to being tied back. I fizzed and rushed with that kiss, quietly thundered to myself. How would I bring myself, at the end, to send all this back to the sea?

But why think of that? I sat to the rock, drawing him down with me. I pushed him back, and lay alongside him, quite unafraid. I roamed over him, exploring the hills and vales of him, the roads and towers, with my small, plump, work-red hands, wondering at all his different degrees of hairiness and smoothness, of warmth and chill, tying and loosing his hair, which was dark as night, slippery as water.

And here was a wonder, that a man so well conformed himself should be so eager to embrace what I had always been told was a poorly made body, laughable, even disgusting. But I delighted him; he traveled my curves, weighed me in his hands, pressed me and gasped with me as I yielded. Open-faced he looked into me, his eyes empty of the scorn I was used to seeing, in women's faces as well as men's. Instead he was only another creature discovering skin, discovering forms of limbs, folds and fancies in the fire- and moonlight, all of them laughable, all gravely serious. He pushed the dampening hair back from my temples, and kissed me again with that wide, that white-teethed, that smiling-serious mouth.

We barely spoke, beyond a muffled cry here and there, a little laugh, a gasp. What was there to say as we did what we did, or even as we floated in its aftermath, curled around each other in the fire's warmth, in the night's cold? Exultant, I watched as my life tore free like a kite from its string and flung itself up into the windstorm that was the future. I had been so small, and stuck so fast in my little round, my puny terrors! Why had I cared so much for people's opinions—people even smaller than myself? Ha! It hardly mattered why, did it, if I cared no longer? Look what I could have! Look what I could do!

The stars teased cloud-veils across themselves and twinkled out brightly again afterward; the ample air of spring spread above, salty, green, teeming with life; the sea lipped and popped at the rock's rim, sighed farther out in its swells and tides and darkness. I turned in my lover's arms and pulled his mouth to mine again.

At last we reached what I knew was our end. He had given me a new body, modeled and magicked it up with his hands and mouth and manhood. For the first time in my life I had been beautiful, and lovable, whether Potshead people thought so or no. I felt cleansed of the rage and misery that had made up so much of me in pettier company, in prettier. I felt freed to please myself, to find my way as I would, in a world that was much vaster than I had realized before, in which I was but one star-gleam, one wavelet, among multitudes. My happiness mattered not a whit more than the next person's—or the next fish's, or the next grass blade's!—and not a whit less. How piddling I was, in the general immensity! And how lovely it was to be tiny and alone, to have quickened to living for a moment here, to be destined soon to blink out and let time wash away all mark and remembrance of me.

We went down together to the cold, stinging sea and swam there; I rinsed his sealness from me, and he my earthliness from him. He came to me and stood against me; I reached barely to his chest, and he held me, and played my hair about my shoulders, wringing the sea from it and scattering it with his big hands, beautifying its messy wet masses by only touching and looking. He kissed me once more, a deep, long, drinking kiss upon my sore lips, involving my aching tongue.

And then he let me go. Naked I followed him, through the seals, up onto the rocks. His skin lay there, all the magic asleep inside it. For a moment as he bent, it trembled below him, and was indistinct in the wash of upflying life. He reached for it, and it woke and leaped to him. He hoisted it up, and it thickened and sagged, and the first lights went from his fingertips into the seal flesh. He fell to his knees, the skin clapped down and the man was gone. How had he ever been? Aghast, I watched the rearing blubber-mass tip itself off the rock, into the crowd of crying mams.

Shivering, still bathed in upflowing magic, I went back to the fire and crossed myself with my bandage. Peace fell around me, and I was alone at Crescent Corner with the sea and the moon- and starlight playing upon each other, and the seals sinking back to their rest. Slowly I hid my new self in my same old blouse and kirtle and boots, kicked over the embers and crushed the heat out of them. I walked, warm now and thick-shod, across the rocks and up the sandy path. At the top of the cliff I stood in the grass under the stilled stars that had so dithered and streaked above me before. I had been ugly once; I must remember that, remember how to be ugly again now that I knew I was beautiful, remember how to be ordinary now that I'd seen the wonders inside me.

I walked home through the unmagical night. I changed into my nightdress in the privy and went into the house, and my old life greeted me there, ready to box me straight back in, to pack me tight among my old chores and irritations. My new eyes looked around at the shadowy kitchen; it would never hold me again as it had. I was here, but I was no longer *trapped* here.

As I went along the hall, Mam grumped from behind her door. "What've you been so long for? Have you the squitters, or what?"

"I fell asleep there." I shuffled onward as sleep-clumsily as I could pretend.

"A person could lie here *bursting*," she said.

"You should have followed and knocked," I said mildly, and caught back a laugh into my throat, at the thought of what her knocking would have led to.

I closed my door and put myself to bed. I did not want to sleep, to see the end of this night, to wake into the humdrum tomorrow and think it all a dream. But as I'd seen, lying beside the seal-man on the Crescent rocks, what did my wants count for? Nothing and less than nothing. I watched the ceiling's swirling shadows, happy to matter so little. When my thoughts ran down at last, with a sigh I wrapped my own arms around myself, and stroked my own damp hair as I sank to sleep.

Life went on as before. The feeling of the seal-man's hands faded from my skin, and the sight of his face from my memory. One day after midsummer it struck me that life had gone on, for quite a time, without its usual monthly event, and that he had left me more than my torn virtue and my new peacefulness.

I looked coolly on this realization. The town would condemn me, and Mam would rant and rail, but I would still have this bab, half magical, entirely mine.

Now that I had admitted it, I felt the child growing inside me. But I did not become spectacularly ill, as both Grassy and Bee were now, as they had been for every bab, trying to outdo each other with their suffering. I did not have to sit about green with a puke bowl by me, fighting to keep food down. Sometimes a vague wisp of sickness floated through me, and once or twice the smell of fry-fat brought a lump to my throat; any but the weakest tea tasted foul to me, and the house sometimes had so close a fug that I must go and gasp on the step if I were not to faint away. But Mam did not notice these small discomforts, and no one else watched me closely enough to remark the difference.

And then the discomforts went away, and there was only the knowledge, the growing weight right deep down in me, the occasional fluttering movement. I waited for someone to notice, for voices to snap and eyes to turn on me. But there had always been a lot of me, and I was not much larger, only firmer. The outward change was hardly to be remarked, beyond what Mam always carped about, beyond what men like Garter O'Day watched sidelong when they had the chance. The months went on, and the weather closed in, and I sat by the fire curiously unfrightened. I would go back in my mind to the night I had had with the seal-man, to the dark of the spring moon; I would listen to the movements of his child in me, and it would all make a sense of sorts. There was no need to tell it, to surrender it up for gossiping, to cheapen it so. Let people realize when they would; it was no concern of mine.

Deep in the winter when the ice knocked in the harbor and Potshead pulled in its elbows under the snow, Grassy and Bee both were brought to bed of their babs. Mam went up to stay with Grassy, so as to tend to them both without having to take that slippery hill every time, leaving me at home with doddering Dad trapped in his bed unable to speak, or possibly even to think. Then only, with the larder as full as it could be and no reason to venture from the house and be seen, out popped my belly, and for a few days I was clear as clear a mam-to-be. And no one came, and Dad did not care. And then, one afternoon while he slept, in my own room I paced back and forth, and held to the bedpost and exclaimed myself through the pains, and after not very long a labor, I brought forth the being that had swum and somersaulted in me these last months.

I wrapped it and lifted it and held it against my own heat.

It was corded to me still; I crouched over the chamber pot and waited for the followings to follow when they would. I stared at the bab's face in a wondrous terror, as it pinched and frowned and then gasped up a breath. The shock of that, of having a life of its own, woke it, and it opened sticky eyelids. I thought it must be blind; I had never seen eyes of that smoky, stormy blue.

I unwrapped it to see if it was well formed, to count its fingers and toes, and I discovered that I held a boy child. There now, I thought. There's two good men in your life. I covered him quickly, to stop any more of his warmth escaping.

I gasped and rocked there and held him fast against me; if I could have, I would have taken him back in through my bosom, and carried him about there warm and next to my heart. This was not the child I had planned, as separate from me as a badge or a brooch. I wanted to hide him, to keep him from harm; no one yet was aware of him, and I wished that no one ever need be. Must I let Potshead at him, as they'd gone at me? Must Mam pass her judgments on his tiny head, and my sisters gape and prod at him, weigh him in their practiced arms, hope aloud that he would grow up handsomer than I had? Could he not grow entirely himself, unharassed and unshaped by their scorn? How could I watch as they pressed and pummeled him, as he shrank under their blows, and grew extra flesh, as I had, thinking to protect himself but only offering them an easier mark? How could I engineer for him to find his own shape—small, slender and fragile as it might be, or wild and fierce and rude? Already I could feel his purposeful working inside the cloth, his feet bracing against my arm. His face knew nothing and yet he was discovering already how to breathe, how to yawn—and sneeze!—how to surrender to sleep, one hand resting its little warmth against his cheek.

Dad made his noises in the other room, needing me. I woke from the spell of the bab, rose and laid him in the hollow of the bed. I pinned cloths around myself and dropped my skirts to cover my drizzled legs. And I went out to Dad; it was toileting he wanted, and my new body went slowly about the tasks of that. I was glad to care for him, and to have tended him so long; now no one was better equipped than I to serve that bright tiny being in the other room, so helpless, so entirely mine to help.

If it had not been winter, and if I'd not been so ugly and friendless, I would not have been able to keep the bab hidden. But no one visited, except Mam once or twice, to fetch more sewing things and to leave me laundry that she could not manage up at Grassy's in such volume. She only cared whether Dad was clean and quiet and taking food, and the house in good order; whatever else I did was my own business. And my boy, while Mam visited, was whisper-quiet, or the squeak he uttered was straightaway followed by a cat's outside the window, and my secret stayed close.

My son did not flourish, though. I could not think where the milk went in him. I fed and fed him and he took and took of me, but the work of breathing, and of filling breech-cloths and of grasping the air and his own face and my finger, seemed to consume all that he drained from me, and leave none for growing. He slept well, he cried little, he grew to see me and to smile and make movements of joy when I came to him. He learned to lift his head on his narrow stalk of a neck, and catch my eye and laugh at my congratulations. I bathed and wrapped and carried him about and sang to him; I encouraged his every little move or murmur. But he stayed small. First he shrank a little, then he grew back to what he had been at his birth, but he did not grow much beyond that. He would be round-bellied with milk when I put him down to sleep, and slender as ever when next I picked him up.

One day I dared the hill myself, leaving my boy sleeping milk-sodden in the house, and Dad, the other great bab, full of dinner in the next room. I visited both sisters, and neither was pleased to see me, and Mam bristled when I walked into Bee's.

"You have shrunk to nothing, girl! Have you forgotten how to cook? I hope your dad's in better flesh, or I'll have something to say, I will."

I saw both babs, Bee's girl and Grassy's boy. Great pale lumps they were, flushing with rage and distress. Their hands could tear your ear off, or your lip, or whatever they took a hold of, they were so strong. But mostly their *weight* impressed me; my arms ached after only a few minutes holding them.

I tottered and slithered back down the hill, my ears ringing with the racket of those houses, the older children fighting to be heard and the sisters and Mam hectoring and the cries of those two monstrous babs.

I went past sleeping Dad to my room. My little one lay there small and saintly, with his ghost of black hair on his pale brow, mauve shadows painted around his eyes with the kindest and most delicate brush. He was *nothing* on the bed compared to the babs I had just seen and held. Even awake, even laughing to see me, he was not half as alive as they, and he was not half their size.

"Fairy child!" I crouched beside the bed, and watched him sleep. Everything about him was delicate, and very nearly transparent, where Gladys and—what was his name?—Horace, where Gladys and Horace had been solid as clay. Like cream forced into sausage skins, they were. My boy was finely made, far and away finer than them. I stood and picked him up, and sat with him on the bed, searching his lax lovely face, the creases of his tiny mauve hands. He was fine, and foreign, and he did not belong here. I held him close, not crushing, not waking him, letting him sleep, and I suffered. I had never felt such feelings before. I would do anything for him; I would do anything. Anything that was asked of me, that would increase his happiness or health, I would do, and willingly. So I told myself, rocking him, the winter sky white at the window.

The spring thaw began. Mam stayed away uphill. My little one—I called him Little Prince, and sometimes Ean, hardly a name at all, not much more than a smear of sound—grew older, but no larger, and now he seemed to be in pain, squirming and struggling in his wrappings. He began to cry, not lustily like Horace and babs of that make, but softly, as if each bleat were forced out and he were apologizing for this little noise he made.

Some nights I was sure people in other houses must hear him

crying, though his voice was so soft. I took him out and away, and round about the cold country we would go, the sog of it and the snow patches, the black earth splashed with the white of the moon, the sea turning in its sleep. Always by the time I reached Crescent Corner he was stiller, and one night as I walked back and forth with him at peace in my arms, on the very rocks where we had made him that spring night, I wondered if there were a way to take something of the Crescent back with us to the house, to put by him, to ease him when we could not come here.

And my gaze fell to the weed that straggled from the fresh-piled tide wrack. The kelps and dabberlocks lolled like shining tongues on the rock. Perhaps that strappier stuff would do, or the egg wrack higher up, with its bubbles? Then there was that other kind, harder to see in the stark dim light, like furred string, finer than the others. I laid the bundle of sleep that was my little prince in a hollow in the rock and unraveled some weed clots and tangles, some long lengths. And I began a loop-and-looping, which, when I turned after a certain length and went back along the loops, pulling more weed through and through them, became one edge of a small blanket.

Before too long my fingers tired of being the wrong instruments for this task, and I cast up and down and found the perfect bone of some fish or seabird, with a broken-off end making it a hook, which I smoothed on the rock so it would not catch in the weed. I collected more makings, and I sat there piled about with them, taking here the fine-furred weed that sparkled wet under the moon, and now and then a strand of bubbles, and back and forth, back and forth, I knitted and knotted my son's peacefulness up out of the night and the sea-stuff. When I had finished a perfect square of blanket I covered my bab with it, and wrapped him around and gathered him up, and walked wearily home through the beginning dawn.

The seaweed blanket achieved its end, for a time, but as it dried, it soothed Ean less—though I could revive it, I found, by sprinkling it with fresh seawater or, even better, by soaking it in a bucket of the same.

But my little one's distress grew, and though I knitted up another blanket, so that one could soak while the other kept him calm, still he began to be never quite comfortable, never quite comforted. He drank and drank from me, all my milk and more. I was worse than slender now; women stopped me in the street to ask what ailed me, to scold me for not eating. And still the little prince of my life would not grow, but only slept or lay awake listless, making his small speaking-sounds, as if remarking, low and constantly, how this was not his world, however hard he might labor to exist here.

I could see all too clearly what I must do. Deep in my deeps I felt the dread of it, the knowledge I fought against with my soaking of blankets, my wringing of breech-cloths, my hours of feeding him. I knew we could not go on this way.

Finally it came time to do the impossible. Mam had come by that afternoon, throwing about orders for me to begin spring cleaning. The only door she had not flung open was mine; if she had, she would have seen the little prince in a nest of damp weed on my bed, the clean breech-cloths beside him where I'd pitched them, having snatched them from the fireside when I heard Mam greet Pixie Snaylor outside.

Spring was coming. If I did not act, others would have to

know of this bab; Mam would have to know, and my sisters, and the town. Ean had lain unhappy for weeks, his little face creased with pain. His body would not strengthen itself by moving anymore, would not lift its own head; he only lay close, his miniature arm around my neck, only lay still, dreaming of better places, his tiny nostrils breathing the sour air off the seaweed around him.

Night fell and the full moon rose. I unfastened my crossed bands, rolled them up and pocketed them. I picked my boy up, and I wrapped him close, and I took him down through the teeming night to Crescent Corner. Only a few seals greeted me as I came down the cliff path, but more bobbed out in the water, their heads like shawled women's.

I knelt with Ean, unwrapped him and kissed him. Fresh weed I took from the lip of the sea, fine as lace. I bound this round him as he gasped, around his tiny goosefleshing chest that would not breathe enough, that would not broaden and fatten like my niece's and nephew's. Two *X*'s I made on him, front and back, to make sure he always fled witches and men, to keep him safely in the sea.

I kissed him again, and then I wrapped him head to toe in clean breech-cloths like a shroud; he moved inside them, inside his sleep. Around the cloths I wrapped a weed-blanket, freshly wetted. I sang all the while, one of the odd-tuned lullabies I had made for him without intending—it had come up out of me, as they did, one long winter night or day, just for this little one and no other. The song and the sea-sound came together; the seals waited and watched, bobbing. I sang and I sang, and I tied him into the blanket. And as I tied, the leaves of the weed clung and clamped to the white cloths underneath, and the woven stalks sank in; my singing and my weaving and the seal-gaze and the moon and water all worked together to combine the weed, the cloth and the bab. Magic rose from the rocks and the sea like locusts from a summer crop; power welled up in me like tears, and was held in check as tears must be held, for this business must be done right. I must make of myself a pure channel for the magic to tumble along at its right pace, in its right depth exactly.

When my boy was quite sewn away, down I carried him—already he was heavier—to the narrow curve of sand that showed here at the lowest tide. The seals had nosed a little closer through the water; I sat and took off my shoes and hailed them: "Are you ready, beautiful women, to take charge of my Ean?" I knotted up my skirt, lifted the bundle, waded out.

I laid him on the wavelets, held him there awhile, unable to move for fear of what I was about to do. I glanced up from my armful, the sea rocking cold about my knees, lapping at one elbow and one hand. The seal-mothers were still some yards off, but I could hear their breath, and I could smell it; I could see their whiskers bristling; I could feel their attention to my song and my activities, like cords stretched tight between us, heavy with sea-water, drenched with starlight.

I gave Ean a little push toward them. I let him go, and he sank, and I could not see him below, only water-shine. In a panic, I bent and wet the front of my dress, reaching down. I pushed him again, and he was smoother, and at once livelier. At my finger-tips moved all the vigor I had longed for him to show while he lived with me. This heartened me to strike up my song again. Ean wriggled; he sprang away from me; two of the seal-women dived to meet him. I straightened and stepped back, my cold wet hands to my mouth. I imagined their meeting underwater, the two large beings and the one tiny.

I backed from the wavelets, watching. The water busied as they brought my son into the group of them. His round head bobbed up among their larger ones, and his sleek side shone as he threw himself over in the water in a game, to their amusement. He broke my heart with his celebrating—how little he needed me, how perfectly happy he was now, as he had not been before, in my house, at my breast! I was glad of his gladness, and that he would be cared for, but how would I live without him, the little prince who had ruled my days and nights?

Empty-handed, empty-armed, I watched my son play among his new mams and be taken away. It was heavy toil to watch, the heaviest I had ever done, yet I felt I had to stay and see all there was to see. He grew littler and littler, leaping among them, till he was no more than water-gleams on the darkness. They too shrank, until they were only mistakes of my eyes among the waves. Then I crouched and hugged my bare knees, and laid my face on them, and I was incapable, for a long while. All the years to come crowded into that time, and I lived them, long and bitter and empty of him. The rightness of what I had done, and the wrongness both, they tore at me, and repaired me, and tore again, and neither of them was bearable. I did not know how I would ever lift myself from that crescent of sand and that water's edge, and make my cold way home.

I spent a wretched spring. I did not go down to the Crescent; I did not want to recognize my son among the young and to remember that I had had him, that I held him no longer, that I never would again.

I cared for Dad; Mam seemed to despise him now, and did very little for him. When he slept, though, and I had got the house more or less in order, I went to my bed and hid away in sleep, for to be awake and unoccupied was to be filled with a leaden and unending sorrow.

"At *this* time of the day!" Mam cried, throwing open the door to my room one afternoon. "What kind of lazy lump lies abed midafternoon?"

"A tired one," I said.

"Tired? What have you got to be tired for? Come up to Grassy's and Horace breaking through a new tooth and you will know what tired is. Your bab's the peacefullest of all this lot, and the least bother. You should be ashamed!"

She could not embarrass me out of bed, though; I was too sunk in mourning. I hardly knew which I missed worse, my son or the solitude in which I'd enjoyed and suffered with him. I hid my head under shawl and bedclothes, and readied my sticklike arms for if she should try to drag me out bodily, as she had done before.

Instead she only stood closer. "Are you dying of something? Are you ill?"

"Perhaps I am," I said dully. "Perhaps this is what dying is."

And that struck us silent. Quite cheered, I was, at the thought of an end to my suffering, and I closed my eyes ready to welcome it. From Mam's breathing I could tell that she gazed on me less happily. Perhaps she wondered how her world would be without me, how much work she would have to take on.

Summer rose to its peak, and fell away, and still I did not die. Indeed, I found myself able to sit in the sun against the laundry wall for longer and longer each day, without too great a pain descending on me. The time came in the autumn when, unbandaging myself, I knew that all the seals had left Crescent Corner on their great migration. I washed, and tied the bands on again, and stood a long while staring at nothing. Next day, midafternoon, I escaped the house and walked a little, out into the town, unpropelled by any particular errand.

"Look at you," said Moll Granger. "Hardly more than a bundle of sticks."

I gave her a wan smile and kept walking, so as not to be scolded again, or questioned, or given recipes for sustaining foods.

I was leaning over the sea-rail, lost in the sight of the sea, which seemed to have grown wider, and greener, and more mysterious in my absence, when a child's voice piped behind me: "Oh, look, Mam; she's not fat anymore!"

It would have been wise to pretend I had not heard, but I seemed to have forgotten whatever wisdom I'd once had, and I turned to see Mattie Kimes, her hand out toward her son, who had paused in his running to stare at me. "Come, Donald!"

"Does that mean she's not a witch anymore?" said the little boy, gazing at me as if unaware that I had ears or feelings.

"Oh, Donald, you daft one. What a thing to say!" She went to him and seized his arm, all but pulling him off his feet. At the same time, her face fired up with blushing, she sent me a terrible smile, mortally embarrassed, begging me to ignore him.

"But you *said*—"

She snatched him up, so violently that he cried out, but it did not stop him.

"You *said* you could tell she was a seal-witch, because she was fat like a—"

Mattie cut him off with a hand over his mouth, swung him around out of my sight, strode away.

As if determined to hurt myself, I glanced about, at two small girls smirking at me on Trumbells' step, at the curtain whisking across Havemeyer's upper window, at a woman scurrying away along the seafront, both hands to her mouth, in search of someone to tell what Donald Kimes had just said—Fisher's wife, perhaps, for the tale would travel fastest that way.

I strode off, myself, not caring where I went, deciding no more than to move myself on from that place and moment. By the time I was able to see anything but Donald's bright face or Mattie's red one, to hear anything other than the little boy's sharp, innocent voice, I was well out on the field road.

Along to Crescent Corner I went, empty though it was of seals, and down the cliff path. I loosened the bands as I stepped out onto the flat rocks, and I searched the sea around, but no seals came up to me, none came out; only the usual wings beat about me, the wings of the earth, the wind of them. I paced about, wishing that wind would take me up and away. I unlaced my boots and kicked them off, hoping to make myself lighter for the rescuing.

No scorch or smudge showed on the rock where I had lit my fire last spring; no special power blazed up where I had lain and loved with the nameless seal-man. I had been such a fool in my momentary bliss, thinking that things would change for me! All I had known since then was grief; to pay for that night's pleasure, my heart had been cut out and thrown into the sea, to be grieved after forever. I had thought myself all-powerful, above caring what others thought in this town, but look at me now, shrunken, miserable and stinging at an insult from a child's lips, parroting his mother—parroting, perhaps, the whole town. I was not above caring; I was not above longing for relief from this unending shame, from this relentless loneliness.

My rage grew cold, and I sat to the low shelf of rock above the fire site. I could not stay still; I reached out and plucked tiny black periwinkles from the damp rock seams around me, and began to lay them in a design. If I'd been crossed, this would have been only idle play, but with earth-breath flowing up into my foot-soles, out from my shoulders like wings, it took on a different force; each little shelled animal I laid down in a line or curve or corner set a knot in the rock beneath, from which trailed a trembling strand in the upflow. This knot and strand remained even when the snail wobbled away; it was as if I burned this design into the rock, and the smoke of the burning trailed forever into the air above.

I do not know how long it took; as I placed and straightened, the sea-sound washed away my sense of time and care of time. There was only care of placement, a fierce intention to make this shape rightly.

When I was done, there lay outlined—in parts with the black shells, in other parts only with the knots and filaments they had left—a roundheaded, faceless figure. She had arms but no hands; her two round breasts each bore a periwinkle nipple; her legs came together, then separated, not into feet, but into two lobes of a fishlike tail. This blunt personage regarded me, and I her, while one by one the periwinkles crept off, leaving her burnt to the rock, burning into the wind. I turned to face the sea, to feel the real breeze blow through the up-pouring mysterious one; I watched the sun coast slowly down and tip-touch the horizon. The periwinkle girl held firm to the rock behind me, streaming upward, changing everything.

Dad died not two weeks later, his lungs filling up and drowning him. With the first winter storms Mam sickened too, beginning with her stomach. Then her mind began to go. She took to her bed as if she never intended rising again. Both events brought with them a great deal of quarrelsome sister business. Bee and Lorel and Grassy Ella felt free to descend on me almost every day, with or without an armful of bab and a trailing of older children. They scolded me and their eyes went everywhere, looking for new evidence of neglect and carelessness that they could tell to each other. Give them a funeral and they blew in like thunderclouds—the noise of them! The combined ill will! I had forgotten how they took over a house, how they took over my mind. With their pecking and remonstrations, my own will disappeared, and I went about dully, obeying this one's commands, that one's counter-orders. I drudged through the winter, and as I shivered through washing myself those half-frozen mornings, joylessly I registered the return of the seals to Crescent Cove as spring approached. I all but forgot what I had done there, the lure I had left in the rock.

It was after a thorough nitpicking by Bee, as she swept out the door into the well-puddled slush, that Arthur Scupper's children came running up the street, crying: "Come to Fisher's! They've found a mermaid! Come and look!"

Bee stood out from the step to stop them. "A mermaid? But the boats did not go out today!"

"She walked into town, with not a stitch on!" cried Hex Scupper. He ran on, then called back over his shoulder, "Up from Crescent Corner!"

"A mermaid!" Bee exclaimed after them.

I hid the shaking of my hands in my apron. "What can they mean? Perhaps it is only some kind of malformed fish."

"A fish that walked into town?"

"Let us go and see, then."

I went to Mam's doorway, pulling on my coat. "What're *you* want?" she said. "Fetch that daughter of mine."

"I am off down Fisher's a moment, to see a sea-girl," I said. "I will lock you in, just in case you take a mind to follow me."

She glared and did not know me still—her knowing had come and gone a great deal lately. I could talk nonsense to her, or insult her outright, and she would forget a moment after.

I locked the door and Bee and I set off for Fisher's, falling in with a crowd of others who spilled from their doors, donning coats and pulling on shawls. I was glad of Bee, for she could take care of the talking—which she did, for along with all the other betrothed or married women, she had a great deal of anxiety to spill out, about this mermaid. I went quietly among them, nodding at what they said and making the right faces so as not to be noticed.

We met Doris Shingle, coming up. "Aye, she's fair," she said. "Fair strange, you ask me. Foreign-looking—as you'd expect, I suppose, for she's not of this country."

"Has she seaweed hair?" joked Abby Staines. "Has she sucker-fingers like an octopus?"

"None of that," said Doris. "Her sea-ness is quite gone. She's fingers like you or me, only finer. And her hair is finer too, and as straight as if you took and ironed it."

Pensive men we met too, who would not be drawn so much. Their silence did nothing to improve the wives' tempers.

Then we were at Fisher's. They had put the sea-girl in his back room there; two doors led to it from the main store, and the whole town was filing in one and out the other very slowly. Those coming out were some of them eager to tell us everything we were about to see; others sidled away, or went head down, and would not be pressed. The ones that did speak each had a different story—she was fair enough, she was ugly, she was the fairest thing ever made; her hair was like silk cloth, like rats' tails, like a horse's floppy mane; she was sulky, she smiled like an angel, she was the most radiant creature; she had swum from Spain, she was clearly of the sea, she had nothing about her of the underwater. I hardly knew what to expect when finally I pushed and shuffled into the back room with the others.

Fisher's women had got the poor thing into a dress, but it did not fit her well; its puffed sleeves sat sadly out from her shoulders, and her long shins dangled below the hem, with the fine small bare feet that looked as if they would not hold anything up of substance. In the window light her skin had a greenish cast, and the dress was a particular yellow that set it off badly.

"She looks *ill*," Hatty Marchant whispered to someone, behind my shoulder.

I was crowded along by those eager to enter, everyone breathing and murmuring. Mag Fisher was seated by the girl, looking about fiercely.

"Has she a voice like us?" someone ventured at last from behind me.

"I've a voice," said the sea-girl, and I heard that clear enough. Her voice was low, and of course lovely, and held an accent of some kind, I thought. I wanted immediately to hear it again, to make sure.

"Will she be staying?"

"That's enough of questions," snapped Mag. "I've answered everything over and over. Go and ask those who already know. I won't have the girl badgered."

"We're not badgering *her*, Mag. We're badgering *you*." A wicked titter ran among us.

This was how it would be, then: the women pretending this was everyday, that she was not much of a girl to look at, while her enchantment went to work upon the men. I could see it, their eyes fixing and following the length of her hair, of her limbs, of her slimness under the awful dress, their lips parting. I began to see the size of what I'd accomplished that evening at the Crescent. What chance did these men have against my faceless, heartless periwinkle girl? Poor defenseless fools. And poor wives and mothers! They were no more than encumbrances now. They could titter and screech and weep as much as they liked, in the weeks and months to come. They would not be paid any mind.

Was she beautiful, the sea-maid? *Fair strange*, Doris had said, and I thought that was a fine assessment. I had seen her face before, of course, or very like it: the portrait in Strangleholds' attic, the Spanish dancers on my brother's postcard. Their hair, like hers, was neat dark wings either side of their faces; their eyebrows too were drawn clear-edged against skin that bore not a freckle or a fleck. This girl's eyes, like those others', were wide and dark; her hands were long, the fingers slender and longer than the palms. Her mouth was like my own, only beautiful; looking upon it I could see why whoever-it-was had asked could it speak, for it seemed to be made only for people to admire, for ornament: curve-edged, bruise-colored, plump, heavy. I looked about me at the small mouths, hardly lipped at all, spattered with freckles, little pinch slots into the women's worried, or disagreeable, or frankly afraid faces. Any man seeing this maiden's lips would want to lay kisses on them; he would want to roll in the cushions of those lips, swim the depths of those eyes, run his hands down the long foreign lengths of this girl. Oh, I thought, women of Rollrock, you are *nothing* now.

Next morning there came a knock on the door.

"Who is it? Who is it? Are they here already?" Mam cried

weakly. Lately she had been trapped in memories of her wedding day, terrified that she was running late for the service. Her anxiety had grown much worse since she stopped being able to raise herself from her bed.

"Oh, you've plenty of time, Mam," I said as I passed her door, hurrying through from the back. She was beyond being explained to, brought forward into the present; it was easier to talk to her in the language of her delusions.

I opened the door. It was not, as I had feared, one of my spouting sisters, or a child of theirs come to ask favors. Able Marten stood there, his coat flapping in the spring breeze, his hair out sideways, loops and locks of it, crimson almost, it was so dark with grease. Just the sort of low fellow I'd thought would walk into my trap.

"What are you up to, Able?" He had been one of the teases, up at the schoolhouse. He had poked my belly once with his grubby finger: *Here's a nice fat chicken*, he'd said. *Plenty of flesh on this one*.

But now he was tall and a young man. "I've a word with you?"

I let him in, waved him toward the fire. He perched himself on Dad's sunken chair. It was a startling thing, to have a live young man in the house.

Cautiously I sat opposite. He leaned forward at me. "You go down Fisher's yesterday and see that mere-girl?"

"I did, as did everyone."

"I went down again this morning. A lot of us went down, for another look at her."

Good. They were well and truly fascinated, then. "And she had slept well, in her land-bed?"

"She had not," said Able. "She had got out, and taken her coat, that Fishers had retrieved, from the cupboard where they hid it—she bled all over, fighting her way in to find it. She took herself back to the sea, and Fishers all sleeping so soundly above, you'd have thought they had seven pints apiece in them, even the women."

I was only relieved that his sneering was for Fishers, not for me. "That was careless of them," I said gently.

"Very careless," said Able self-righteously.

"So now she is gone, and we can all go back to living as we lived before yesterday."

"Like heck we can." He would have uttered worse than *heck*, had he not wanted a favor of me.

I tipped my head and refrained from smiling. "Well, *I* can. What is wrong with you?" Able held my eyes a long glance, but I made sure they told him nothing. "Come along, Able. You have never come uptown to gossip with Misskaella Prout before. What is it you're after?" I wanted to see him in discomfort, begging.

"Well." He was not embarrassed at all, the insolent thing. "People say you have the gift. I wondered if you could fetch me a seal." And when I did not answer, he added, "A woman *out* of a seal, I mean, like that one yesterday."

"I know what you mean."

"Can you do that?"

I looked into my hands, still a little earthy as they were from pulling radishes. So different, this was, this bald question, from the nightful of sea-shush and magic, and the bull seal hefting himself up the rock.

"Because if you can't, I'm wasting my time." And he scraped his feet forward and took hold of the armrest to push himself to standing.

I let him start on that bluff, then said, "Why would I?"

"What do you mean?" He plumped himself down again.

"People are uneasy enough with me—if I start bringing up sea-wives, they'll take against me good and proper."

"It could be secret."

"Could it?"

"I could tell a tale. I could say she came up like this first one, by herself."

I gave a little snort, examined my earth-smeared apron. "And once you have her, what then?"

"What then? Why, I'll be happy then. And you'll be well paid."

"Oh, and that'll be all, will it? No other men will want a pretty, when you start parading yours about the town?"

"They've got the girls here, no? They don't need one. I am driven to this; none of these bitches wants me."

"None?" I said. "I don't recall your ever asking me."

That was amusing, to watch him wake to me, then blush, then look about at everything else. "Listen," I said, full of scorn. "Every lad in town is spelled stupid by that maid. That's a fairy lass you're talking of there, Able; you see her, you want her, and one of our girls hasn't a chance against her."

He grinned. "That's part of the charm of it," he said. "That other lads should want her, and only have our island girls to choose from. It'll send them mad."

"And where do you think they will come in their madness? Right where you have come in yours: up to my door."

"This is not madness; this is a well-conjured scheme. Listen." And he mentioned a sum of money.

"Why, that's paltry!"

But he raised his hand. "I know. I would give you more up front, but I will need the rest to set up our house and to pay the parson to wed us."

"Parson Rightley? He'd as soon marry you to that hearthstone there as to seal-kind. You will have to go abroad, Able, for the formalizing of it."

"Curse it, yes I will." He thought awhile, then mentioned half of the previous sum. "But," he said, waving aside my laughter, and he promised me this and this of his earnings in the two years coming.

The effect within me as he laid out these terms was a great relaxing, of a tension I had not even known I was suffering. It was one thing not to want a husband, I realized; it was quite another not to *need* one for the roof over your head, for your meat and bread, for the shoes on your feet and the coat on your back.

"And this you would pay me," I said, keeping my voice hard, "even should she escape you, find her coat and run off back to the sea? Or sicken to a burden, like my mam there, or my dad before her? Or die on you, childbirthing or otherwise? Or catch some land-disease that she cannot fight off? The effort is the same for me, whether she stays or goes, Able. And you might gain not very much, if you don't take care. But I cannot have your caretaking, or luck, or acts of God's hands, be a part of the bargain. I can only extract the girl into your keeping. You undertake, do you, to pay me the same, good luck following or poor?"

"Every penny," he said, "I promise."

He put out his hand, the way men do to make a bargain.

I looked at it. "I don't know, Able," I said. "Give me a day and a night to sit with this, with the gains and the losses to me. It is no small thing."

He pulled back his hand, annoyed. "How could you be *worse* off?"

I met his contemptuous eye. "Do you want this, Able?"

He looked aside and clicked his tongue.

"If you want it, you'll perhaps think twice before insulting the person who can get it for you."

He cleared his throat, watched the floor between his boots.

"Come back tomorrow. I'll tell you yea or nay."

And I showed him out, my face serious, my heart as light as a floating feather.

In the night, though, Mam slipped her moorings worse, going from wedding day terrors to a full fight against all her imaginings. Such a strength came on her, most of the night I spent pinning her down, dodging her fists and feet and trying to calm her; in the end I had to tether her to the bed, and even then I could not bring myself to leave her to find some sleep myself, for fear she would struggle free.

Morning rescued me from that nightmare at last, and I sent for a sister and for the Widow Threading for one of her sedative teas. Through the fuss of all that I saw Able loitering in our lane, unwilling to come knocking while others visited. I sent Lorel off, to go and tell my predicament and our mother's to Grassy and Bee, and once she had gone out the lane end I gave Able a sharp look and he toddled across to me most eagerly.

"I will do it," I said, "what you asked for. But my mam's beginning her dying now, and you must wait until she's gone, for I won't have the strength."

"Will she be long about it?" he said.

"She might go tomorrow, or fight on another month yet, is what the widow said. Can you keep yourself in your trousers that long?"

That sent him away blushing.

Two weeks more Mam dragged on. From that night until the very end she fought away food, fought away sleep, struck out at any person who came near her, snarled and bellowed. And she nearly sent me mad along with herself; in my exhaustion and fear of her, I reached a point where I could barely remember a more human Mam, a woman with sense behind her eyes, and from whose mouth came recognizable words. One night in her struggles she pulled her shoulder bone right from its socket, though, and the pain of that injury tamed her somewhat. She shrank and weakened quickly then, snarling less and weeping more, and finally one dawn I woke from where I had collapsed asleep with my head on my arms on her bed, and found her dead before me. I watched her a long time, waiting to feel something more than the enormous relief of her leaving; then I rose and sent for my sisters.

As soon as Bee arrived, I claimed the need for fresh air, and set out to Crescent Corner. There they all were, sleek soggy mams and furred sprightly babs, carpeting the rock and all but covering what little sand there was. Down the cliff path I went, and hurried across the rocks to the blunt sea-maiden I had drawn. I loosened my bands so that I should see her clearer, and the seals lifted and cried to me. Each dot of her outline still streamed with invisible smoke. But her work was done, with the coming and departure of the mere-girl; all further transactions with the seals I wanted to conduct myself. I bent and extinguished her, dot by dot. It was like crushing out small coals with my fingertips and knuckles. She had not been very finely worked, but still I cursed the number of burns I must sustain to erase her. Clumsily I reknotted the bands at my shoulder, and walked home shaking both hands to ease the pains I had given myself unmaking the spell.

We buried her. My sisters agreed that I should have the use of the house, which was only fair, seeing as I had been nursemaid of both our mam and dad, and otherwise one of their child-crowded houses would have to take me in. But they took their time deciding, holding long and pleasurable discussions in my hearing about what should be done should I ever marry, or should Billy return with a wife to settle. The most they would promise me was that I could live there as long as these things did not happen. If either did, they said, all this talking would have to be done over again. Perhaps I could be maid to Billy and his foreign wife that they had invented? Perhaps we could pay the sisters rent, me and my unimaginable husband? I said not a word; I would not give these bargainings energy by protesting. Whenever they asked me my opinion, I would say, "You work it out among you. You decide what you think is fair. I'll not live with any of you resenting this decision." For how could I *care*, even, with my fortune staring at me from over their shoulders, in the form of Able and whoever else would traipse along behind him? Let them go on; let them have one last boss and blurting-out of righteousness, before their world went to splinters. I would end up best off of them, though they talked of me now as their burden, to be shared out among them, and shrugged off if they could.

We waited a few weeks more for the moon to come to the full.

Able brought clothing and some boots for the girl, and a bulge in his coat pocket that must be my money. We went early, so as he could carry her straight off on the Cordlin boat that morning, and marry her respectably as soon as he could.

I was entirely prepared, starved but for bread and teas and only the tiniest meat these last three days. *You're looking well,* Bee had said suspiciously the day before when she had met me unexpectedly down the town, so anticipation of the magic must have gone to my skin and hair and carriage too; I could not keep it a secret. Even a man or two had glanced at me, taken aback, this last day or so. What was it about me, I could see them wondering, that I was not so ignorable as usual, not so repellent?

I was like a banked-up fire. I was glad of the bands crossing my chest, containing what was in me.

I met Able at Lawson's stile, so we should not be seen together and commented on. We walked out unspeaking, not at all the way any other lad walks out with a girl of Potshead town. Soon we stood at the top of the cliff at the Crescent, looking down on the many silken bodies lying ashore like poor-piled bolsters, sandbags, jelly bags.

"Which one of these, then, is your wife?" I laughed, hands on my hips. Someone flapped her flippers below; some seal bab croaked and yowped after his mam, and the mother crooned back, somewhere between dog- and person-sound.

"Does it matter?" he said. "Aren't they all equal of beauty inside that lard?"

"I don't know," I said, and laughed again. "But beautiful or ugly as a sow's backside, you are only getting the one. If she ends up the Misskaella of seals, that is your trouble, and the price remains the same."

"There's worse than you," he said kindly, because he was feeling kind toward everything this day.

"There is, and worse we might see. Be prepared." I had no fears, not really; but I could not, now we were so close, resist testing our bargain yet again, just to watch it hold. Several ways I had begun to spend that money in Able's coat, that the wind was bouncing against his belly. New boots I would have first, not Hardbellow's clumpers that all of Rollrock wore, but something Cordlin crafted, of softer leather and sweeter style.

"Come, then," I said. Now that we were on the point of this, I did not want him turning to straw on me, or bringing to mind some nuisance pronouncement of the parson's. I waved him to the head of the path. "Lead me the way." If he decided at the last chance to run, I wanted to be behind him to block him, slap him, maybe, bring him to his senses—or rather, keep him from *coming* to his senses, for this was not a sensible enterprise. I wanted to keep him dreaming and dazzled. I wanted him foolish and greedy and fixed ahead on his magical wife.

"Which, then?" he said as I ran into the back of him, stepping down onto the sand. "Near or far? Or middle? Which shall I choose for my Ivy?"

"I'm not to know—whatever takes your eye. Pick a healthy one, a nice specimen, a model of its kind. There. Or what about that one?"

"Gad, they stink, don't they? Will I have to train her to the toilet?"

"Have I ever trained one?"

"You might have, for all I know."

"Did you ask Fishers whether they had to clean up any mess of her?"

He made a face. I slapped his arm. "Dolt. As if you'll care, once she rises up naked from her trammelings. Come along now, Able, make your pick. Let's get on."

At last my expecting and gesturing brought him to heel, and he concentrated, walking where he could among the slumped bodies, some of which cared as he passed them, nosing after his smell, fixing him with their dark-wet eyes, others who lay only stunned, sacks of sun warmth, barely more alive than the rocks they lounged on. Off away among the crowd of them, the bull heaved himself up, but it was not our intrusion that bothered him but another bull, rearing from a little gang of them that sulked in the shallows. They closed to duel, clumsy lumps of rage that they were; how could my springtime lover have emerged from such a beast? And little Ean, son of that spring moon, where was he now? Could I have dreamed it all, the birthing and the nursing of him, the knotting-up of his weed-blankets? I wished I had, but I ached all through me at the thought of him, at the sight of his father's ignoring me, busy about his beast-life. I knew all too well it was true.

"This one. This will do." He had chosen one slightly more brown than gray. He put his hand on her to claim her.

"Let me look at her. All of a piece, is she? Neat as new-made, this one. She's a fine choice. Now stay by. I should not want her bonding with me like fresh hatched duckling, if you are not in her waking sights."

I undid the bands. The seals' attention veered toward me like a change in the wind.

"What's all that?" said Able fearfully, eyeing the crowd of them.

"Nothing to worry about." I tangled the seal's gaze with mine. How much surer of myself I felt this time! A hugeness of mind and a benevolence came upon me as I looked for the girl within the beast, and brought the grains or runnels or sparks of her inward. She began to form pale at the center like an almond in its fruit, and the sealness shrank outward to become fruit-flesh, to become coat. I went very carefully, and sought and sought for lights I might have missed in her. Then I raised my hands into a point, summoned my resources, cleared my throat and clove the sealskin top to bottom.

"Come and stand here," I told Able, and I put him where I was. I went to the head, propped it up with my knee and pulled apart the sealskin there.

Able's face blossomed. "Ivy!" he said joyfully, and put his hands out to her. And up she sat, her black hair tumbling, then spreading on the long shaped back of her and into the wind, her bottom as neat as a boy's. She put her long white hands into his befreckled ones, and stood unsteadily on the coat, which was thick and slippery as yet. She stepped off it, onto the safer stone. She coughed; she coughed out words: "What have you done to me?"

I rolled up her skin; it thinned and dried and dulled a little as I went. I was wobbly from the effort of transforming seal to girl, and with relief that she had come out right, that she was whole, that she could speak, that she was fastening to Able—and he to her, cooing and exclaiming.

"Put on these underdrawers," he said to the girl, "and get yourself modest, before someone happens along the cliff and looks down."

"What is *modest,* Able Marten?" she said as she stepped in.

"Why, it is something you will need to learn of smartly."

I bundled and tied the seal-coat; we had agreed, he and I, that I would take and mind it for now, so that his girl could not easily retrieve it, and escape. Now it was no more than a blanket bundle, though not so heavy as that, and smoother, quite different to the touch. Different to the mind too, with all its lights drawn off it, all its seal-life stifled flat. Quickly I tied my bands into crosses again, so that I should not feel so sharply the skin's suffering there at being so reduced, its hopeless straining after the girl who had stepped from it.

Able had the dress on his Ivy now. He sat her on a rock and showed her the shoes, brushing her small feet clean and remarking on their whiteness, their well-madeness, their lack of use. He slipped the shoes on and tied their stiff new laces, explaining all the while.

"They do feel strange," she said politely. "This all feels strange, to be so bound inside, away from the weather."

"Exactly," said Able. "Warm against the weather and the wind. And the shoes, against stones, you know, on the ground, and sharp shells, and thorns should you walk in grassed places."

"Grass?" she said uncertainly, and looked around. "My sisters might swim out without me," she said, her hands in her skirts. "And our king. Then who will protect me?"

"I will protect you, my maid. It will be my role and duty, and my pleasure also, once we're wed. Come, we must walk to the wharf and catch the boat to Cordlin. I have sent ahead a letter to the parson there; the banns are out this long month, and by tonight, we will be man and wife."

This settled her, though it would not have settled me. *Who the gracious are you?* I'd have wanted to know. *And who says I'm to marry you?*

"Ready, Misskaella?" said Able; he couldn't tear his eyes away long enough to grace me with a glance.

Ivy looked at me curiously, but he did not seem to think it necessary to introduce us.

"Let us go, then," said I drily, to show him I was steering this, not he. "Are you content with the young lady, Able?" I reminded him.

"Oh. Yes and yes! Most content, Misskaella. Here."

And there on the shore the moneys crossed, notes with the wind in their edges, coins with their music. And all was transacted, and I put my pocket away. This was how it was done, then, and this was how it would be, each man buying his misery from me, believing it would be his wedded bliss. Now that Able had his Ivy, no Rollrock man would be able to settle for a red-wife. And all those girls who flung their skirts and hair and laughter about, and curled their lip at me or wore their pity so loudly in their eyes and voices, they would know first and freshly the treatment I had always got from men, the scorn, the overlooking, the making-invisible.

I patted my pocket. "Thank you, Able. And the rest whatever happens."

"As agreed. Hold tight to that coating there, though. Who knows her yet, and what she might do?"

So up the cliff path I followed that pair of clasp-handed lovers. Able was alight with pride and satisfaction, the sea-maid learning to manage her feet and skirts as she went, struggling and reliant as he wanted it.

I walked with them to the waterside, as we had also agreed; seeing me there, folk would not ask Able what he was about. So long as no one fetched the parson, Able and his Ivy should be able to put off without hindrance or protest from any man or woman.

But of course, our standing there together would show me for what I was, for what I could do, and had done. Everyone would know, from this day forth, that I was not just Froman and Gussy Prout's daughter, the unmarried one, the one that came out last when there were no looks left for Prout girls. In part I was proud to have made this seal-girl and this bargain on my own, and out of my own powers. But the idea of folk knowing, and judging, and fearing or scorning me—that gave me the chill it always had.

I held tight to the bundle of money under my skirt band, the only consolation I had. The *Fey* put out, the two heads red and black in the window. The little crowd left a space around me and a silence; the men and especially the women cast glances of *What are you?* at me, and *What manner of evil have you wrought?* and *What will you conceive of next, witch-maid?* I stood in the sun and the blow, with the parcel of the sealskin in my arms. *That can only be one thing, that bundle*, they would be thinking. And the boat chugged away.

Bet Winch

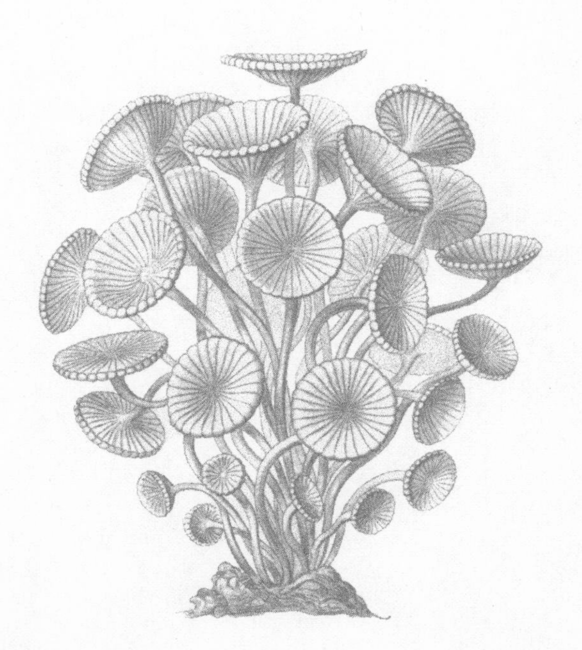

We were about to go to bed when she knocked. Indeed, Geedre was already abed, getting that "beauty sleep" Mam said she needed now. (*You certainly do*, I'd told Geedre. *You need a* lot *of beauty sleep*. Then, while she pinned me down and slapped me, *You ought to be sleeping every hour of the day! Seeing if you can work up some beauty for yourself!*)

Even the knocking was anxious. "That'll be Sophie," I said. "She's been bothering Mam all afternoon."

"Why'd Nase marry her," said Snell, "if he wasn't going to stay home with her?"

"I don't blame him," said Byrne. "Two screaming babs and her twittering."

"Quiet, you boys." Mam came through thin-lipped, opened the door, then stopped the doorway with her own body, hiding Sophie from us. "What is it, Sophie? You can come right in, you know. Don't stand there knocking and making us run to you. You're family now, you know." Which she'd said a hundred times.

But Sophie would never do it; she was too afraid of us, and of Mam the worst. She was afraid of everything. Her wedding day was the only day I saw her happy and settled-seeming.

"Only, is he here? I won't bother you if he's not here."

Snell sat forward and wrung his hands with an anguished look, *just* like Sophie. Byrne snorted and covered his face.

"Of course he's not here," said Mam. "Why would he be, this time of day? He's a wife and two babs." As if Sophie might not have noticed, she was so dim.

"He's not at Wholeman's either."

"Well, that's a blessing. Speaking of which, who's minding them? The babs?"

"Knitty Thomas across the way, just while I look. She's got an ear out."

"Get home, you silly girl. A man doesn't want his wife bleating about after him in the town. If he goes to Wholeman's now, they will chaff him half to death because of you. Go home and don't be an embarrassment."

"Only, he's so late," said Sophie. Snell made a mawkish face, and Byrne rolled around on the floor.

"Of course he is. Why would he want to come home to your miseries? Get home and calm yourself, girl, and prepare to greet him with some cheer for a change. What's that?"

"He wouldn't notice," Sophie said more strongly. "He's been so wrapped up in himself lately. I daresay he's worried about money, as everyone is."

There was a little silence then, before Mam started in again. "Go on home, I tell you. He'll come to you in time. Just getting a breath of air from that house, no doubt. Go on, Sophie."

She all but shut the door in Sophie's face, and then she stood with her back to it, as if she was worried Sophie would push it open and ask again, *Is he here? Is he here?* Snell turned to look at her, and Byrne lifted his face, dewy-eyed and hilarious, from his hands. You can hear when Mam has a thought. She is such a bustler that when she falls still, everything falls still with her and you need to know why.

"What?" said Snell.

"Do you know where he is?" said Byrne.

"Were you *lying* to her?" said Snell.

"Mam?" I said.

But she was off in her own thoughts. Her face went faraway and stony. I was suddenly frightened of her.

Dad came to the hallway door. "Sophie again?"

Mam did not seem to see him.

"That's three nights running," he said.

"Do I not know that." But there was no heat in her words.

"What's he up to?" said Dad—not as if he cared, but as if he might soothe her by speaking what he took to be her mind.

"Has he been borrowing money from you?" she said suddenly, coming out of her calculating.

He took a shocked step back into the hallway. "No! Why would you think that? Why would I give him money and not say?"

"I don't know. Why would you? What was it for?"

"I swear I never. I *swear.*"

Snell and Byrne were all eyes and no laughing now, trying like me to read this.

Dad looked as if he was telling the truth, *sounded* like it, but Mam was making that mouth at him, pulled in at the corners.

She took her coat from the back of the door. Fear jumped up my throat—was she leaving us, the way Frog Davven's mam walked out on them? I was on my feet.

"Where are you off?" said Dad accusingly.

"To fetch that boy and haul him home."

"He's always had friends." Dad stepped out of the hallway again. "He used to go up Fernly's for a session, Fernly with his fiddle and Nase singing. What's wrong if he goes back to that?"

I edged toward the door, looking from one to the other.

Mam put the coat collar up with sharp tugs; she might take her own head off with it. "Nothing. Except he's not *at* Fernly's."

"And you so sure."

"Yes," she said hard at him. "And me so sure." And she was out the door.

"How? He told you?" But she slammed it behind her. He swayed back as if she had struck him.

I leaped for my coat while he was still recoiling.

"She's taken leave of her senses," he said.

I pulled open the door. "I'll bring her back," I said to their three faces, Snell's and Byrne's echoing Dad's on the other side of the room. Then they were gone, and I was out in the night and running.

Mam was already far up the main street. She heard me coming, turned and saw me, made an exasperated movement, hurried on.

I caught up. Her mouth was closed up tight and she stared ahead as if I were not there. I ran-walked along, panting, pulling the coat on, for the cold bit right through my blouse and woolly, my skirt and stockings. I kept up and kept up, and she kept striding along as if she were quite alone, until finally, up by Nickels' place, she said, "You won't like where we're going."

"I don't care," I said.

"You'll care when you see." And she swung right, along Marksman Road.

I followed, afraid already. "I'll not fuss," I said. "I won't get in your way."

"I won't even see you if you do, girl. I'm as wild as that."

The last house reared up, the tallest and finest in the town, and the most frightful. Its gardens lay around it in ponds and rows and mazes of moonlight. The house was mostly dark, but some low windows at the back glowed alive.

When Mam drew up at the gate, I had to stifle a whimper. This was the only moment in which I could choose; I could turn back now or I must go right in with her. But when she was through the gate and on the path, she didn't even check to see if I was following, and that, more than anything—that she might *expect no better* of me than to be such a coward—drove me after her. I closed the gate behind us, just as if we were visiting a person of manners. I followed her up. Some waxy flowers beside the path swayed in the breeze of Mam's passing; they looked as if they ought to have some strong, strange scent, but it was too cold for them to give it up. Then we were mounting the broad steps, with their sweeping balustrades like the welcoming arms of some aunt I didn't want to kiss. Mam lifted the doorknocker, and rapped five times firmly.

I restrained myself from slipping my hand into hers—I was

thirteen, after all. And I had promised not to get in the way. Instead I stood as far to one side as the balustrade would let me. Mam would want to flee, and I must not stand behind her and obstruct her. Or perhaps, if the witch pounced, I could fling myself over into that nicely clipped shrubbery there. I could not believe we were standing on this step. I could not tell what was my heart-thumps and what was the footsteps of Misskaella, coming toward us up the hall of her house.

Her lamp lit the glass in the door; her shadowy figure could have been any harmless person's. The key ground in the lock, but I felt as if it turned in my stomach; soon I would be face to face with that dreadful woman, so ugly and so angry. I had never spoken to her, never even looked her in the eye—I had only ever seen her stalk up the street preceding another cartload of goods and gewgaws from Cordlin. Like the other people watching, I hadn't known whether to fall away in fear or stand and stare in fascination.

Now the latch was lifted, and Misskaella opened the door and shone her lamp on us. Look at her; she was just a person. Perhaps Mam could deal with her as she dealt with any other person, Fisher down the shop, or that craven parson, or Hatty Threading and her ravings in the street.

Sweet-spicy smoke curled thickly from the long-stemmed pipe the witch held, and fumed from her skirts and hair; she must have been sitting in a cloud of it. She was dressed darkly and finely, as she always was; her skirts swung clear of the floor and showed a pair of shiny little black boots, buttons all up them as if they were nailed to her shins. Stout she was, but her dress was tailored to her stoutness; a deal of lacework lay on her bosom to distract the eye from the absence of waist below. Her hands were like a child's, but the nails were better kept than any child's; her hair was piled up and pinned into a soft crown. But for all this she was the witch, and her face was a witch's face, ugly, suspicious, and with a witch's mind behind it, thinking who knew what?

"What is it?" She shone her lamp at me, dismissed me and returned to Mam simmering on her step.

"My name is Nance Winch. I'm wondering if you've had any dealings with my son Naseby."

"Why would I have?" She looked Mam up and down as if any children of hers must be well beneath contempt.

"He has gone missing from his wife and children, three nights running, at full moon. That sounds like your work."

"Ah, *sounds* like it. Which is Naseby Winch?"

"Very tall," said Mam. "Thin. His hair is nearly golden."

Misskaella thought on that, but only to tease us, I felt. She touched her chin with two fingers of her pipe hand. "So many come, you see. It is not easy for me to keep account of them all."

"Oh, I'm sure you never forget to take their money." Mam looked pointedly up at the moldings over the doorway, and at the lace bosom-trimmings. "Just think—is he one of the ones who's paid you, or one who still owes half his family's livelihood for the favor you've done him?"

As Mam flung all this, the witch's face, far from reddening and enraging as I'd feared, broke open, open and opener, into a kind of pleasure. She leaned against the doorpost, took a pull of her pipe, swung the lamp a little. "Let me consider now. Your golden-haired boy, tall, slim, wife and children—though of course he wouldn't mention those to *me*, for I might turn out to have scruples." The smoke popped and puffed out with her words and then rose free and hovered over her forehead. "Hmm," she said, and smoke streamed from her nostrils. "I cannot say, really, that I remember a golden Naseby. No, I really cannot say."

"Can you say"—Mam leaned closer into the lamplight—"that without doubt you do *not* remember him?" I would have found her dangerous in that stance, in that light.

But the witch didn't. She began a laugh, which then caused her to cough. She finished the cough smiling. "You know? I cannot exactly *not* remember him, either. But this is a small town, Missus Winch, Naseby's mother," she said, as if she found the names delicious. "I would have seen him about the place, without a doubt. Only I can just not quite put my finger on whether he has appeared on this step as you and"—she waved a smoky hand toward me—"your daughter?"

"My daughter." I saw Mam try to be rude and withhold my name, but Misskaella looked so expectant there, perched curious above her neat boots like a fat thrush on a fence post. "Bet. Elizabeth."

"Just the way you and *Elizabeth* Winch here have appeared. Or perhaps he was less polite, coming to the back door, if he felt he had something to hide? I cannot recall. I just . . . cannot . . ." And she grasped after the memory with her few free fingers in the smoke.

"And such a *pretty* daughter, Nance," she said over Mam's next question. She cast me a dark look, as if prettiness were something regrettable. She might well reach out the doorway, I thought, and peel off my prettiness like a mask.

She turned back to Mam, spoke very softly, almost in a whisper. "Just as you were pretty yourself, when you married . . . Who is your good man?"

Again I could tell that Mam did not want to give her the name. "Odger."

"Odger, of course. Odger Winch," she said in a breathy rush, and I thought of my old dad, his face after Mam slammed the door, and I felt for his defenselessness, and Naseby's and Snell's and Byrne's—and even Mam's standing there, with the witch extracting humiliation after tiny humiliation from her, the pair of us at her mercy in the night, her whole house behind her, her whole beautiful garden around, calculated, laid out, paid for. "Do give my regards to Mister Winch." She rocked as if that idea were so funny that it *hurt*. She might be a little drunk, I thought.

Mam turned to me. "Come, Bet." She started down the steps.

Misskaella pushed herself off the doorpost, raised the lamp and made a grotesque face of wounded innocence at me. I swung away from the insult and started after Mam.

"Good night, Nance Winch! Good night, Elizabeth!" There were many humiliating notes in that farewell, but the overriding one was of great satisfaction.

By the time I had closed the gate—Misskaella still at her door, rocking, smoking, watching, very possibly laughing—Mam was well along the street. I had to run to catch her. "Where are you going now?" I muttered as we crossed the top of the main way.

"Only out of sight of her, to collect myself. Don't look back."

But I already had. The witch bowed this way and that in the lamplit doorway.

Out we went along the top road. At the first stile, Mam sat, head bent.

We caught our breath. When we were recovered, still she sat and thought.

"You really think Naseby would go to her?" I ventured to ask.

"We should have left. The minute Able Marten bought his Ivy, we should have gone as the Summerses did."

"But perhaps he is just like Dad said, musicking. How can you know?"

"Money, is how I can know. Worrying about money. Sophie is worrying, Odge is making noise. But Floss Granger was down at Fisher's this morning, ordering up a pair of new shoes for herself. *Something a bit pretty,* she says over that book of Fisher's. Floss Granger wears out shoes down to her *foot bones* if the fishing is poor. And those Mace daughters, all of them in new dresses. So the fishing is fine but Naseby's keeping money from Sophie, and Odge is helping him, in whatever enterprise. What else could it be?"

"A musical instrument?" I said. "A fiddle, like Fernly's. Or a cow? He's talked about farming before. A piece of land to till?"

"I'd know. He'd tell me. He'd not be so secretive. He's pulled the wool somehow over your father's eyes. But where is he right now?"

"He might be home by now, sitting at his own table with Sophie."

"Some old barn or shed, out of people's sight and hearing. Think about it, Bet."

"Don't be daft, Mam—this is *Naseby*! Don't you remember their wedding day, both of them so happy? He said it was all his dreams, ever since he played at house with us, out above Six-Mile—"

I stopped, and we stared at each other.

"Stony Cottage," said Mam, and we both knew it was true.

We cut across to the Crescent road, all but tumbling slantwise down the field; the cows were like islands, and we ran across the grassy sea between them, the stony. Once on the road, we put our heads down and strode, not speaking. I didn't want to believe it, but if Mam did, how could it not be true? But Naseby, my big sweet-tempered brother? "How could he bring himself to be so cruel to Sophie, and to little Tom and Myrtle?"

She put her hand on my arm. "We don't know yet. We don't know *exactly* and for certain. Wait and see."

The north road swung up over the cliff almost gaily, and we walked it up into the teeth of the wind, and it battered our hair and flapped our coat collars. The sea on our left tossed moon twinkles about, rushed and smashed at the cliffs, drummed in the road underfoot. The hill to the right was a different sea, charcoal gray; all its sproutings blew against the stones; the two hawthorns on its top leaned worried by the wind. Then the road dropped away and Crescent Corner lay like a fallen moon eating up its own light, and beyond was the smaller, messier cove, where the caves were.

Around the top of Crescent we strode. "I used to come here as a girl," Mam cried to me, "and walk about, and dream of running away. I thought I could make anything of myself, back then. Rollrock felt so *puny*! I was after something better and brighter." Her teeth flashed in the moonlight. "And then I mistook Odger for that thing—he *was* better and brighter to begin with, while we courted. But he did not stay that way, and after a time I could not revive it in him, and the rest has been the same dull round-and-round that you know of so well."

We nearly missed the little path beyond the Crescent cliffs. It looked as if it led off into nothing, that path, into a last step out into night air and then, after a gasp and half a scream, into the swill and rock-forest below. But no, it ducked in under a lip of rock there, and along and along, then down and doubling back it wove—so constricted that Mam used hardly to be able to fit down, following our tiny feet to cram herself into Stony Cottage with us and pretend to sip a cup of seawater tea and nibble the edge of a sand-and-weed cake.

"I will show that Odger," Mam said as we followed the gray thread of path all around Cave Cove, the wind swiping at us like a cat's paw at a mousehole, never quite hooking us out.

We crept up on the mouth of the cave we'd called Stony Cottage. I rather hoped we would find it empty, for then we could use it ourselves, to get out of the weather awhile. But just as Mam was about to poke her head around and look in, the wind dropped for a moment, and in that moment Naseby cried out, all strained and joyful, "God, woman, what are you doing to me!"

Mam stepped across to the mouth, her hand back so as I wouldn't follow and see. "She's doing what your wife Sophie ought to be doing, I daresay."

A dreadful silence fell in there. A girl's voice questioned, but the wind blew up and stopped my hearing the words.

"Come on out, laddie-boy," Mam said. "You've a wife and babs after your company."

Nase said something.

"Where else would you be?" she said. "Where else is there to hide?" I was glad she didn't give me the credit for having guessed the place.

Then he was there, pale, naked, bending over her in the black entrance, a clump of clothes hiding his boy-bits. "Mam, Mam, you won't tell, will you? Mam, I can put her back. Right away, right now. Her cast is just up over the meadow. No one need know. Sophie need never know."

"Please, Naseby Winch," said the girl, her voice all pleasant music. "Let me go home. My sisters will miss me."

"Dress yourself," Mam said to Nase. "And you? I suppose you've no more than that blanket to make you decent?"

"She can put her *skin* on, Mam! She can be gone! I shall run and fetch it."

"You won't," said Mam. "It does not suit my purposes. Here, she can wear my petticoat."

She stepped into the cave, and I moved forward and looked in. Nase was excruciated, cringing there, shivering, his back to me, his skinny backside—what was that wife feeding him? The seal-girl was seated on the blanket, watching my mam work her petticoat out from under her skirt. She looked quite unfrightened, and very beautiful, and the smell! Like a summer sea, it was, a breeze off living salt water, a waft of warmth, while all else was echoes of the cold noising sea.

Mam held out her petticoat. "There you go. That will wrap you more than once, such a mouse you are."

"Mam!"

"Come along now, come along."

"Mam!"

"Too late, Naseby. Don't waste breath begging."

"Please, though!"

"It's time, my lad, to face the size of what you're doing. It's more than a dally in this cave house, lad. It's more than a hot moment between this lady's legs. There's me, you see, and Sophie, such as she is that you married her. There's Tommy and Myrtle, hanging off your loyalty. Throwing you in, assuming you feel any shame, that's five, at least, people in this town that will never lift their heads again, because of the ridiculous picture you've just painted before me."

"All the more reason, then—"

"All the more reason to *dress*, boy!"

The seal-girl stood, tall and not trying to cover anything of herself. "If you would only give me my coat," she said reasonably to Naseby, to Mam. She even cast me an appealing look, before Mam put the petticoat over her head.

She did not fight or protest; she watched as Mam pulled the petticoat down, maneuvered her arms free of it, then brought it up to tie under her arms. "She is like a doll," I said. "She just lets you."

"Oh, they'll go where they're pushed, these women, if there's no prospect of escape to animate them toward the sea. No wonder the menfolk like them. Pah, you're swimming in this dress, girl! Well, you will just have to swim." She tied the ties ferociously tight. "Come, then."

"You are taking us to Sophie?" said Nase frightenedly, buttoning his pants.

"I am taking you to Dad."

"What for?"

"You go," Mam told him at the door. He went, and Mam ushered the maid out, the petticoat blowing up around her, giving us a fine view of her neat bottom and long legs, her tiny feet hardly showing ahead of her ankles.

"What does Dad need to know for?" Naseby bellowed back to Mam along the rock wall.

"I've to prove to him. I said this would be the way of it, and I've to show him."

A long argument came out of his mouth. Some of it blew over his shoulder to us; the rest broke against the rocks or was swept up the cliff by the wind. "—telling—Sophie—anyway—"

"Move along, the both of you. I want my supper."

All the way home Nase pled and complained. Mam didn't answer him; he seemed to have taken himself beyond her caring; this time she would not come aiding him.

After a while the girl caught him up and took his hand. I thought he might have the decency to throw her off in disgust at himself, but he clutched the hand as he walked unsteadily on.

"My eldest," Mam muttered beside me. "You think they are gems and pearls, your little ones; you pour yourself into them, watch them grow, wait for them to make you proud. And then all of a sudden they are just as besmutched and low-motived as everyone else, and worse than some of the Potshead people you've always despised. The bab you carried and bore and fed tosses away your good name for a night or two's tumbling in Stony Cottage with Miss Long-Limbs here, Miss Moves-Like-Enchantment. Look at her! She's finer in my petticoat than I was in my wedding dress."

I walked alongside Mam's disgust, in a daze myself, across the town. Nobody met us; Naseby looked aside at each house, though, cringing at who might come out, or who might pull aside their curtain, hearing our steps in the street.

We came to our door. "Go on," Mam told Naseby, when he hesitated.

"Please, Mam? I will take her back. I will find her coat and—"

"Lift the latch, Nase. It's too late for any of that now."

"Curse you, Mam," he said, nearly weeping.

"Curse yourself, boy. You brought this down entirely on yourself."

He opened the door, and we went in. It was so quiet inside, so warm! I closed the door behind us and we were stiff-still, all three of us. The front room was empty, the fire low; Dad must have sent the boys to bed and gone to do work out the back. Naseby wrung the seal-girl's hand. The girl, the nameless girl, radiated beauty there; our house looked like the house of peasants, and Mam and even Nase looked wrinkled, reddened, worn out from rough living, peasant work and the endless scouring of the wind.

Mam took off her coat and handed it to me.

"Excuse me." She edged around Nase and the girl. Through to the kitchen she went. There was the scrape of a bowl taken from the shelf, the clack of the ladle in the pot of kale-broth we had had for supper; Mam liked to see us all fed and then be left in peace to her own meal. "Odger?" she called out. The bowl clunked to the table, the spoon rang down beside it, a chair was pulled out and sat in. I realized how motionless we were, here in the front room, and tried to break the spell, hanging up Mam's coat and then my own.

Dad came in the back door. "What do you want, woman!"

Mam must have made some gesture, for he filled up the doorway there, came out to us. His face as he stepped into the room? He knew. He had known all along.

He saw me realize, my face between the two faces. "Where did you find them?" he called back down the hall.

Mam gave no answer but a pointed clink of her spoon in her bowl.

"Where did she find you?" he said to Nase.

"Cave Cove," he said.

"Anyone see you, coming here?"

Naseby shook his head.

Dad would have said more, if I'd not been there. Instead, he started back along the hall, turned to make some reassuring sign to Nase, saw me again and was gone into the kitchen. Leaning on a chair back, his shoulders around his ears, he spoke a word to Mam.

"No," she said.

He spoke louder. "There's still a way. Nobody saw you, Nase says—"

"Sophie must be told," Mam said. "And I don't care who else. I really don't, Odge. It's time Naseby faced his follies. And time you admitted his uselessness."

I realized I did not want to leave the front room, which was full of the seal-girl's wonderful wild smell. It was as if the whole ocean had pooled in here, fish and salt water, weed and whale, seabirds slicing through the fresh air above. Could a *girl* fall under a seal-girl's spell? A little knifing of fear cut me free, and I forced myself up the hall to the kitchen doorway, to the comforting sight of Mam eating supper, perhaps tireder-looking than usual, but to all other appearances living through an ordinary evening.

Dad twisted in his chair to look over his shoulder. "Go to *bed,*" he said, as if it were the last straw for him to see me.

Mam glanced at me unperturbed. "She may as well hear; they may as well *all* know. Wake up your sister, Bet. Get the boys out."

"Don't you *dare,*" snapped Dad.

"And then go out in the street and bellow it about town. Tell all creation."

Dad's shoulders sank and he shook his head and turned back to deal with her. While they looked hatred at each other I slid forward into the kitchen, and peered back along the hall to see if Nase would bring his girl through.

But no. I had never seen two people so close-wound together; certainly I'd never seen Nase hold to Sophie so.

"Look," said Dad to Mam behind me, as if he were bringing a whole new complexion of sensibleness to the conversation.

"Look, he *knows* he's done wrong, the lad—you've only to look at him. She can be gone by morning, and all this over, his lesson learned."

"And Sophie never know," said Mam in a dead voice.

"And Sophie never know!" he said, as if that would be wonderful, wouldn't it?

"Just you, and I, and Nase, and Bet there know."

"Just us! And we would never tell—"

"And Nase when you fill him with kickwater, and his whole soul falls out his mouth onto the table—who would know then? Who would be standing by?"

"That need not happen, Nance. I'm telling you, he knows the enormity of it—"

"And *this* one?" She nodded at me. "When all the girls are sharing secrets and she has this juicy one to share? Who'll be there? What other little gabmouths?" I was insulted, but she was right—she knew us girls and what went on among us.

"Then tell her not to, Nance. Impress upon her. I'm telling you, none of this need happen!"

"Well, I'm not sitting twitching the rest of my days, hoping it won't, are you? Oh, you are, I can tell, you fool."

"What are you saying? That we bring Sophie down here to see?"

"Did I say that?"

"Should we troop up there, then—is that what you want? Him and her and—I don't know, all of us? You want Geedre and the lads to come too?"

"Nor that, did I say. All I said is, Sophie must be told. I don't care how you go about it, but I'll not have this hidden. That's my part played. Sort it out yourselves from here." And her spoon moved in the broth, rang again against the bowl.

Dizzy from the scent of the seal-girl, I went and leaned in the mouth of the hall. I closed my eyes and they all melted into the sea-smell: Geedre flat as a sleeping fish on the other side of that wall; Dad and Mam either side of the table, which was like a slab of rock or the side of a sunken ship; Nase and his girl there like two twined strands of sea-ribbon, tilted in the flow. I opened my eyes before I should drown, and there was the house again, walls and air, the tintype hanging there of Great-Grandmother Winch, in her baskety chair, just as cross as ever.

Now Dad almost spat. "You sit there so *smug*." I had never heard that thickness in his voice. Fright blossomed up my spine. Would he strike Mam? I had heard of dads who did hit mams. I turned in the doorway so as I should be ready to run forward and grab him if he tried.

"Nothing smug about me," said Mam calmly. "Do you think *that* pleases me?" She tore bread, ate a piece.

"Stuffing your face," said Dad.

"I was hungry," she said around the bread, as if she didn't notice how far she had pushed his temper. "I was hungry *before* I set out."

"You don't know everything," he said quietly.

"Did I say I did?"

"You acted like it. You always do. You think you are so sharp? You think we're fools, me and Nase, that can hide nothing from you?"

"Well, Nase has done a poor job, certainly." She was not afraid at all. Perhaps she did not *care* if she goaded him to hitting her?

Dad growled; after a moment I heard the words in it: "You would shame our son, would you?" His voice was squashed from him hunching over at Mam.

She did not lean or shrink from him. "He has shamed *himself*, in my book."

"And would you shame me the same?" He brought his palms to the tabletop, his shoulders up around his ears again.

She gave a little laugh. He had unsettled her. A short silence passed. "If you *did* the same as him, you would shame *yourself* the same."

He pushed himself up from the chair like a spider launching itself high onto its legs, and sidled around the table. He wore a joyless grin; he looked entirely a stranger. He caught Mam's arm above the elbow. I cried, "Let her be!" and leaped to her side and took her other arm.

But, "Hush." Mam watched him, and rose from her seat, and went where he drew her, slowly, resisting him, but going with him still. I held to her, and followed.

He forced us, crept us, through the scullery, out the back door, from the dim warm lamplight into the moon's bright frosting of everything. We crossed the moony flags to his toolshed. He let go of Mam, and I went close and held her, shivering. My father, eyes wide and teeth bared, opened the shed and backed into it.

Some weeks back, he had built a cupboard against the side wall. I had watched him build it. The door opened to the back of the shed; I had told him how foolish it was. *It cuts off all the light*, I'd said. *You'll never find anything in there!* He had only smiled and done as he pleased, and now I saw why. He had only ever intended keeping a single object in this new safe place, and he needed no light to find it. Now he reached in, and drew that thing out among us by its narrow white hand.

"Come out, Helena-Grace," said Dad, his voice softening, saddening. Mam jolted and trembled; I held her tighter and tighter. I squeezed my eyes shut, as if by not seeing the woman emerge, I could make her not be there. The summer-sea smell rolled out the shed door; Mam gasped, and so did I, at the loveliness of it, at the awfulness.

"We can close this now," said Dad to his sea-maid. "You need never go back there."

Now it seemed cruel to hide my eyes and make Mam endure the sight alone; as well, the smell promised cleansing, and horizons, and sky, a flying-out from this, a floating-out, an altogether larger, fresher way of living than we'd so far been cramped up in. I looked around in hope as much as in horror.

Side-on to us, Dad kept grinning, kept eating up Mam's distress. The sea-maid watched us more calmly. One breast announced itself through the fall of her hair; a patch of blackness sprouted at her cleft, as unconscious as the breast of how it should be private. She was narrowly built, yet what curves she had were full, and her narrows were beautiful too, her wrists and hands, her ankles, her neck. Her face was as lovely as that other's, Nase's girl's, and just as unaware of what it was doing to our mam, to our family; she looked out on us with the same shy lack of enmity or vanity, expecting neither harm nor welcome from us, and needing nothing. I wished I was her, in this little group of us, rather than myself clinging to my mam, rather than my dad waiting gleeful and horrified for Mam's rage to crash down, rather than Mam herself, shuddering in my arms like a lidded pot on the point of boiling and gushing over, drowning the fire beneath it.

Dad bore the girl forward by her hand and elbow. They made a monstrous bride and groom in the doorway of their church, our shabby shed. The seal-girl moved all long and relaxed like a queen or a heron, or indeed like a bride trailing a heavy train behind herself.

Mam and I shrank across the flags before them. We retreated just as stiffly-slowly as we'd advanced, into the house, through to the kitchen, back up against the kitchen chairs, Dad thrusting the maid at us all the way.

And now I saw a seal-girl's face, straight on and lamplit, for the first time. Not quite human, she was all the more beautiful for that. Her dark features sat in the smooth skin like a puzzle of stones and shells; I wanted to look and look until I had solved it. The mouth began hesitantly to smile, full-lipped and shapely.

"Pack your things, Bet," said Mam. "Everything you will ever need. Wake your sister and the boys and tell them to pack theirs."

I peeled myself from Mam, and hurried to the bedroom.

I shook Geedre hard. She was wide-eyed in an instant, and I hissed Mam's command in her ear. "Light the candle," she said.

The boys complained more when I woke them, but as soon as they heard what had come upon us, they went silently to the task of gathering all they owned that they could carry.

"But where are we going?" Geedre said softly, casting about for what to take. "And for how long?"

"Forever, is my thinking."

She stared at me across the candle.

"Looking at Mam's face," I said. "So take it all, coat and boots and all."

"That *smell*!" said Byrne, awestruck.

"Don't breathe it," I said. "Block your nose, or you'll be bewitched. I nearly was myself."

"Bring your blanket," Mam said, pausing at the door as we gathered. "Sophie has few enough." And she was gone again.

"Sophie?" murmured Geedre. "We'll never all fit at Nase and Sophie's."

"Nase won't be there," I said hollowly.

"She must mean just for tonight," said Snell, "and the boat in the morning."

We all paused silent at that, looking among ourselves, disbelieving one moment, knowing it was true the next. Then Geedre snatched the blanket from the bed and folded it quickly, badly, as if she were stealing it.

We carried out our bundles to the front door and stood there hugging them, our hairs all awry. The sea-smell poured down the hallway from the kitchen, almost a wind. Nase and his girl sat at the kitchen table, their chairs pulled close together. Dad held his sea-maid on his lap, a shield between him and the rest of us, between him and Mam. Naked still, she had laid her arms loosely about our father's neck.

Then Mam obscured them, stepping from the bedroom into

the hall. Snell went and brought her to us with her bundles, and I did not look toward the kitchen again.

Mam searched and silenced each of our faces; she seemed both greatly tired and freshly flowered. Then she proceeded among us, and we gathered in after her. She opened the door and walked out onto the step and down into the street, and all we could do was follow.

Dominic Mallett

A clump of us lads was fighting on the northern mole. The wind carried the first bite of winter in it; the water fussed and jostled on three sides of us.

I had Harvey Newsom down and was sitting on him. I'd no advantage of weight, but he'd clouted me on the side of my head, and my rage was pumping from that. And he was laughing at me—that made me stronger, and him weaker. His bright red cheeks and his orange curls glowed against the wet black cobbles. He flung up names: *piece of tripe* and *cat meat* and *fingerling*. His mouth was a mess of half-grown teeth, like all of our mouths lately. I sat over him shaking his shirt, punching his shoulders into the ground.

Then he stopped, and looked up at me sharply through his watery eyes. I saw the next insult occur to him, saw him hesitate, saw him throw caution to the winds. "Your dad is old as a granddad," he said. "And your mam has hair like a man's, and the biggest arse in Potshead."

Well, it didn't matter what size I was then: I laid into him and didn't stop. His words poured power into me, poured size, made a brute of me, a brute with fine fast sight, seeing openings and throwing my fists and feet in, my knees. At first he kept laughing, delighted to have enraged me, and then he was too busy to laugh, trying to cover himself—and then, when he saw how much I still had boiled up in myself to deliver, he began to beg for mercy.

I felt I would never finish with him, but I could also feel tears coming, and only my mam was ever allowed to see me cry. I leaped up, gave him a couple of kicks for good measure and ran away along the mole, his words on fire in me, hissing and crackling, pleased with themselves.

The truth was, I had never noticed, before I heard it from Harvey's fat face, that my mam was round and small, when everyone else's mams were lean and tall; that her hair was not black silk like other mams', but red curls, as men's was if they let it grow; that her skin freckled like a dad's if she caught any sun, rather than honey-goldening as most mams' did in the summer. It was only as I ran up the lanes with a sob ready in my throat that I properly saw these differences, and felt dismay that they could be used against me. And why *was* Mam so different in shape and color? Why *was* her way of cooking, and speaking, and houseworking, different from the other mams'? I had never realized, so I had never asked.

I ran up home. I flew in, and straight to her at the sink in the scullery; I flung myself at her bottom as if I would cover it forever from the taunts of such as Harvey Newsom; I grasped her waist and buried my face in her. I was cold and windblown and full of rage and terror; she was warm and solid and smelled of home.

"Oh my gracious! What is this?" She dealt with the plate she was washing, then put her warm damp hand to my head as she turned in my arms. "Are you hurt, Dominic?"

I shook my head in the cushion of her front.

"What, then? Are they teasing you, calling you names?" She laughed somewhat through her sympathy, at my passion.

I shook my head even more fiercely. I could not have held her tighter. I didn't know what to want, whether to hide myself away inside her, or to squeeze her down to a size where I could pocket her and protect her forever from any insult or other boy's laughter.

"Are they calling *me* names?" she said with even more amusement.

I pulled away to look at her, my face fallen open in surprise. How could she know that? And how could she not mind?

Out sprang my tears; up burst the sob I had been containing, and another followed it, and another. I wept spots and splashes onto her pinny and skirt. My father came from the yard. "What's up with the boy?" And she explained to him above me—I did not look, did not want to see the agedness of Dad that Harvey had drawn to my attention. They talked it back and forth between them and chuckled together, not at me but at the source of my tears, so that I knew, even as I sobbed, that we maintained our own customs and conventions here in this house, and that all was well in it, that nothing could injure either Mam or Dad, and certainly not the lip of Harvey Newsom. I was relieved for them, yet still cast away from them somehow. No matter how hard I clung here, or how soothingly they spoke overhead, I could never make Harvey unsay what he had said, so closely to my face that I had felt his spittle on me. I could never unhear his words. I could never repair my mind to close over what had been opened up in it, the questions and the worrying, and the shame.

My dad and I sat before the fire. I was closer to it, right on the hearthstone, soggy with heat; my dad was more grown-up in his armchair. Mam had nipped down to Fisher's, and then the rain had started; we were listening to it ticking against the window, wondering if it would worsen and strand her there.

It worsened. Drops collected on the window glass and streaked down; the patter and trickle on the roof slates, sounds that had been so cozy when she was here in the house with us, were alarming now that she was out in them.

Dad sat forward, hands on his firelit knees. "I should take her coat down to her," he said.

"I can do it." I sprang up.

But he stood too, and pressed me back onto the hearth. "I will. Can't have you catching cold."

With a whisk of his own coat and a bundling of Mam's he was gone. He passed the window, downhill, in the cold gray afternoon.

I was too hot now. I climbed into Dad's chair, and the sting when I sat back against my heated shirt and jumper made me gasp. I sat and waited and listened for the two of them outside. The house around me was one large comfort in the middle of the rain.

When they came back, I peered around under the chair's wing

to watch them fuss and exclaim at the door. Dad took Mam's milk bottle that she had bought, and she shrugged off her coat, and exchanged coat for bottle. The raindrops fell from both their hems to the rug there, and her hair straggled crimson on her cheeks. They were laughing about her having to be rescued, and how quickly and hard the rain had come on. "Specially to wet *me*, you would have thought, Dominic! See how it's stopping, now that I'm home and safe in the dry?"

She carried the milk away to the kitchen, and Dad shook out and hung up their coats. I slid from his chair as he crossed back to the fire. I sat in Mam's chair, which was smaller and of smoother cloth, with flowers. He resettled himself, and I waited for him to say one of the things he always said, *Two old codgers by the fire, then*, maybe, or *Oh, it's a wild night to be out in*, which he would say whether it stormed or sat perfectly fine outside.

But he sat silent awhile, searching for his thoughts in the fire and smiling on them. Then he saw me watching, and his smile grew serious.

"When it comes to marrying, go to the mainland," he said. "Get yourself a Cordlin woman, like your mother. That's the proper kind of wife for men like us."

Men like us? Could he not see my legs stuck out here, the ankles only just off the seat? Could he not see how I had to lift my elbows almost level with my shoulders to rest them on the chair arms? Still, I was proud that he would call me a man in spite of these, would regard me as like himself; he charmed me with the idea of the two of us fronting up at life together in his mind.

I was so pleased and preoccupied with *men like us* that I let the rest of what he said stay mysterious. It would never come to marrying, for me; I would always be a boy, running and fishing and fighting and mucking about in coracles. I would never want more than that.

"Harvey Newsom is a turnip," said Neville Trumbell.

We were up on Whistle Top, with the whole town below us, and no one coming up the path. There was a springish wind about—maybe its warmth, and grassiness, and sea salt had made so much talk fountain out of me.

"Everyone knows," Neville went on. "Newsoms will say anything to hurt you. They've all got that nastiness. Their dad was always picking fights up at Wholeman's—you know that. That's why he has to drink at his home."

"It's true." I admired how Neville could dismiss Harvey's words, how he did not let them stay and burn in him. They had never stopped burning in me since Harvey had said them.

"Everyone knows too about the mams. All the mams were like your mam once, and like our dads. They were of a piece, women and men the same."

"They were?" I could not imagine such a thing.

"Oh yes. Didn't your dad tell you? Or your mam, more likely? Course, she wasn't here then; your dad went to mainland and fetched her in. But she was from an old Rollrock family—Trenchers, they were. She knew what she was coming to. Back in our dads' times, it was, and our granddads', some of us. None of these other mams were about then. They were in the sea, being their sea-selves."

I stared down upon the rumpled little jigsaw that was Potshead, with Meehan's cherry tree coming into blossom in the nearest yard. I did know that, about the mams; I had heard and known about it all my life, that older world, that angrier. But somehow I had never properly listened and thought and put it together.

"Where did they go, then, the red ones?" I asked. "What happened to them?"

"Oh, they left," said Neville. "All of them, of their own accord, in a great temper."

"What did they have to be angry about?"

"Nothing," said Neville. "They were just like that, says my dad. You'd only to give them *Good morning* and they'd go off at you like a cracked hen. They hated everything and everybody. We're well rid of them, he says."

"Hmph," I said. "But my mam is not like that."

"I know." His face was clenched to hold a grass stalk in his lips the way some old men hold their pipe. "I said that to him once. *Dominic's mam is peaceable enough*, I said. *But look to Misskaella*, he said. *You cannot get much fierier or fiercer than that*. He said your mam must not be full red-woman. She must have seal in her somewhere, he reckons."

"You think?"

"I don't think, no. Or why would your dad have gone all that way to get her, if he didn't want her pure? That was the whole point."

I nodded, though I had no idea. I'd no idea about any of this, and I did not like to think of my mam and dad being passed about as ordinary Potshead gossip and legend.

"Besides." Neville's whole face changed, grinning, becoming boy again. "I like your mam's arse. She makes a change, to walk along behind, the way she flubbles."

I sprang at him with my fists, and he parried me, laughing, and that was the end of that conversation.

I was rising twelve when my dad died, one dark winter. He took the heart out of us, Mam and me, for a good while there; we washed and buried him, and then we sat about. Though the island thawed and seeped around us, still we stayed frozen, she and I. We could not be apart, each alone with this changed arrangement of things; we could not be together, knowing what we had lost with Dad.

People who were not Malletts, their lives went on around us, and they had never looked more peculiar to me than they did from within the cold shell of our mourning. The rude red men strode about, the dark silk-haired women with their soft smiles and their sea-singing moved vaguely about the town, and all of them seemed foreign, as did the boys, my fellows, who were mixtures of their mams and dads. Some were completely red after their fathers, and others had hair that fell flat, or that drink-of-water build of their mother, or her big dark eyes, or something of her floating manner. Whether red or black, they seemed quite distinct in nature from me, they were so energetic and enterprising, they laughed so easily, and brought such passion to anything they talked about.

I was out of doors in my restlessness, in a little crowd of such mixed boys, when Nicholas Kimes brought his new wife up from Crescent Corner. Some of us wanted to watch the actual extraction of her, out of the seal-body, but that crow Misskaella had scowled and cawed at us to be off before she and Kimes went down there, and some lads would not go against her. They held us back from the cliff top, who might otherwise have spied on the magic over the edge. Brawn Baker had said you could feel the moment if you held yourself attentive enough, so we sat quietly in the grass against the wall and waited for that. Some said they felt something, a prickling of their skin and such, but nothing they claimed could not be sheeted home to the chill of the spring breeze, or the thrill of being here, so near to what was forbidden.

And all of us were surprised alike when Nicholas's copper curls showed so soon, in the sunlight at the top of the path. He walked slowly, leading his lady. She was learning to balance and to walk as she came. She wore a land-dress, a plain shift, somewhat stiff in its newness. Her hand was locked in Nick's, and she leaned to him in all her movements. The salt-and-seaweed breeze blew her shining hair, but could only lift strands of it, not the full weight, which fell as far as her thighs. Behind these two the witch struggled up into view like a block of cliff face come to life, stone-footed and clumsy yet.

As the three of them drew near, only the seal-woman seemed to see us—and then she looked to Nick to explain us, to give her our names. When he did not, but only gazed wondering and wordless back into her beautiful face, she seemed to accept that too, that we were to be nameless for now, a crowd of gawpers to be passed on by. So on they went, as solemn a procession as if they came out of a church, as strange as if they had straggled off a shipwreck.

In my present deadness of heart, it was not so much the seal-woman who impressed me as Nick himself being so enchanted. I wished I could be as distracted as he, as readily taken up with another person. And there was no doubt she was beautiful; they all were, of course, but this one was fresh-risen from the sea, fresh-peeled into white wonderfulness. My skin goosefleshed at the sight of her, at the knowledge that magic had brought her. I could see a day when I might want a woman as willowy and bewildered as that, with such silken hair and such dark eyes, and such an inclination toward me as this one had toward Nick. The lads either side of me must have been thinking the same thing, the way they joined me in my silence, gazing after Nick and his bride walking, bound fast together and passing into their new life.

Fearsome Misskaella, her wrappings trailing, rocked along stiff-legged behind them, her red and white hair wisping from where she had quickly knotted it up out of the way while she did her magic work. She was the only red-woman on Rollrock besides my own mother. I was not, like these other lads, born of seal-maids. And I was not to marry one, hadn't Dad said? *Men like us*, he had said, separating me off from these boys. Placing us above them, was he? Or did he feel, as I felt—sitting back so that, beyond Misskaella's rags, I might see more of the new bride's cloak of black hair, shivering at the sight of it shining and sliding across itself—that neither he nor I would ever be fine enough for such wives as this, long-limbed and foreign from the sea?

We upped and followed, but timidly, keeping the three leaders always in sight, but never in hearing.

"How much does it cost you?" Salmon Cawdron whispered.

"No one will say," said Neville. "You must bargain with *her* on the price. All I know is, Jerrolt Ardler took three years gathering the money, and not a drop at Wholeman's did he drink all that time, and still he owed her more besides, after she brought up his Abigail."

"It costs you your full life and manhood, says my dad," said Howth Marten.

"Yes, there's lots of Rollrock men still in debt to Misskaella, with a pack of sons needing food and clothing on top of the price."

"Look at her, though!" We knew by his tone that Salmon was not talking about the witch. "She is not *goods*, that you put a price on—a sack of *flour*, a box of *tins*."

"Oh, the price is not for *her*," said Neville. "The price is for Misskaella's bother. The price is the bringing. The money is about what happens on the land, although the reward comes from the sea."

That night I made Mam something of a meal, bread and some cheese, a little smoked fish, and while I assembled it I told her what I'd seen, of Nicholas and his new wife and Misskaella going by. She was always quiet since Dad died, but this night as I spoke and served she spread a different silence about herself, and when I noticed the bright sound of my words ringing in the hollows of it I stopped speaking. I poured the tea and brought the cups to the table, pretending not to notice how present she was in the room, how she was more motionless than usual, fixed on me with a watchful seriousness I had not felt from her in a while.

"Only I had never seen a mam straight from the sea like that," I heard myself apologize.

"Oh, she is not a mam yet," said Mam. "At least, not on land. Though she may have pups and pups that she's left behind, living in the water."

"That's true," I said. "Some of the stories say that, don't they, how they are torn apart between the two kinds of children?"

"Stories?" she said. "If only they were but stories."

I sat and nudged her tea toward her; perhaps I could send her back to quietness with this reminder of all the wearisome tasks ahead of her, the lifting and sipping, the endless chewing, and all the time the absence of Dad at our elbows, the room echoing with his un-uttered remarks, his un-laughed laughs.

But she kept her hands in her lap and only watched me. "I've been thinking," she said. "Rollrock is no place for me without your dad. And no place for any young man who has a choice about it. You remember your Aunty Ames, and your grandmother, that visited from Cordlin?"

"A long time ago." I sat over the plate I had prepared myself, wanting to begin on it.

"We will go and be with them, I think," she said. "I am sure they will have us."

I stared. Her words, each one small and sensible in itself, would not come together except to mean one thing, and that seemed outrageous, impossible to me, given the shape of our lives to this point. "We would go to Cordlin? You and me? And be mainlanders?"

She smiled at how dazzled I was. "It will be an opportunity for you, Dominic. Perhaps you can become something other than a fisherman. Not that your dad was not quite happy on the sea, but who knows what awaits his son?"

I pushed her teacup a little closer to her. "While it is hot," I said, to bring us both back to the present, to this meal, in case we had already dreamed more than we could ever hope for. In another part of my mind I was thinking, Of course, of course. How *right* it will feel, with everyone red, Mam not mismatching anymore! This at least was a pleasure I could imagine; the rest was too enormous, too out of my experience, for my mind to regard with more than blank surprise and excitement.

"I will write to them tonight," she said. "It can go on tomorrow's boat. We will wait to hear from Aunty Ames before we make any plans. I've no reason to doubt she will take us in, but it's best not to court disappointment."

She picked up her tea and took her first sip, as if the action did not weary her in the least.

After Rollrock, Cordlin town was an enormous whirling fairground of a place, full of strangers and strange objects and animals, machines and habits. I grew up there, and up, and up, into a gawkish boy, and then I filled out and was a young man. I made my mam proud, as she lay in the last of her several illnesses, by getting myself a job at the market; I wore a white apron down to my ankles and pushed a trolley back and forth all day, loading up crates of vegetables and fruit, buckets of flowers, boxes of fish layered with ice. I was happy enough there, though part of me knew that my Potshead fellows would think little of any living not made on the sea. I had some money and some mates, and once I put on flesh and muscle I found that girls quite liked me.

By that time I had just about forgotten the day Nick Kimes's wife had walked past us boys on the Crescent road. No, it was the girls right here in Cordlin who had my attention, and after one or two small heartbreaks I found myself Kitty Flaming, who worked in the market office over the books, with whom I was comfortable right from our first conversation at the market employees' picnic, and with whom I settled to regular walking out, and dancing, and picture shows, and the other kinds of entertainments that young couples get up to about a port town like Cordlin.

I was very pleased to have Kitty as my sweetheart. Mam and Gran and Aunty Ames loved her, and she was a fine-looking, proud girl who knew exactly how to dress and behave for any occasion and any group of people, whether they were above or below her in station or exactly matched. She'd a straight eye and a good laugh and such energy, she fair whisked you up and carried you along with her, whatever place or project she was set on. She swept me toward the altar without ever once mentioning it; she let everyone else do the talking. "When are you going to marry that lovely girl?" they said to me. "She'll not wait forever, you know." More and more often they said it, as a year went on, and then another year.

We strolled by the quayside, the sunshine softening toward autumn. We'd just met and parted from Jeannie Grace, who had told us of her brand-new engagement to my friend Thomas Parsnall. *It's hardly news to anyone*, Jeannie had said, *and yet everyone seems surprised, and takes pleasure in it, and looks at you properly, as if they had never seen you before*.

Now I said to Kitty, "People say *we* should be married, you and I."

"To each other, you mean?" she said with a wicked smile.

"Of *course* to each other."

"Hmm," she said. "Which people are these, who say this?"

"Let me see—Aunty Ames, Tom Geoghan and Mister Bryce at work. Windy Nuttall, your Uncle Crowther. Everyone."

"Really. How funny of them. I daresay marriage is not on your mind at all. I hope you tell them fair and square what to do with their opinions?" Her face was raised to meet the breeze, a look on it as if she never wanted to do more than enjoy that freshness on her skin.

I was full of doubt, in an instant. I walked along beside her, listening to her words again in my head. "Do you not want to marry me, then?" I said eventually.

"Who's asking *me*?" she said, pretending astonishment. "Isn't it up to you and those *people* to decide?"

I took her hand and walked close beside her. "Come, Kitty, don't fool with me now. Will you marry me or no?"

She shrugged, looked away toward the Heads. "I probably will" drifted back over her shoulder. I was about to throw away her hand and stamp off when, "Don't you think?" she added. And she turned and looked at me, sweet and sly, and into her kiss, a quick one because we were in public, she put all that she was not admitting in her words: surprise and excitement and a little terror.

We walked on, and everything was different, just as Jeannie had said—outlined in gold, things were, in the late sunshine, funnel- and mast-shadows crisply black on the sunlit storehouse walls. Every gull flew in a more purposeful arc, or arranged its folded wings more importantly; every stone and plank went toward making a different stage of life from the one that had passed on from us, moments before. "This is the day you tell your grandchildren about," I said, and Kitty squeezed my hand.

We reached Cobalt's store and turned back. "One thing," Kitty said. Again she looked away from me. Between the Heads, the clouds hung puffy, gleamed golden. "Your house on Rollrock."

"You want to live on *Rollrock*?"

"I most certainly do *not*," she said. "I want you to rid yourself of that house. It gives me the shudders just to think of it there."

"Why, ever? I've not been back in years!"

"Still, the house is there, and it's a place for you, among those men and their . . . what they've married. I never want to go there, and I never want you to think that you can go. Go *back*, you know, and belong."

"I've never for a minute!"

"I know you've not," she said a little gentler. "But that's not to say you never would, while you had that house. Will you sell it, please, Dominic? To settle my mind?"

"Why on earth would you be afraid—"

But she *was* afraid. She was not sweet and sly now; she was all grave attention to me. "It's the one thing I worry about with you, your connection to that place. Will you sever it, for me? For our *sons*, should we have any?"

I saw then how far she had taken this in her mind, while outwardly she had seemed carefree, accepting of everything about me. I saw, in her thoughtful, firmly held face, that she was prepared to forgo me, if I chose not to do as she asked, it mattered so much to her.

I took both her hands. "Gladly," I said. "It means nothing to me, that mad isle. I'll sell the house tomorrow, and buy you a ring with the money."

She examined my eyes, saw how serious I was behind my smile and smiled back with relief.

Well, it turned out not to be so straightforward, of course. No one in Cordlin wanted a Rollrock house. Men laughed, and women looked at me sideways at the very suggestion.

"Twenty years ago, maybe," said Aunty Ames, "you might have sold it. But no one wants to take their family there while all the wives are those sea-madams."

"I should say," said my employer Mister Bryce, "that your only hope would be to go to the isle yourself, and see if there is any young man about to make a marriage who could use it."

"I could write to Fisher, I suppose," I said to Kitty, "and have him ask about."

"Yes, do that," she said, and moved on to talking of the arrangements for our betrothal supper.

I sat to write that letter with hardly a thought, and I wrote swiftly, laying out my greetings to Neepny Fisher, who I'd heard had taken over the store from his father, Jodrell, and to his wife and family, and moving briskly on to frame my request. It was only as I watched the words *and all its contents* fall out of my pen onto the page that I felt a tremor of doubt. I sat there and stared at them awhile, and then I wrote on, to the end of the page and the end of the matter.

I put the letter in the post next day, and when I had finished work I went by the market's office. "Wife-to-be?" I said in the door.

Kitty looked up from her calculations and smiled with happy surprise, and blushed a little.

"A quick word?" I said. "I'll not disturb you long."

She pulled up another chair for me to perch on near to her.

"I have sent the letter to Fisher."

The happiness vanished from her face, and she was all business. "Good. How soon will you hear back, do you think?"

"Maybe Tuesday night's boat? I'm not sure. Neepny may not be as ready to do a favor as his dad was. But I wanted to ask you. There are two chairs in that house, armchairs, my mam's and my dad's. I remember we covered them with sheets as we left. It's not that they are valuable, and they're probably not improved from years of sitting there unused, through winters and summers."

"Can you have Fisher send them, perhaps? Crate them up and put them on the boat?"

"I thought of that. And then I thought, what a clumsy lad Neepny used to be, and a grubby one, and would I want him manhandling them? And I thought, perhaps I should look the place over—the old house—for anything else we could use in our married life? And also, my dad's grave has gone untended all these years. I should like to visit, I think, just to tie off these ends in my mind, do you see? Also, if I go and look Neepny in the eye, he may take better care on the sale, in getting me my price. I would only go a day or two, and then I would be finished with the place forever. And we would have those armchairs, brought across carefully. I don't even know if we could use them, but to have them in our home, Mam's and Dad's side by side . . . I think I would like that."

I had bent farther and farther forward in my seat, so that now I must look up to see Kitty's face. She regarded me most soberly awhile. "Two days," she said. "Two chairs. Yes," she said. "It is nice to have some keepsakes." She examined her lap, turning the folds of her skirt there and smoothing them. She looked up; she nodded. I loved her in that moment. I saw how easily our married life would run, how agreeably. "When would you go?"

"Wednesday morning is the next boat. Mister Bryce would give me the time off, I'm sure. It is his suggestion, this arrangement, after all."

"Saturday is our supper. Can you be done and back by then?"

"Oh, I should wait until next week, then, so as to help you here with the supper!"

"No, no," she said. "Get it over and done." And she flashed me a cautious smile.

On Tuesday at the market I bought some mainland flowers to put on Dad's grave, kinds never seen on Rollrock, I was sure; they would have bemused him, but that was partly the point of them, to show him how far I had moved on from the isle, from our little lives there.

On Wednesday morning, I and my flowers boarded the *Fleet*

Fey, and I sat before the wheelhouse as we chugged across the harbor, and out between the Heads top-gilded by the rising sun. As the land fell away behind, the breadth and depth and mystery of the ocean struck me as it had not for a long while, and the tininess upon it of people, and people's crafts. The waters heaved and rolled and sank beneath me, and I remembered how, when small, I had regarded the sea as a single vast beast, many of its moods and intentions hostile toward us on our little island, or in our little boats.

I remembered our boat ride, Mam's and mine, from Rollrock to Cordlin, as a great sea voyage, at least a day long, so it surprised, even alarmed me how soon the island rose from the sea, how quickly Potshead spotted and sprouted on the slopes, and then grew thick in the cleft of them as we rocked around the western headlands. I hardly felt ready. But what was I afraid of? I was a Cordlin man now. I would transact the business of my house and the chairs and then be gone again.

The town seemed smaller and poorer than I remembered it, more beaten into the hill by the weather. Clancy Curse detached himself from Fisher's wall with exactly the same idle-seeming movements as I remembered from my childhood, and caught the ropes and wound them about the bollards in the old familiar way. He was quite a small man—they were all shortish, the men who met the boat, though I remembered them as giants, their heads among the clouds, full of wisdom and weather and long-gotten experience. But no, they were little nuggety fellows, and some of them bowlegged, their skin gone to leather from years of wind and cold aboard the boats.

"Is that you, Dominic?" one of them said. It was Shy Tyler, my own age but crease-faced from work and weather. He smiled and shook my hand heartily. "What brings you back?" He eyed my flowers. "Have you come a-wooing?"

"These are for my dad," I said. The strange bright things shook in their cone of newspaper.

"Of course they are. And you'll see to the selling of the house while you're here?"

"Why, yes! You know of that already?"

He grinned. "You want to keep things secret, you don't tell Neepny Fisher. No, we've several young fellows squabbling over your place, don't you worry. You'll want to catch up with Neepny now, I daresay?"

"I might visit Dad first, and see the house for myself, before I talk to Neepny."

"You'll stay over? Come and have supper with me tonight. I've a wife and son now: Fametta, loveliest ever to step out of the waves, and little James, spit image of my old dad."

I suppressed a shiver on Kitty's behalf. I knew what I should answer.

"Are you married yourself, Dominic?"

"Nearly."

"Oh, it's grand being a married man." Shy slapped my arm. "And having a boy, there's nothing like it."

"I'd be very happy to meet him," I said. What harm could it do, congratulating a man on his son? And I might hear some stories to take back to Kitty, to make her laugh, and marvel at island life.

I went up through the town. Everything was so much as I remembered, and yet so much littler, that I was charmed and horrified both. Kitty would certainly hate it here, how cramped it was, how quiet, how empty of bustle. And she would see as odd, rather than as pleasing in their familiarity, the sea-wives' touches on the houses. Stones and shells and tiny dried-weed baskets, useless for anything but decoration, lay arranged on many windowsills. The curtains the wives favored were swept aside one way; a Cordliner would laugh at those, how the houses seemed to be looking slyly sideways. Cats stalked about everywhere, or lay curled on steps or fence tops or in windows, patched strange colors from their interbreeding. And little gardens grew in pots and sheltered corners, crammed with the plants that the seal-women liked, which were not airy and flowery like mainland potted plants, but brought to mind coral, or oyster clumps, or other kinds of sea-growth.

The church was a relief, absent of any of these unsettling details. My father's grave, instead of the raw wound in the turf that Mam and I had left those years ago, was now the gentlest-grassed mound, and the headstone was speckled and patched with lichen. I took my flowers from their wrapping and laid them at the foot of the stone; the breeze buffeted their fragile heads, and their colors and shapes were just as odd and overly bright for this green and gray place as I could have wished. I crouched beside the mound, never one for praying and unable to speak to a Dad transformed into mound and stone. The wind wagged the cypress trees at the graveyard gate, and a blackbird happened by, as neat as the Cordlin undertaker, but with a curious eye, a bright beak and a cheerful spring in his step.

I crossed the town to our old house. I turned the key, remembering it in Mam's hand as she locked up the day we left, and I pushed open the door. Look, I must duck my head now, just like Dad, to avoid the lintel!

Inside, the air was so dead and yet so aswarm with memories that my knees almost gave way. I wished, momentarily, that Kitty had come; if I had had to show and explain all this to her—this town, Dad's grave, this house—it would never have affected me so strongly. As it was, the house embraced me, immediately and completely. Cordlin, it seemed to say, had been only a distraction, all noise and color and rushing people. Cordlin had beguiled me and built extra layers of talk and work, money and society, onto me, that were now stripped away. Here on Rollrock was the stillness I remembered from before, the small silence of the house within the quiet of the small town within the vast airy wordless limitlessness of weather and water. At heart, I was not a Cordlin man, betrothed and businesslike; I was a carefree boy following my fancies around Rollrock's lanes and field walls, too young to realize that anything was amiss.

I left the front door open. I opened all the windows. The same ones stuck as had always stuck, and I knew just where to apply the force to lift and lower them. At the back, I opened the door to the yard—the grass had grown high out there, and then been beaten down by rain or wind. The air drawn through the house by my opening it up felt like the first deep breath I had taken since Dad died and we left the island. I closed my eyes. The distant sea-sound only made the quietness quieter.

The small rooms echoed unfamiliarly without their rugs. Back in the front room, I pulled the sheeting off my father's armchair. How small it was, how modest, when once I had thought it a throne, and had had to *spring* from the floor to board it! Now I lowered myself to sit there, and the dead fireplace sat with me, and my mother's chair dreamed beside me under its own dust sheet.

It's not that they are valuable, I heard myself saying to Kitty, of these two pieces of my innermost soul. Look what I had become: a chattering busy townsman with a childhood I only laughed about, and encouraged others to find amusing, this backward isle I had come from, these unworldly folk! My dad had loved it here; my mam had loved the place along with the man; I had lived my first twelve years here, and the island's cobbles and wall flints had left their imprints on me, its hills and dales, its moles and beaches, and the peaks and hollows of the sea all around. Now in the silence, the armchair's wings dampening even the sound of the sea, the voices came back to me, woken by Shy's accent down at the quayside. Dad and Mam sighed and admonished and laughed, and the bright chipper cries of my playfellows cut through the different airs of crisp winter mornings, and blowsy summer afternoons. And I was glad Kitty hadn't come, for if she had, I would not have heard those voices; I would have gone on not knowing who I truly was, and the place I truly came from.

I stood up out of my father's chair and left the house, closing but not locking the door behind me. I climbed the hill slowly, taking in everything, remembering everything, reawakening to the childhood I carried within me, but had long denied.

I reached the highest house, the witch's mansion. There the grass was grown up and beaten down just as at home. The windows were closed and curtained, and many of the curtains were pressed to the glass in square-cornered shapes of furniture, as if someone in their madness or terror had piled up the house's contents to keep some force from breaking in. The garden, that I remembered as so neatly laid out and kept trim, was now a thicket, trees and shrubs burst well beyond their borders, clotted with fallen flowers and ornamental fruit and underclothed with weeds.

A man climbed into the street, walked along it toward me. It was Emmett Marshall, dad of Risby Marshall that had been my pal in school; Risby and I had saved each other from many a beating by the bigger boys.

"Well, if it's not wee Dominic Mallett!" said Emmett. He laughed and stuck out his hand to me. His teeth were longer than I remembered, and his hair was entirely white. "How are you, my boy?"

"I'm well, Mister Marshall. Just across from Cordlin a little while, to visit my dad and do some business on the house."

"You want Misskaella?"

"Oh, no. I only happened up this way. She's passed on, I take it?"

He looked puzzled, then laughed. "Why, no, she's in as fine a fettle as ever she was, the old gooney," he laughed. "Only she's not lived here since a good year now." We looked up at the ivied walls, the furniture pressing at the windows. "Filled it to the rafters with treasures, she did, brought from the mainland—furnitures and pictures and a kitchen of pans, a great oven never been lit. No more room in there for her own self! She lives down Shore Cottage now."

"What, the old boat on the beach, below McComber's place?"

"Oh, she has made it good, a neat little bothy sodded over the top. Spread it round with her rubbish, mind—she cannot seem to stop with the collecting, wherever she resides—but she's comfortable enough. Comfortabler than she ever was here; this conjured the worst in her. There-awhile she was bringing foods across, none of us had heard of them. Fish eggs from Russia. Some terrible vegetable from Siam that she could not eat; she put it on her rubbish pile, and the seeds took, and it ran all over her back field. Down in the bothy she is calmer, and now that her sisters are died—though that last one visited but once a year from Cordlin—she has less reason for that show-offery, that throwing of money at silliness. It sits now, her wealth; she still asks it of a man, to bring up his wife, but she cares less about spending it."

I looked at my feet, shook my head. "I used to be so afraid of her, when I was tiny."

"Oh, you want always to be wary of a woman like that, lad. However high you grow." Marshall gripped my shoulder. "Are you coming back to us, then, Dominic?" he said warmly. "Have you finished your mainland wanderings?"

"No, no, Mister Marshall," I said. "Matter of fact, I'm about to be married there, to a Cordlin girl. I am just sorting out the house here and I shall be off for good, I should think."

He twinkled on at me awhile, and then he took and released a big sigh. "Well, congratulations on your marriage, lad. And it's grand to see you, and see you so tall and well, after all this time. You're always welcome here, you know that, don't you? Whether you have a house here or no."

"I do, and thank you, Mister Marshall."

He walked off along the street toward his house, and after a last look at Misskaella's imprisoned furniture I gave myself a shake and went the other way. At a brisk pace I strode up the path beyond Watch-Out Hill, to the windiest place on the Spine, to the wildest, out of the sight of any Potsheader. My hair blew sideways and my coat beat hard at my knees, and the delicate wonderings that had afflicted me in my parents' house were wind-washed out of my head, and my conversation with Emmett Marshall too; I was stupid with cold and with rushing air, and my only thought was what was I doing here in such discomfort, when I had so much business to attend to back in the town?

I filled the rest of the day in conferring with Neepny Fisher, which entailed as well a great deal of greeting, and of repeating my situation to, the customers of his shop who interrupted us. In sum, as Shy had said, there were several likely buyers for the house; Fisher himself was interested in it as somewhere to place his father, who was growing too cantankerous to have around the store.

I extracted myself midafternoon with Neepny's boy Juniper, who helped me carry the armloads of wood I would need to build crates for the armchairs. He was a good lad, sweet-natured and eager to help, and although I was well past wanting company I was glad of him, for without him I never would have got those crates so far along before I was due down at Shy's. He looked like Neepny entirely, with his red hair and freckles, but his manner was quite different from boys his age I had observed in Cordlin, much quieter and more attentive to his surroundings. As he fetched and carried for me, I heard Shy again: *Having a boy, there's nothing like it,* and I could see myself as father to a boy like Juniper; it was not too much of a stretch. It was really the first time I had thought about fathering. I had taken for granted that I would have children, and would have them with Kitty—that was what marrying was *for,* mostly, wasn't it?—but I had never pictured such times as this, working at some practical task with a small, interested person at my side, perfectly trusting of me and eager to help in any way he could.

Juniper's mam I had barely glimpsed down at Fisher's, barely heard say more than "Nice to meet you, Dominic Mallett," the way they do, using your full name, and low-pitched, as if they have secrets with you. One or two other wives I had passed in the street, and once I had heard a snatch of singing from inside one of the houses that had pulled me up short, flooding my head with childhood and sea-mystery. But when I went to Shy's that night for supper, I properly met his wife Fametta, and their son James was of an age where a visitor is some kind of grand new toy, nothing to be afraid of, and if I were not to be rude I must spend quite a deal of time gazing into one face or another. And very odd I found that, coming from plain unmagical Cordlin as I did, and used now to seeing faces that were put together of pallor and freckles as mine was, and framed with red curls. And though I tried to keep Kitty's revulsion in mind as the correct way of regarding these two people, in fact I found them pleasant. Quite apart from the beauty of Fametta's face and figure, and the simple but ingenious way she had fixed up her hair, her smile and quietude calmed and charmed me. In little James's face were blended both of his parents', his pale eyes from Shy, his clear skin and silky hair, hardly more than black down yet, from Fametta. He pulled himself up to standing at my knees, and he burbled smilingly up at me, and his parents took great delight in every sight and sound of him.

And Shy talked, impelled by the joy he had found in the married state and in fatherhood. He reminded me of things we had seen together, and done, and heard of in our youth. I was surprised to remember times I had forgotten, or to find that I remembered them differently from Shy, and must quarrel amiably with him about the true events. The beautiful woman cooed to the charming child nearby, and knowing that just such lovelies ruled each home and hearth around me, up and down the town, I began to think that Potshead life was perhaps not so small as I had once thought it, and not so unnatural as Cordlin people feared. *It is all so familiar,* I thought toward Kitty, who sat warily in my mind all evening, noticing everything and disapproving of most of it. *What is to be frightened of, in this woman, this child? You only hate them because you do not know them; you have not seen their harmlessness.*

"So there is no hope of you returning?" said Shy on his doorstep as my visit ended.

"No, my wife will want to stay in Cordlin," I said. "And she will have no work, being married, so we will need the money from the house, toward a Cordlin house for ourselves." I thrust my hands into my coat pockets, and we both of us looked everywhere but at each other in the dimness.

"Goodbye, Dominic Mallett," said Fametta. Baby James was a sleeping bundle at her shoulder. Her face floated like a beautiful mask in the night, her lips full shadows, her eyes dark pools, each with a moon gleam on the surface.

"Goodbye, Fametta," I said. "It was lovely to meet you."

I set off home, but the clap of the cold sea air had woken me, and at the end of their street, as I heard Shy's door close behind me, instead of turning uphill I turned down. I walked easily through those lower lanes, confident that I would not meet anybody at this hour and glad of the peace of that. Down to the seafront I went, and along it north past the mole end, and on to where the paving ended and there was the choice whether to struggle up through the dunes to the Crescent road or to slither down to the firmer sand of the beach. Down I went, and set out along the silvered sand past the ripples that broke the moonlight into pieces, and the wider waves that curled over and crushed the pieces to blackness.

It was a fine feeling to walk fast and breathe deeply, to leave Potshead and people behind me—and more-than-people, or less, or whatever the sea-wives were. I rescued Kitty from the place deep in my mind to which Fametta and James had banished her. *Look, there is all this of me, too!* I exclaimed to her. *And perhaps it is unusual, but is it quite despicable?* I wished dearly that she were here beside me so that I could talk to her, because in truth she had faded a little, as had Cordlin and its excitements and stimulations, cleared from my mind by Rollrock's simplicity, its straightness and its strangeness, as the tide smooths the day's footprints and drag marks from a beach.

"Hoy!"

I thought I had misheard the sea as a voice, and I looked out that way, in case there should be a person there, requiring saving.

But "Hoy!" sounded again behind me, and I spun, and there,

lit starkly by the moonlight, sat two things that brought my heart jumping into my throat. Thrippence's bothy, a furry black mound high among the dunes, sent smoke slanting from some invisible chimney. And on the steps from bothy to beach sat a shadow mound smaller in size but mightily more fearsome than the bothy: the witch Misskaella, waving an arm to beckon me.

I glanced back along the beach, searched the shadows of the Forward cliff ahead, but no one walked nearby who might be summoned to help me, or even to share this dread. Slowly I paced up the hard wet sand and into the softer, wishing it were more soft and difficult so that I might never reach Misskaella. What could she want of me? Why did I not have the strength to walk away, along the beach, ignoring her? Come now, I told myself, what harm can she mean you, an old woman, sleepless in the midnight? She is probably only in need of some company, and curious about this passing stranger.

"Good evening," I said as I neared her.

She watched me, glinting-eyed. Her dark rags looked as if they had grown out of her rather than being created from cloth and put on. Her face—the face of my childhood nightmares—turned up at me as I drew closer, the moon unkind upon every whisker and wrinkle and mole.

"Misskaella," I said, to show that I knew her, that I had the measure of her. She stared up at me, clearly feeling no compulsion to speak.

"My name is Dominic Mallett," I said. "I come from Cordlin."

"Mallett? You come from Potshead. You cannot fool me; I remember your father. How he looked down on everyone!" She made a horrid noise in her throat, and spat the hawkings off to one side. She reached into the neck of her garment, and worked or scratched at something on her shoulder. "What are you back for, to sneer at us some more? Oh, your little round mam, I remember her too, so lonely and so pure. You think yourself pure as well, I have no doubt?"

"Of course not. What do you mean?" I knew very well what she meant, and I was cross with her for having seen me so clearly. "I am here on business, to make some arrangements, about property."

"About property," she said in exactly my affronted tone, and grinned up at me, showing the terrible state of her teeth.

"Yes, I am selling my house."

"Are you now, my love?" She shrugged and tweaked at her upper garments as if dislodging fleas, or preparing a moment of madness when she might fling off all her clothes and stand naked and appalling before me. "Cutting your ties?" she crooned up at me. "Hoping to escape us forever?"

"I'm sure there's no ill will in it, Misskaella," I said.

"Oh, I'm sure not!" she said sweetly. "Such a nice young man, with his mainland manners. Have you anything for me, Dominic Mallett?"

"I'm sorry?"

"'I'm sorry?' Look at him. People bring me gifts. People leave me offerings. Sometimes it is a nice fish that they catch, or a loaf their wives have made. A blanket for the winter? A leg of a lamb for my supper? People here," she said, "respect a woman like me and know how to keep her good-tempered."

"Forgive me," I said. "I was only walking by, taking the air. I didn't have it in mind to visit you; if I had thought about it I would have guessed you were asleep."

"Oh, they bring their gifts while I sleep, just the same," she said. "That is no obstacle. How *is* your sainted mother?"

"My mother died, several years ago."

"Ah, ah . . ." Even she would not make merry with a mother's death. "These things happen. So. You are wanting for companionship."

"Of my mother, yes. But I have friends, and an aunt."

"Friends, and an aunt." How foolish she made my words sound. "There are some things that friends and an aunt cannot provide you, as I'm sure you know."

"I am to be married very soon," I said, perhaps too hurriedly.

She laughed. "Oh, I see you understand me. She is all red hair and sharp words, your betrothed?"

"Not sharp at all," I protested, though in truth, by contrast with Fametta . . . "She is a fine girl, and kindly too."

"Kindly." Misskaella pushed out her mouth, as if kindliness were a very suspect virtue. "And you've tested the limits of her kindliness, have you?"

"Why should I do that?"

She straightened and looked at the sea beyond me. "Oh, I don't know. It is useful to have the measure of these things, don't you think?"

I wished I could run away from her; I did not like the way she pulled my words apart and laughed at me through the shreds.

"Let us try an experiment, shall we? Help me up." She took up the stick beside her and put out her hand, a filthy claw, beyond which she was such a mass of flesh and cloth that I felt sure I could not lift her.

On the second attempt, my hand sliding on the greasy fabric of her sleeve, her claw painful around my wrist, I managed to pull her to her feet. She swayed there, steadying herself with the stick. I could not believe she would not topple, her bare feet with their ragged toenails were so small.

She set off as though I were not there, and quickly I stepped aside to make way. Her rising had released from her clothing a strong sour smell from her body. I stifled an exclamation and followed her, straight down the beach toward the water swimming with moonlight. What did she mean, *testing the limits* of Kitty's kindness? Would she throw herself into the waves, maybe, and expect me to save her? Why did she think Kitty would care about the fate of a mad old woman, and one so closely allied with the sea-wives she despised? Perhaps I should flee, back along the beach—look how hard Misskaella found walking! Surely she could not catch me up. But what might she do instead—lightning-strike me? Throw up a magical stone wall in my path? I lagged behind her, to one side, and veered slowly toward the town.

And then I stopped, unable, from surprise and something else, to take another step. Some of the moon shadows in the sea revealed themselves to be swimmers, and as they gained the shallows I saw that they were seals, several now plunging forward out of the waves. A long string of their followers led out beyond the surf, north around Forward Head toward Crescent Corner.

She sang, the witch, indistinctly against the wave noise; I

held myself back bodily from walking closer to hear the words. Her feet squeezed darkness into the shining sand. The ripples ran back to the sea, ran back and made splashy ruffles against the chests of the three leading seals, which forged toward Misskaella like dogs to their master. She put out her hand and moved her fingers as if scattering seed for birds. The seals came up around her; beside them, above them, she was neither so enormous nor so strange as she had seemed before.

I tried to step backward, preparatory to fleeing, for what if she should set those beasts at me somehow? But her song, whatever it was, held me, its sense unfathomable, its play both horrid and beauteous, unlike any tune I had heard before. Another pair of seals coasted up on a wave, and then began their caterpillar-rippling on the firmer ground; all my skin came alive and rushed about on my trapped body, but Misskaella tottered among the beasts quite unafraid, her feet and calves shining wet, the hems of her rags dragging in the water and dripping moonlight upon it.

Matter-of-factly she chose a seal, one that lay between her and the water. She tucked her stick under her arm. She pressed her hands together and bent from the waist as if begging, as if praying, as if bowing reverently. She sang, she sang, and the song was no less senseless than before; it was like tethered kelp on the tide, its ribbons reaching and reaching, never obtaining what they reached for. The chosen seal rolled onto its back—I felt that roll as if I were seal myself, though I stood slender and fearful here on the sand. An invisible knife pierced the flesh under the beast's chin and pulled a dark line down its body. I cried out, my voice feeble, quite without magical force, as the seal opened bloodlessly, parting like giant lips. But instead of teeth appearing and a tongue, the skin convulsed, and from its darkness and its glistening a girl sat up. Misskaella put out a claw to her, and the girl laid her long white hand in it, and allowed herself to be lifted from the shrinking seal flesh. She was as white as bone, as narrow as a sapling tree; her hair tumbled black from where it had been pressed in a mass to the back of her head. It fell and spread, darkness and gloss together like the sea waves, like the sea-rinsed seals.

I took several steps forward, then stopped myself. I was a-hum with Misskaella's song, mazed with the light off the girl, the sight of the shape of her, swaying so tall beside the hunched fat witch. Out of her coat and onto the silvered ground she stepped, guided by Misskaella. She stood among the seals, afraid neither of them nor of the crone before her, and seeming not to feel the cold. Her coat, no more than thick cloth now, shriveled and curled on itself beside her shapely feet.

The sea fell silent, as it sometimes does. Out from the creak and slither of the seal-bodies came Misskaella's voice, low and crafty. "Dominic Mallett?"

With halting steps I approached the two upright people, one shadow, one shining, among the prone wet seals. Kitty Flaming, I told myself desperately, my wife-to-be. Kitty. But the words were nothing against Misskaella's singing; Kitty was nothing, a frail flag blown to tatters by a magical wind. Her face blurred and faded in my memory, while the seal-girl's grew clearer and clearer in the moonlight, serene, dark-eyed, full-lipped, a pale oval, her night-black hair moving around it, breathing of warm sea. She watched me soberly, fearless, unsmiling; she could no more look away than

I could. No one, no woman or man, had ever regarded me so steadily, so trustingly. Kitty herself never looked at me this way; always her own next purposes and plans moved somewhere in her eyes and readied words behind her lips. This girl only waited, her whole being, her whole future, fixed on me.

I felt as if I had been doused in cold fresh water from the sweetest spring. It had washed away the anxious, busymaking man I was before, whom Kitty had been satisfied with; now I felt worthy to face this purer creature, unsullied yet, uninjured by the world. She put me at peace in a glance, and I went to her eyes, to her mouth as a swimmer lost in the night ocean makes for the only light he sees. The rest of her I all but ignored—the fine breasts, the narrow hips, the shadowy cleft of her, the lean legs leading to the sand-swirled half-buried feet, her black fall-and-fall of hair shifting around her like a frayed silk cloak. All those things I registered, but they were for later. Misskaella grinned, off to the side, the old crow, she sang and laughed at me, gloated over my plight. She too I ignored, falling into the dark eyes' attention, longing to press my lips to those full, slightly open and uncertain ones—but restraining myself, until we should be alone together, unobserved by witch or weather.

"What is your name?" I asked the seal-girl.

She answered with the sea, with her comrades' huffing and whining.

"What *is* her name, Dominic Mallett?" said the witch. "It's for you to give her one, to use here on the land. What would you like her to answer to?"

I listened in my heart for the right name. I put out my hand,

and her warm palm met it; her warm fingers intertwined with my cold ones. "Dominic Mallett," she said, just as Fametta had, but more curiously, experimenting with the first words to come from her new throat, to pass across her new tongue.

"Her name is Neme," I said, because I wanted to see her tongue move on an *n*, her lips on an *m*, again.

"Neme?" rasped Misskaella from the glare off the moonlit sea. "There, then, her name is Neme." And I took the girl's other hand, and we stood spelled together on the sand, the seals moving about us like monstrous dark maggots, helpless, harmless, huge.

Next day I rose, and dressed what felt like an entirely new body, an entirely new man, in the ordinary clothing of the old. I kissed sleeping Neme, and took up her skin that had lain folded all night on the blanket chest, and tucked it into my coat. I went out into the world, which greeted me wet and windily, full of a cruel and exhilarating light.

Up the town I climbed to Wholeman's inn, and peered in at the window. Wholeman was at work in there, wiping down tables. I knocked on the window, then met him at the door.

He squinted up at me. "I know you, I'm sure," he said, "though it's very early for a welcome-home drink."

"That's not what I'm after. May I speak with you a moment?"

"Why, certainly! You're Mallett's boy, aren't you, that his mam took off to Cordlin years ago?" He stood back for me and I stepped in. The empty room smelt of men and pipe smoke and ale; it had no ornament beyond mounted fishes and a stag's head on the walls.

"That's me: Dominic Mallett," I said, with the smile of a man who has had his name whispered in his ear all night. We shook hands. "And I have come into a fortune."

"You have? Well, you're very welcome to spend it here," he said with a laugh. "Oh," he then said as I pulled Neme's skin-parcel free of my coat. "It must have been *quite* a fortune, to persuade Misskaella out so late in the season."

"No, no," I said. "I found my lady on the beach last night, just this side of Forward Head, singing on the rocks there." This was the story Misskaella had advised me to tell. *I owe you money*, I had said foolishly, not even looking at her, because that would mean tearing my gaze from Neme's. But, *Let me give* you *a gift*, the witch had cooed, *just to see what that feels like*.

"*Found* her?" Wholeman took the skin from me, and looked up wide-eyed. "Singing on the rocks? For the taking?"

"She is at my house now. She has agreed to stay awhile."

Wholeman shook his head slowly. "I have heard of such luck, women coming up by themselves," he said, "but I've never known a man to have it, not in my time."

"Well, now you have, Wholeman," I said. "But my fix is still the same as every man's, to keep the skin where she cannot find it, for she says she does not trust herself to resist the lure of the sea, if she knows of the skin's whereabouts, or finds it accidentally. Do I remember, you used to have a locked room out the back here?"

"I did and I do. Shall I hang this there with the others?"

"Would you? And what do I owe you for it?"

"Owe me? Why, a little custom now and then, that's all."

"No fee, for the keeping? Are you sure?"

"There's enough debt in this town without my taking men's pennies for a bit of hanging-space I'd not use otherwise. If you don't owe Misskaella, you are one of the few who doesn't. You must drink twice the amount for your good fortune." But he was laughing at me, and he clapped me on the arm. "I will put it away safely right now, lucky man."

Next I went to Fisher's store and bought milk and foodstuffs, and a dress that Neme might leave the house in without shame, and so on. There was no means of keeping my luck and my decision secret there either, any more than there had been at Wholeman's. Fisher was much more excited by it, though, than Wholeman, and brought his wife Darely out to tell her the news directly; he expressed hearty congratulations, and was in awe of how well things had turned out for me, that I had not had to pay as others had. Darely, more quietly, asked whether I had hidden the skin, and did I intend to marry Neme, and when would I bring her to meet the rest of the wives? She helped me buy underthings for Neme, and forced the loan of a cardigan and coat on me "to keep the poor maid cozy"; she asked after the state of my firewood and food, in between Neepny throwing questions at me as they occurred to him: "What will you tell your betrothed, though, back in Cordlin?" and "How will you keep yourself? You will have to get a place on one of the boats."

They sent me away laden with gifts and necessities, even coming to the door to see me off. Darely wrung her hands as if she wished she could come with me and see my new wife settled.

I climbed the hill much encouraged—relieved, in fact, that now I had company. Potshead was full of Dominic Malletts, each devoted alike to his strange wife, each intent on keeping her, and keeping her happy as far as he was able.

Back at the house I showed Neme how to dress, and we breakfasted, amid many small adventures of discovery and misinterpreting. I took her down to Fisher's then, and to Shy Tyler and Fametta's, where she was welcomed with many embraces and exclamations. Fametta and Darely promised to care for her while I attended to my Cordlin business. They talked of wedding preparations, and gatherings of the wives to welcome Neme among them, and I nodded, and thanked them, and felt a little panicked. This was the day my mam and dad had brought me up to avoid, yet here it was, folding me compliantly into itself as an octopus folds a fish toward its mouth.

Then I took Neme and we walked, out beyond Crescent Corner to Six-Mile Beach, where you can stride the sand forever if you've a temper or a mood to pound away. We walked, and sometimes we talked, about my predicament and her new life, and about the people we had just met, and the little I knew of them, from long ago. How different it was from conversing with Kitty! With each utterance Neme and I must seek ways to make sense to each other, speaking out of our different pasts, our different worlds above and below water, our different beings. Kitty and I had always been turning over matters and objects familiar to both of us; by comparison, that had been like talking to myself, I was so easily understood. From here, on the beach, with Neme questioning me and her slim foreign hand in the crook of my arm, the conversation with Kitty seemed a dull one, revealing nothing, taking neither of us anywhere new.

I told Neme of my intention to go to Cordlin and tell Kitty face to face what had happened.

"But, Dominic Mallett," she said. "Once you see Kitty, might not your love for her rush back upon you? I fear you will stay and marry her as you said, simply because you are there and in sight of her. Just as you could put her aside and love me on first sighting, won't you be able to put *me* aside, when she is there before you, ready to kiss and marry you?"

I stopped on the sand, openmouthed. "You think me so fickle?" I said. "You think I have had . . . nights such as we have just had, with Kitty? You think my loyalty and love shift so easily to whichever woman is before me?"

"Why would they not?"

I had to explain to her then that men were not like bull seals, with their many wives, that we mated one to one like bird pairs and many other animals. "I can never put aside the thought of you," I said, "now that we have met."

Into my hand she pressed a sea-penny, one of those shells worn flat on one side, grooved on the other like the inside of a person's ear. "Hold this in your pocket while you talk to Kitty," she said, "and remember me." She folded my fingers around it, a measure of doubt still in her eyes.

"I will," I said. "Don't worry. How can I tell you so that you'll believe me? This is different, this is a proper love; I am helpless against this, whereas Kitty, I now discover, I can take or leave."

"Who knows what else you may discover?" She pushed the hand with the shell in it into my coat pocket.

I dropped the shell there and took Neme in my arms. I tried, with all the warmth that I wrapped her in, with all the force I could summon to an embrace, with the length and depth of all my kisses, to convince her—as I was *beyond* convinced, as I knew in my bones, to my deepest innards and my heart of hearts—that I was hers, flesh and soul of me, for as long as I lived, that I would not forsake her, because I *could* not, but was helplessly, hopelessly hers forever.

"At this hour?" said Mrs. Flaming at the door. "We are all but abed!"

"I've important news for Kitty," I said. "It cannot wait."

"You young people, you *always* think it cannot wait. Come in, then, into the parlor." Annoyed, she looked, and inconvenienced—and this was as kindly as she would ever look on me again. I watched her hurry away up the hall, and then I stepped into the parlor, which was aglow with the new electrics that the family was so proud of.

Every candlestick, every silk flower, every landscape on the wall had once held and increased the glamour of my love for Kitty, but now each object only seemed to speak, and rather smugly, of well-earned comfort and a kind of terror of not being thought tasteful. Look at those drapes! How many layers of cloth did you need at a window, how many tassels and fringes, to keep out the light and the cold, to thwart prying eyes? I crossed the room slowly toward the screened fireplace, the mantel loaded with pictures and figurines. I felt as if I carried the weight of it on my own back. How had I made sense of such things before? My little time on Rollrock had emptied my head of rooms like this, the detail of them, the fuss and filling of spaces. What more did you need than a chair and a fire, and another chair with Neme curled up and dreaming across at you? What gave lovelier light than a spirit lamp, which left some mystery to linger in the darker corners?

Kitty's hurried footsteps sounded in the hall; dread flooded my head and churned in my stomach. Then she was there in the doorway, and I lifted my eyes to hers. Her face was fresh and unguarded, as if she had been asleep, her hair hastily gathered up, fine curls falling from it. She had never looked prettier. She was pleased to see me, and surprised, and amused. She thought I had come because I could not bear to betake me to my rest without seeing her, holding her, asserting our bond once more.

I might reassure her with a smile. I might cross to her and embrace her—I knew exactly how she would feel, the bold curves of her that had once excited me. I could choose, coldly, to undo everything I'd done on Rollrock. I could confess to it, or I could keep it secret; I could invent an excuse to return to the island, give Neme back her skin and send her home to the sea. I could do my duty to this woman before me, and no one in Cordlin need be any the wiser.

I couldn't put it off a moment longer. "I have taken me a seawife," I said—softly, as if it would hurt her less that way.

All pleasure went from her face—I would never see it there again. She gave a little cry—"I knew it!"—and bent in the middle as if struck. Softer and flatter she spoke: "I should not have let you go." She straightened, took a few steps into the room, then retreated and sat in the upright chair by the door, and put her face in her hands. "Tell me," she said into them. Then she looked up at me, haughty, white-lipped. "What has happened."

"She came up from the sea." I pressed my shoulder blades against the mantel. "Of her own choice."

"Saw you standing there, did she? Could not resist you?" I could see how Kitty would be as an old woman, with this roundedness gone from her face, with this bitter tightness about her mouth.

"I found her on the beach." I saw Misskaella bending to the seal praying, the flesh splitting deeply, shining wet in the moonlight.

"What were you doing on a *beach*—pacing up and down and hoping? You were supposed to be selling a house, crating up two chairs, not wandering about the island looking for trouble!" I could see how she would have scolded our children, the thin line of her lips.

"I had done all I could do that day. I had had supper with Shy Tyler and Fam—his wife, their little boy . . ." My voice faded on the disapproving silence.

"So," she said. "You are here to tell me that you don't want to marry me anymore." She raised a hand and dropped it, almost with a slap, to her thigh.

"I wish I *could* marry you," I said sincerely, "to avoid you the embarrassment—"

"I wish you could too, for better reasons than that." Her voice was low and harsh. "I wish you could marry me out of love for me, love that you said you felt, and that was firmly enough set before you stepped aboard that boat to Rollrock. You are not the man I thought you, if you can be pushed so easily from the path we had laid out for ourselves."

"I am not the man *I* even thought me," I said. "What can I say? I am bewitched." I saw it cleanly, truly, then, for a moment: Misskaella's work, Misskaella's fault.

"You are *stupid*," she hissed, "to have let yourself be enchanted. To have put yourself in the way of it. *Two chairs*, you told me. *It will be so nice for us to have them, side by side, Mam's and Dad's*. While all the time, I should not be surprised—"

I had crossed the room to her while she spoke. "Kitty, it was not like that! There was no forethought, no scheming against you, I promise! I am as surprised as you!" Though I should not be, I realized. Why else would Rollrock be so afraid of that witch, if not because she could snare us like this, whenever she chose?

Kitty's eyes were dead; her lips pressed together. The freckles seemed to hover just in front of her face like a cloud of russet insects. "Yet you emerge from *your* surprise with a bewitching woman, and an island full of men clapping you on the back. While I come from *my* surprise with what? A crowd of people to explain to, a meal to pay for—a *cake*, for goodness' sake! And the knowledge that I've been made a fool of, that my sweetheart all these years was never mine. A mermaid had only to crook her finger at him, and he'd be gone."

"I swear, Kitty, I never wished for this! I never had such thoughts in my head!"

"Oh, this is not a matter of *heads*, Dominic," she said with something of a laugh. "Of reason, or logic. This is not civilized. This is barely *human*!"

Her tears surprised her, and for a moment her rage and horror fell away and her face held only pure distress. In that moment I could imagine loving her again, and I regretted that I could not use the power I had, to take her in my arms and set my affairs to rights once more. I had tight hold of the sea-penny Neme had given me, in my coat pocket; I squeezed it as if I wished to crumble it to dust there, and my attachment to Neme with it. At the same time I wished I could wring magical properties out of it, travel upon it as they say a witch can sail upon a nutshell if she chooses, out of this suffocating room and across to Rollrock where I belonged. The thing was done; I had betrayed Kitty and confessed to it; now I only wanted to be gone.

She fought to contain her tears. Another fell, and she all but smacked it away from her cheek.

"I won't ask you to forgive me," I said.

"Good!" She flashed me a hot glance. "Because I won't, ever. All the people I have to face and tell! Not to mention what you have done to *me*!" And she knocked at her chest with a fist, as if trying to wake a heart stopped within.

"All I can say is, I am sorry this has happened to us."

A silence fell in her struggling breathing. What had I said? She raised her eyes to me and they were as dry as if they had never wept, and never would again, even as her cheek carried the sheen of the tear she had struck away.

"*Happened* to us, Dominic?" Her voice was deep with scorn. "Let there be no mistake about this, Dominic: nothing *happened* to us. *You* did this thing, to *me*. You chose that creature above me; you left me embarrassed in this town on the very eve of our betrothal celebration. Don't tell yourself it *happened;* don't console yourself that way."

She glared up at me. There was no point in my protesting that indeed this *had* happened to me, had *been done* to me, as I was just beginning to see. On Rollrock, in Neme's arms, I had thought myself to be waking from a state of confusion, my engagement to Kitty being but one aspect of my uncertainty; I had seen my destiny laid out before me strange but clear, frightening but full of beauty. I did not want to let go of that revelation in favor of this new one, of myself as Misskaella's puppet.

"Do you know?" Kitty's eyes glittered.

I bowed my head to receive whatever blow she would next deliver on me.

"I am *glad* you found her in time. I'm *relieved* that you showed me you are this sort of man, before I was locked to you forever in marriage. These years we were together I was well fooled, Dominic. Perhaps I wanted so strongly for you to be what you could never be—honorable, you know, and loyal, and with some strength of mind, some integrity—that I missed all kinds of tiny clues that I should have noticed, glances at this woman or that, which I thought were quite innocent, words you said that I might have read another way."

She paused as if to let me protest again, to deny it. But she was so entirely mistaken, and so energetic in putting together her mistaken view, and so *trapped*—as I had been—in Cordlin life and the Cordlin mind, that I could not see where I should begin in countering her. Besides, I did not want to; I had done what I had done. I deserved every chastisement she heaped on my head.

"It doesn't matter," she went on. "Everything's clear now, and I see you for the weakling you are and the traitor, and the toyer with my affections. You can go," she said, rising. "And I will thank you never to approach me again, or any friend of mine or member of my family."

She left the parlor and stood aside from the doorway to let me pass out into the hall. Her face was chalk, her body iron; the slippers she wore had a rose embroidered on each toe, and the dressing gown an arabesque on each lapel, but neither detail at all softened this general impression.

I paused before her, looked her in the face. She held her gaze aside from me as long as she could, then flicked me a glance. "Go," she said. "I don't want you here in my house."

"I'm sorry to have hurt you, Kitty."

"Well, that is very gentlemanly of you, I'm sure." Her voice was loud in my ear as I turned aside from her scorn. "But I am still hurt, and I will stay hurt longer than you will stay sorry. Go and find your consolation in that monster's arms. Be sorry there. The spectacle of your sorrow makes me *sick*."

She might as well have spat on me. She brushed past me and pulled open the door. The front porch was electric-lit too; I had often rung the bell and stood there in that golden glow, waiting for the family to admit and welcome me, looking forward to the sight of Kitty dressed for dancing, hurrying down the stairs.

I stepped out; I turned in time to see the door close with quiet finality on me. She left the light on until I closed the gate, perhaps to make the point that she still held to a system of civilized manners, however far I had left it behind.

I walked away dazed. I took out the sea-penny and pressed it to my lips, tried to drink up some sea-scent from it, but it smelt only of my nervous sweat. I put it back in my pocket and walked on.

I had left turmoil behind me in that house. I had never made myself so unwelcome in a place, and I stung with all the things that Kitty had said. I was shaken, unable to tell which of her words were true and which were only her bitterness coloring her view of me. I felt I hardly knew myself. Perhaps I had *never* known myself very well. Could I really be so evil, and have remained ignorant of it?

I grasped after the thought of Neme for some consolation, but she scarcely seemed real; Kitty was so hard and bright and vituperative in my mind, her voice clawing away my confidence in myself, that I could not think past her to gentle Neme, to the moment Neme had handed me the sea-penny on the beach, to the nights Neme and I had had together. A mermaid, Kitty had called her, and a monster; how could I want to be married to a monster?

But Neme was no such thing. She was my Neme, spelled to me as I was to her, awaiting me on Rollrock, in that humble, isolated, sparse-furnished home where I belonged. She was all I had, and all I needed. I walked through Cordlin to my aunt's house, where tomorrow, before I left, I would deliver the same news as I had just imparted. As I walked I breathed out Kitty, and Cordlin, and the mainland fuss and frippery I had furnished my life with, and I breathed in the simplicity I was returning to, the cold wind straight off the sea, the smell of the spirit lamps, the tang of woodsmoke—and, at last, the damp-seaweed smell of Neme's hair. I closed my eyes and buried my face in it; I felt her slim arms around me, heard her low voice, so absent of hatred and accusation. *Find your consolation in that monster's arms*, Kitty had said. But it was not consolation I was after, it was truth, the truth of myself, a man who did not pretend and strive after this fine house or this rare object or that impressive friend; a man who was complete, and steady in himself, and clear as to what he was, however shameful or regrettable that might be.

That is what I told myself, walking closed-eyed through the Cordlin night, running my thumb tip over the ridges of the sea-penny, recalling to my lips the touch of Neme's warm, silken skin.

Daniel Mallett

Mam paced back and forth, the blanket dragging behind her like turf pulled free of the ground and fashioned into a rough cloak. From one window, she went past the closed front door to the other. I did not try to hear words in what she muttered, in her odd bits of song, a whine here, a whisper there. They made as much sense as the swish and scratch of the blanket, or the hiss of her foot-soles on the gray boards.

She paused by one of the windows, fenced off from me by the chair backs, a seaweedy hummock of shoulders and then her head against the glary cloud light, her hair pushed and pulled a little, some strands waving in the wind of her warmth. She applied herself to the view and was silent, and I stood in the hallway, listening to her upsetness.

I knew better than to ask her what was the matter. Often enough she had told me in the past: *I come from the sea, and I miss the sea.* How could she miss the sea? I would wonder. It was right there at the bottom of the town, for anyone to visit! I would suggest, when I was smaller, *Shall I take you down to the beach, Mam? It's not far. We could bring your blanket and freshen it up in the water.* I had suggested this even in November sometimes, with snow drifting down outside. *No, my darling,* she would say. *Thank you, my darling, but no. There is nothing you can do.* And I had heard the same from many other lads, that their mam was low, today or this week or these last several months, and whatever they tried they could not raise her. They had sat her in the sun, brought her any kitten or duckling they could find, walked her on the shore up and down, and nothing would console her.

I went to Mam, stood at the sill as if I too were interested in the day outside. The same lanes as ever slanted away, the one up, the one down. The same front steps shone whitewashed like lamps along the lane. The same tedious cat sat in Trumbells' window, now blinking out at us, now dozing. And through the gaps and beyond some of the roofs, the sea rode to the horizon, dark as charcoal, flat as slate, with neither sail nor dinghy nor dragon to relieve its emptiness.

She turned and turned her silver wedding ring; sometimes she would do this till the flesh reddened around it. She pressed and turned, as if working it free took quite some effort, though the ring always slid loose between her knuckle and finger joint.

I laid my hand on her darker one. She looked down from the view.

"What is it, Daniel?"

I took her hands one from the other. I turned to the window again, and brought her ring hand over my shoulder and down to my chest. There I held it and took from her the task of turning the warm silver, moving it much more gently upon her finger than she had been doing.

She laughed very softly, deep in her throat. "Sweetest boy." She kissed the top of my head and then laid her other hand there. And so we stood, she cloaked with the blanket and me wearing her like a cloak, turning the ring on her finger while outside the steps glowed and the cat dozed and the sea sat flat behind it all, nothing of anything changing.

First the mainland was a black fingernail's edge between the pale sea and the pale sky. I pulled Dad's sleeve as he talked to Mister Fisher, who was crossing the Strait to buy some tins and vegetables for the store.

"There it is, yes," Dad said to me, and gazed at it to satisfy me.

"Don't you be fooled, young Daniel," Fisher said around Dad's front. "It may look like the land of promise, but Rollrock's best, home is best."

Dad squeezed my shoulder, invisibly to Fisher. Did he mean me to listen carefully to Fisher, or to ignore him and flee to mainland as soon as I ever could?

We stood at the rail in the biting autumn wind. Mam had combed me with hair polish this morning; I had watched in the mirror as she made two slick curves of my hair, either side of a raw white parting. My whole head had felt scraped and cold, and now the wind had chilled my scalp and ears to a numb helmet.

Slowly the land rose and unrolled out of the horizon: two rounded hills with others either side like attendants. The sea slopped and danced below us. The sky blued up stronger as the sun ascended, and shapes emerged on the land, forested parts and fields. Roofs and roads glinted. Then the black cliffs lifted and obscured all this awhile, before splitting apart head from head to show it all again, closer and more dazzling between them.

Nothing, I thought, could be more exciting than chugging between the Heads. Cordlin Harbor spread out wide either side, serene and glossy after the tumbled sea, after the beating of the waves at the cliffs' feet. Rank after rank of boats were moored alongside the piers, and others lay looser about the more open water, each ketch and trawler kissing its morning reflection, each little pleasure boat. Cordlin town lay thick around the harbor and on the nearest slopes, thinned away higher up the hills to single cottages and barns like drops of milk around porridge in a bowl. Closer windows winked at us, and the great granaries and wool stores stood with their barred windows and red and white brick-work, and I saw for the first time how humble my home island was, beside this center of wealth and commerce.

"We will catch the bus," said Dad to me. "It goes right from the pier. See it there?"

"So we'll not see this town, so much?" I said. It seemed so rich in sights, with its wall of warehouses along the front, its several steeples beyond and its flagged castle at the top. Shining trucks and motors glided along by the water.

"Can you not let the lad at the fleshpots of Cordlin Harbor, Mallett?" laughed Fisher. "Even to the extent of a raspberry lol-lipop at Missus Hedly's shop?"

"We've business." My dad shook his head and smiled. "Knocknee Market will have to be excitement enough for the boy."

All the jollity fell from Mister Fisher's face. "Of course. You're not here for treats and dillydallying, are you?" He gave me a guarded look and Dad a worried one. "Best of luck with that, Dominic."

And when the boat was tied up by the pier, among the shuffle of passengers toward the gangplank Fisher let his hand fall heavily to my shoulder, as if he were seeing us off to a funeral, or to a surgeon whose treatment it was doubtful we would survive.

The bus was a marvelous shining thing, painted cream and green, a crest on the side of it and a number plate behind. People, Cordlin people, people who rode buses every day, sat in it waiting for Dad—and me holding fast to Dad's hand—to climb on and pay our fares, and sit in the glossy red seats.

The trip to Knocknee was all new sights and events, one piled on the next so that my telling of them, which at first I tried to rehearse to Mam in my head, fast became garbled and then fell to silence. I hung on to the windowsill, grateful that Dad looked over me, and would see the important things, would collect any details that I might miss. Presently the overwhelming town with its too many faces, its too many curtains and gates and grand trees and window boxes, sank away and we were flying among fields, and this I could follow more easily, the fields in their emptiness, and the hills in their billowing roundness being much like the sea, which I was well used to gazing on.

The engine must have been right below our seat, it shook our bottoms so. I turned to Dad: "Such a noisy way to get about."

"It is indeed," he said. "Noisier than a boat, and certainly noisier than a man's own legs. But fast," he added. "And fast is what we're wanting, to reach inland and back in a day."

Once we were at Knocknee—which was less grand than Cordlin, but busy still with the market day, and just as overwhelming to a Rollrock lad—my dad went through the crowd, asking this person and that a question. I could never quite hear what he said, but it made their eyes slide aside, their heads shake and their bodies turn away. I ran about after him, and the running, and the noticing of everything—dogs, red hairs and red faces, improbable piles of vegetables, excessive rows of meat butchered and hung—eventually tired me, and chilled me to shivering. Dad put me on a bench against a wall of the market square that was lit with the weak autumn sun. "Wait here while I search on, Daniel; I'll be back to fetch you when I've had some luck."

Before long someone else was put there, at the other end of the bench, someone in skirts, and with a great deal more hair than I had. I had got my breath by then, and was beginning to thaw out in the sunshine. When we had caught each other glancing several times, "I know what you are," I said to her.

She stopped swinging her legs. She looked at me and narrowed her eyes, which were pale like a dad's. "Well, what?"

"You are a girl-child," I said.

She gave a small hiccup of a laugh. "No joking!" she said. "Good thing that you told me." And she swung her legs some more and looked about at the legs and bums and baskets and bustle. "I'd've gone on thinking myself a jee-raff for who knows how long."

"You are, aren't you?" I said. "A girl?"

She looked me up and down. Her breath was white on the air,

air that smelt strongly of the smoked-meat stall nearby, and not at all of the sea. "Are you touched, or what?"

"I haven't ever met one before," I said.

She snorted.

"It's true," I said. "We don't have them on Rollrock."

Her face got more startled, and prettier. "You're from Rollrock Isle?"

"I am," I said. "My dad brought me over this morning."

"For the first-ever time?" Now I was interesting, and she seemed to have stopped disliking me, which was good.

"First ever," I said.

"You've been on that one island all your life."

I searched her face for why she should sound so astonished. "I have," I said. "And on lots of sea around it."

"I've never seen the sea yet," she said. "My mam and dad won't take me. Say it sends men potty. Is your dad potty?"

"Of course not." I looked about for him. None of these legs were his, none of these hatted heads, fuzzy-rimmed against the sunshine.

"Are *you* potty?" said the girl.

"No!"

She laughed at me, but not unkindly. What a *lot* of hair she had, and it was not straight and silky like a mam's. If you took that band off, undid that ribbon, loosed it from those plaits, it would stand straight out from her head, or possibly get up and walk right off her, or catch fire from the combination of so many hot red strands together.

"You might be anything," she said, "with your great eyes."

I turned from her embarrassed, and again she laughed. These girl-children were certainly unsettling.

"What brings you, then," she said, as if she had a perfect right to know, "you and your dad, to Knocknee?"

"My dad has business here, he said." Again I searched the crowd, for I rather wished he would burst out now, perhaps with something for me to eat, some mainland fancy.

"Cloth, maybe?"

"He has to find someone. A girl, like you."

"Do you *really* not have girls there, on Rollrock? Is it all potty boys and men?"

"We have *women*," I said, stung. "We have very beautiful women, all our mams."

"Ye-es." She narrowed her eyes at me again, and breathed more breath-smoke. "That is your specialty out there, isn't it?"

"What do you mean?" I stiffened further, not knowing how insulted I ought to be.

"I'm trying to remember. I've heard mams talking. There's something about those Rollrock women, isn't there?"

"Maybe," I said. "But they're our mams, so don't you say anything that might get you popped on the snout."

"Well, they must be unusual, to've begot an unusual like you," she said sensibly, looking me up and down again.

"They're usual for our town," I said. "Perfectly usual." And I turned back to the crowd, to the sun.

Dad came then and rescued me, for finally he'd had some success with his questions. He knew where to look for the girl now.

He took me there, and it was a very smelly part of the town;

some kind of offal was piled and straggling in the drain outside her family's house, and inside, in a wall corner, lay a cat that at first I was sure was dead, until it lifted its mean triangle of a face and showed me eyes whitened by some dreadful town disease.

Dad talked to what I thought at first was the girl's grandma, she had so few teeth and was so weathered—but it turned out to be her mam. She watched my dad as if he might snap at and bite her, as if he were there to trick her and she ought to be very careful.

The girl herself was orange-haired like everyone here, but she was not so clean as the market girl, or so slender. She had something of the twitching of the mam about her, and a sneaky manner that was all her own. She sat listening closely, pursing her lips, her glance flicking from Dad to her mam and back again. She had tied her pinafore strangely; as well as the straps crossed on her back she had brought the waist ties around and crossed them over her stout front. It gave me a very uncomfortable feeling to look at her; who would *make* a pinafore with such long straps? It was as if her head was on backward. She ignored me as too young to be of any account, and I was glad of it.

They were talking about money; the mam wanted some, and Dad was saying how Rollrock oughtn't to have to pay, giving board and accommodations to this girl as we would. He seemed to be buying this girl, buying something she could do. Truth told, she didn't look capable of a lot, she was such a funny, gray-fleshed lump. She looked like the sort to sidle out of any job going.

Dad took a deep breath. "You have eleven of her, Missus Callisher. Aren't you glad to get the burden of even the one of them off your shoulders?"

"This one eats mouse rations, for all the size on her," snapped the mam. "Why don't you take one of the taller girls, my Gert or my Lowie? Thin as pins, they are, though they put away food like heifers."

"You know why: this is the one with the touch on her, who can be taught up to be useful by our Misskaella."

Misskaella? What did the old crow have to do with this, flapping around Potshead, coughing and snarling?

"Useful for what? Useful for catching mermaids, is what. And stuck on blimming Rollrock Isle the rest of her life, for nowhere else in the world needs mermaids fetched." She slid a glance at me. "I don't want grandsons with *tails*," she said. "Granddaughters with *fins*."

What was she on about? I thought they both must be mad, she and her daughter.

"We will pay for a yearly journey home, how about that? Boat and motor bus to visit you every spring."

The mam sucked at the inside of her discontented face. "And no one to marry."

"She might well meet a man here, one of her visits. I don't know, Missus Callisher. These terms are reasonable. I'm sure Trudle would be very content, a room of her own in the old woman's house, and a livelihood."

The girl Trudle gave a kind of a whinny, and was no less ugly for laughing. If anything her face looked more weaselish, creased up like that.

Her mam shook her head. "She'd be happy on a dung heap, that one. She's touched more ways than the one."

"Ask Fan Dowser how touched I am," said Trudle in a rasping voice.

Swiftly the mam stepped over and smacked Trudle's head. The girl rubbed the spot and glared up at her.

"Very well, take her," said the mam with great carelessness. "Don't come blubbing back to me, though, what she gets up to with your pretty lads." She shot me a look, her lip curled but fear in her eyes. "As I say, there's not a lot up her top. Why a person cannot be touched *and* have brains, I do not know."

" 'Tis straightforward enough work," said Dad.

"Hmph. Nothing of this nature is straight. Go fetch your box, girl."

Trudle insisted on dressing up for the journey in some ancient hand-me-down ruffles and a big dark blue bonnet, her weaselly face in the middle. Dad transacted with the mam, and we left.

I was glad to be out of that house and away from that woman, but unhappy having Trudle with us. She walked in a funny rocking way, her legs wide under her stoutness as if she had wet herself. People watched us go by, breaking off conversations to do so. My dad preceded us, Trudle's box on his shoulder, a bed coverlet pillowing up in the top of it. He walked quite fast, making Trudle rocky-rock along ridiculous. It was a nightmare, this big town and the hurrying, people's glances and opinions peppering us, and the late sunshine flaring coldly along the damp lanes. Trudle did not speak and nor did I; we only struggled along separately and together. I would have liked to walk with Dad, but I could never quite catch up with him.

Then the crowds cleared, and the bus was there alongside its shelter. The door was just shutting, but my dad hoyed and waved and ran, and the driver opened it for us again.

Trudle bustled up first. She chose a seat halfway down the bus and sat very straight and pleased there. She glared at Dad when he made to sit by her, so that he came with me to the seat behind her instead.

"That was close," he said as the bus's starting threw him back into his seat. "Any more bargaining with Missus Callisher and we'd have been stuck here the night."

I could smell Trudle, the oldness of her clothes, and the fact that she had not bathed in a while.

"I see you got talking to a maid, there in the market?" said my dad politely when we had recovered our breaths.

I nodded, watching the last of Knocknee town whirl by: a cottage with a yard full of uncut branches, a dog with a plumy tail, water shining in boot-printed mud.

"What was that like?" he said.

I shrugged—it had not been like anything, and I did not know what to think of it, what to say.

"How did you find her company?"

I slid my bottom back, to sit straighter in the seat. Cows flew by, some of them watching us with their great heads raised. "She was fine, I suppose." Did I have the right to like or dislike such a stranger? Today I was just a big empty trawler hold, with the world's fish and sea-worms tumbling into me. "We only talked a little while."

There's something about those Rollrock women, isn't there? I saw the girl's narrow eyes, her hair wires glowing around her head.

Suddenly, sharply, I wished I were among *those Rollrock women;* I was sick of this adventure. I wished I was tiny again, and curled in Mam's lap with her singing buzzing and burring around me in the quiet room, Dad gone to fish or to Wholeman's.

Trudle looked out the window all across the mainland countryside. She did not seem to feel the need to talk to us; indeed, she might have been traveling quite alone, for all the notice she took of us. When we reached the wharf she boarded the boat ahead of us as if she owned it, and she stayed upright and cheerful-looking all across the Strait.

As soon as we had disembarked at Rollrock my dad sent me up home. Mister Fisher gave me a lemon for my mam, and I dug my fingernail into the rind and sniffed lemon all the way up the town, to clear out the Trudle-smell.

From what I later gathered by overhearing, Trudle was given over to Misskaella just as promised and no fussing. And after that the two of them went about a pair, like a flour- and a tea-caddy. They both wore witch-dresses, tight to their arms and waists, then springing out like flower bells, nearly to the ground—cages and flowers, as I had seen on the women in Knocknee and Cordlin, very *presenting* of themselves. The one's hair was dirty orange in the sunlight, the other's mostly frost, only a few reddish stains in it to hint at what it had been. And Misskaella kept her thinning hair short, while Trudle grew hers, making the point that she alone had such color, and could bear about such quantities of it.

Misskaella never was polite, never greeted you even if she met your eye, and Trudle learned the same ways fast, or at least toward mams and children. For men she would raise what might have been called a smile if it had not been so sly and ambiguous. She enjoyed teasing our men, anyone could see. They would rather have not seen her, but she would keep planting herself in their way and greeting them. "Mister Paige," she would say, but it would come out *Pay-eeshsh,* too lingering, and Paige would seem to dodge and weave without taking a step in any direction, would seem to bow and touch his cap brim without taking his hands from his pockets.

But mostly Trudle followed her mistress about the town and country around. We had been frightened enough of Misskaella on her own; now there were two of them, the small caddy tripping after the big one, taking on and amplifying the old witch's herbaceous, privy-aceous smell. Two bells on feet, they clanged fear into our spines; two ragged flower shadows, they crept along the sky on Watch-Out Hill. Or they would be on the south mole, Misskaella peering out to sea or up to town, Trudle bent bottom-up collecting fish scales for their magics. Or the two of them would be horrors together on the field roads, glowering ahead, pretending not to see us boys as we hugged the wall opposite, greeting them feebly as they passed us by.

Come a fine day, the mams would go down together to wash their crying-blankets in the sea. They would sit about on the rocks at the start of the south mole, with their feet hooked in the knitted seaweed. The water would rush in, and swell up and fizz in the blankets, and rush away again. They were always happy then, and we boys liked to be among them, clambering about at our own play while they talked, mixing their languages to make each other laugh. They sat so solid, and watched the crowding sea so attentively, you could imagine them staying like sea-rocks there, all night even, searching the black waves as the water and knitted weed bobbed and sucked around them.

Misskaella would stump up and down along the mole, Trudle would skip there, both women with bunches of seaweed in their belts like strange sideways tails. The mams, each moving her blanket slowly across her knees to examine the weave and wear of it, ignored them except to call out for a length of weed now and then. Some boys were always among the mole-rocks playing; these would take the lengths of weed from witch to mam, and the mams would pinch their cheeks or kiss their heads for their trouble.

It was a fine sunny morning then, early, and the mams had ooched and ouched over the stones in their bare feet and flung their blankets wide onto the water and now were settling on the rocks around, when what should come in at the pier uncommonly early but the Cordlin boat, and what should fall off it but some Cordlin people, picnic people, baskets with them and the ladies with parasols, and the gentlemen with gentlemen-type hats on and boots that shone like mirrors.

Straightaway the ladies walked across from the pier and along to the south mole. There was not much of a breeze, and their voices were as clear to us as if we shared a room: *Are these them, then? Are these the . . . creatures? The seal-ladies?*

Why, I believe they are. What are they about, do you suppose?

Quite clearly washing of some kind. Washing . . .

Yes, washing what, *exactly, Davina?*

Well, let us go closer and see.

The mams' talk had quieted; they lifted their faces curiously to the visitors. I sat among the mole boulders, so that the Cordlin ladies walking the path were a little above me. Such complicated clothing they wore! And all their bright hairs, brown and gold as well as red like some of us boys', were so fancily packaged and structured on their heads! I followed their gazes to our mams below, the crying-blankets floating all about them, their faces not composed at all the way the town ladies' were. They held their entire selves out, all their thoughts and feelings, as if on a platter for the ladies to take as they would. They did not seem to realize that the ladies might laugh, or not understand. The mams held to their blankets, some still stroking the weave as if examining it, even though their eyes were not attentive to the task. The wavelets rippled the wet blankets and made them twinkle in the sun. Some of the mams' bare shins showed, dappled by the sun, greened and shortened by the water.

A silence fell among the Cordlin ladies too. Misskaella and Trudle stood far off at the mole end; if Misskaella could have hopped into the sea and swum away I'm sure she would have. All us boys glanced at each other, some of us making faces, some just waiting.

Finally one of the ladies, an older one with pink clouds powdered onto her cheeks, came to the edge of the mole. "What is it you are washing there, my good woman?" she said in a clear, commanding way to the closest mam, Bessie O'Day.

"Our blankets," Bessie said, her voice so plain after theirs that

I was embarrassed for her. "And we are not washing them," she went on, "but soaking them. And mending." She waved toward the witches; Misskaella folded her arms and turned away with a flick of her weed-tail.

"What kind of blankets are these?" cried the pink-cheeked lady. "I have never seen their like."

Bessie began, but her older boy Sumner jumped up among the mole-rocks. "No, Mam," he said. "No, Mam. There's no need to say." He cast a look over his shoulder at the Cordlin woman, then explained up to them: "They have a special use, in the homes here. But it is private."

Private. I did not know that word, but immediately I grasped its meaning as a warning to the ladies.

The pink-cheeked lady eyed the blankets in the water. "What are they made of, though? Can you tell me that?" She sent a look around her friends that seemed to ask, *Who do they think they are, having private things?* The friends tittered.

"Seaweed," said Sumner.

"Seaweed!" exclaimed another woman. "How ingenious. This is a craft that they bring from the sea?"

"Hush, Elgin!" said one of them. "Whoever heard of seals *weaving*?"

Sumner pointed at Misskaella. "She makes them. She knits them. Our dads buy them off her."

"Don't frighten them away!" called a man's voice. All heads turned to watch him hurry along the seafront, along the mole, carrying a box on a stick—or several sticks, it was, bound together. He walked nearly to the Cordlin ladies, set his stick ends down and surveyed the mams and blankets, then lifted the sticks again and hurried farther along the mole. "Here is better. There is a subtler light, a more artistic composition." And he pulled the sticks apart to make a stand for the box thing. It had a circle on the front, like a flat black eye.

"Oh no," said Sumner, but softly, as if he knew he had no power over this bustling person from Cordlin. He turned to glance up to Wholeman's, where some of the dads were, all unsuspecting because the boat had come in so early; he sought out someone at Fisher's, but all the men there were in conversation with the *Fey*'s captain, their backs to us.

The man unfastened the box and pulled out the front of it, folded like a concertina, and shook out a black cloth over the box and legs. I could not take my eyes from him, he was so energetic and mysterious. What might he do next?

But then Misskaella whistled.

"Oh, what is that?" said the ladies.

"What? They're not done," said Os Cawdron down from me. "They're hardly even begun."

But Misskaella had not whistled to signal the end of the washing. The dads on the wharf turned. They saw the box man and came running. Up at Wholeman's men pushed out the door and along the rail, and two of them spilled under it and began to run down.

"Oh dear, Mister Thornly," said one of the ladies, "I think they don't want you taking photographs of their women."

Ah, photographs—Mister Paste up at the school had told us about those. This, then, was a camera—a box for keeping light out, with an eye for letting light in.

"Now, excuse me, sir," called out Mister Bannister, rounding off the seafront onto the mole. "We'll have none of that."

The camera-man straightened from his fiddling with the box, and watched our menfolk hurry at him. They stopped a few yards away, and the townswomen slightly clustered and clutched together at the sight. Beside these Cordlin clothes, our fathers' dress looked dark and not quite clean; beside their small smooth faces, our dads' were crumpled, darkened also. But that is not dirt, I protested to myself; that is sun and wind and weather—and whisky, for a couple of them, I admitted.

The man stood hands on hips. "But I came here specifically to make a photographic record."

"And I'm sure we're very happy for you to do that," said Bannister, smoothing down the air while some of the men bristled behind him. "But we weren't expecting you so early, and the women were planning to have this blanket work done before the boat came in. They're not respectable, and we don't want you taking unrespectable pictures back to mainland, do we?"

"We certainly don't," said Bern O'Day crisply, and a touch threateningly.

"And showing them about," said Bannister. "And Cordlin people thinking we let our wives get about like that, all bare-legged."

The mams eyed each other's water-thickened shins, exchanged baffled looks.

"What is wrong with legs?" muttered Oswald, bending his head to look at his own. The sunshine fizzed in the red bristles on the back of his head.

"We don't wish to offend, I'm sure," said the pink-cheeked

lady loudly. "But Mister Thornly here is both an anthropologist and an artist. I think you can rest easy that he will make no inappropriate use of his pictures."

"Can we, now?" said Corbell snakily, back in the crowd.

"I'm sure we can," said Bannister, smoothing the air again.

"It is his project," the lady trumpeted on, giving a little flick of her parasol as if to say she would not allow herself, or any of her people there, to be trifled with, "to document all the customs and habits of the people of these isles, for posterity."

"I think your wives are beautiful!" said the camera-man. How white he looked after our dads, like a man made of china—and how could he think they wanted to hear such a thing from his mouth? Misskaella was walking slowly toward us from the mole end; Trudle danced along behind her as if bored. Everything was so unusual, I did not think it improbable that Misskaella would pick up the man, or his photographic camera, and smash one or the other of them on the rocks.

"And while they are engaged in this traditional . . ." The man looked at the blankets properly for the first time. "What is it, exactly?"

The younger lady said very distinctly and flatly, "They are soaking and mending their private blankets." I heard the tiniest snort from the lady next to her, and another of the younger ladies turned my way to cover her laughter, saw me looking and brought her parasol down over her face, where it shook a little. Very suddenly I wanted to snatch and throw that parasol, or poke her with its sharp point, or wallop her head free of its little ornamental hat.

"Private blankets?" said the camera-man, as if all the wind had gone out of him. "Well, then, I suppose . . ."

"Oh, but I'm sure this has never been recorded before!" cried one of the young ladies, from sheer mischief—just look at her swaying there, her wide eyes.

"Of course not, Georgette," said Missus Pink-Cheeks, putting a heavy hand on Georgette's arm. "Because it is *private*."

"I'm only saying, it is a valuable anthropological record—"

"Hush, now."

And the camera-man folded his black cloth—very precisely, and you could tell from the folds that he always folded it exactly this way. When he was done, he collapsed his camera into its box and gathered its legs together.

The dads' shoulders had dropped, and Job Cress and Michael Lexly were walking away back to the boat. Misskaella had stopped halfway to us. The mams sat quietly, watching the ladies, and all us boys glanced about like chickens looking for seed, keeping an eye on everyone.

"Well, where is a good prospect for capturing some scenic views of the island?" said the camera-man. "If you've no objection to *that*."

"Watch-Out Hill, I should say," said Bannister.

As he described how the man should reach there, the Cordlin ladies took a last look at our mams there in the shallows with the blankets nodding and bubbling all around them, and drifted after the menfolk.

Seal-ladies. Why had they called our mams seals? They had strange ideas, mainlanders, and they were not shy to spread them about.

John Abut trickled out of the group of dads and round to Misskaella as she moved up again, to resume her usual pacing beside the blanket menders. "Be as quick as you can," I heard him mutter to her, "and get them out of sight."

"*I* did not bring the *Fey* early," she said. I was glad I was not Abut, the look she gave him.

"Of course you didn't. But we don't want any more busy-bodying, that's all. Cordlin people making fun."

"Why should you care?" said Misskaella, quite loudly, though the Cordlin people had already wandered too far along the mole to hear. "Why should it matter what Cordlin people think, when you have the most beautiful wives in the world?"

One cold, windy afternoon a gaggle of us took shelter in the back of the pub. The first snow had fallen, but that was days ago, and it was only rotten bits lying in the shade of walls, nothing useful. We had made a man of what we could find in the yard at the back, but he was not much more than a snow blob, it had gone to such slop—although we had given him a fine rod, the brace of a broken bar stool that Wholeman had put out the back for mending, so you knew at least he was a man blob.

Anyway, it was beastly cold and the wind had begun to nip and numb us, so we came in the back door, and it felt like heaven, just the little heat that had leaked out into the hall from the snug. No one was about, to tell us to hie on out again before our ears turned blue from the language we might hear, so we milled there thawing out and being quiet.

I had hold of the lid of the chest against the wall and was

about to see if I could haul it open, when Aran Bannister said, "Hey, lads," in a soft voice that made us all look up. He stood at the storeroom door, its padlock in his hand.

"How is that?" whispered Raditch. The door stood a crack open. All the bigger boys were stilled, frightened by the sight—and perhaps by the smell that spilled out, seawater, sour and cold.

"Wholeman must have left it," said Raditch. "Wholeman must store other stuff in there."

"What stuff?" said Johnny Baker. "Would there be food, mebbe? Would they notice a little gone? Peanuts or something?"

Aran's frightened look changed to hopeful naughtiness, and he pulled the door wider. We crowded forward to see, but none of us went in. There seemed hardly room for us.

"Lemme see!" Kit Cawdron pushed among us to the front and stopped there, baffled. "Why, it's full of . . . coats, are they?"

"Of course they're coats, you gosling," said Aran. "They're the mams' coats. *Your* mam's is in there somewhere."

"My mam's coat is on the hook at home, thank you very much," said Kit. "Why would she wear one of these?"

"Hush, Kit," said Raditch, "or the dads'll hear and belt us. You should shut this, Aran, and lock it properly." But he craned his neck just as hard as the rest of us.

"It's her seal-coat." Aran bent to Kit and spoke most carefully and quietly, as if Kit were very stupid. "From when she was in the sea. That she shook off to have you and Os."

I stared in at the things. Now I could see their shapes better in the dimness. I shivered. "I don't like the way their heads go."

"They're more capes than coats, aren't they?" said Angast beside me. "They've no arms, that I can see."

"No, they come in at the bottom," breathed Toddy Marten at my shoulder. "That's not like a cape."

"They're not capes *nor* coats," said Grinny sturdily. "They're skins, off seals, and so they look like seal."

"Off our *mams?*" said Kit, disbelieving.

But I knew it was true. With a thump like a storm wave's onto Forward Beach it came true for me. *I come from the sea,* Mam said. I had always thought she meant from a boat there; I had imagined each mam of ours had her own boat, that she stood at the helm of, her hair streaming on the wind, her face joyful with being afloat and in command. But no, it was this; I could tell from the sea-smell, and the other with it, of animal. It was exactly the smell of my mam when she lay with her tears-blanket. Except that she was warm then, whereas this smell pouring from the door chilled us, froze us all together in a lump.

Deep in among us, Johnny Baker hissed, "Can anyone see the *peanuts?*"

And that unfroze our solemn-ness, him thinking of his stomach. A couple of snorts sounded, and a *John-ee, show respect!*

"Come, let's have a look," said Aran, pretending to be brave, and some of us followed him in—not many, for the skins filled the room up pretty thoroughly.

"Ain't they strange?" said Angast among the glimmering, glooming shapes. "Like people themselves."

"They're *pretty,*" said Raditch. "All different speckles. And smooth. Have a feel."

"Pretty and smooth, just like a mam," said Grinny from the door. Some giggled, and some jumped on Grinny and started quietly fighting.

"I wish I could *see*," said Raditch. "I'm sure the heads should not look so frightening. What have they done to them?"

"Bring one out," suggested Angast, "to the better light."

I was glad to go out ahead of him; that room was too much for me, the heavy things pressing us, rustling, hung so closely. They made noises as we pushed among them, as if they were alive—they sighed and squeaked and clicked in their throats. And the unhappy smell weighed in my chest more like water than air.

We managed to get one of the smaller ones out. Aran took the wooden ball from where it had shaped the head skin, the hook protruding out the mouth hole. We passed it boy to boy, while each had a stroke of the coat-stuff, sheeny and dark, the markings more faded than on a live seal. And each boy tried the skin on awhile, except Kit Cawdron, who would not. I cannot describe to you the feeling of putting it on. It was as if you found yourself suddenly right down in the slime at the bottom of the sea, with nothing above you but black water.

"How do they *swim* in these things?" said Raditch, elbowing inside so that the flipper flapped.

"It is bonded to them properly," said Aran. "And the water holds them up, *you* know. You have seen seals aplenty."

Jakes Trumbell was the only one who pulled the hood over his face, and we made him stop when he looked out the eyes and lurched at us, for he had dark, mam-type eyes, and it was too eerie.

"It *smells*," he said, taking it off. I sniffed the arm of my woolly to see if the smell had stuck. It was hard to say. The whole air, the whole hall there, was greenish with latening afternoon and seaweedishness. Would Mam smell it on me later? Would it send her into a mood?

"Cawn, Kit," said Aran to Cawdron, "let us see you in it; you will make a great little mam, you're so pretty."

"Not on your nelly," Cawdron said. "It'll drown me, that will."

"Come on; it will suit you so well."

And seeing as there was nothing else to do but persuade him, we set to it, and Jakes hauled out another bigger coat and put it on, and urged some more, and before too long we had weakened the poor lad sufficiently to drape the thing on him, dark and gleaming.

Along the hall the snug door opened. We scrambled to hide what we were doing. Somehow the coatroom door got closed and the coats were hid behind legs and we were all lounging idle and innocent when Batton-and-Johnny's dad passed us on his way out to the pisser.

"What you lads brewing?" he said, taking a step back when he saw all our eyes.

But none of us needed to answer, for he opened the yard door then, and the wind hit him to staggering.

"It's perishin' out there, Mister Baker," said Grinny in just the right voice, dour and respectful.

"I'll freeze my man off, pissing in that." Baker squinted into the darkening yard. "I see a chap who's frozen out there already," he added with a laugh. "A fine upstanding chap, if I'm not mistaken."

And out he went, banging the door.

"He sees so much as a sleeve edge, we are beaten," said Grinny, into the quiet of our relief. "Beaten and put in our rooms and no suppers *forever*—and our mams *so* disappointed."

We had time to hide the coats better before Baker came back. He shut the door and swayed and looked at us, all in our same places. "Don't do anything I wouldn't do," he finally said, and tapped his nose and went off.

And that might have ended it there and then, and everything stayed tip-top and as usual.

Except, "Come, Kit," whispered Jakes. "You looked the perfect mam."

So we hauled the coat out and lumped it on Cawdron again, and Jakes put the other one on, and then they made us laugh, trying to walk about like mams, trying to move their hands all delicate and their heads all thoughtful. Cawdron was the best at it, of course, being so fine-made anyway, and with the coloring. Jakes was funnier, though, being more dadlike, all freckles and orange hair and hands like sausage bunches.

"I've been abed for days, so mis'rable, Missus Cawdron," he said, and the way he leaned and rolled his eyes, and his voice trying to trill and sing—we were holding each other up, it was so funny.

And then Kit joined in and, my, he was good, because his voice was not yet begun to break, and he could really sound the part. "Because I'm to have another bair-beh," he said, and we were just about rolling on the slates there, but as quiet as we could.

"I thought you just had one, Missus?" said Jakes, through laughing.

"Oh'm, I did. But 'twas only a girl, so I took her down and drowned her."

"It is not *drowning*, you goose!" spluttered Raditch.

But, "Grand!" said Jakes over him. "Another sea-wife for our lads to net, come sixteen summers."

"Oh yes, but if only I could have another son like my lovely Christopher there! For it is daughters-daughters-daughters with me!"

And he was just overacting a suffering mam, staggering, with the back of his hand to his forehead, when something behind us, and up from us, caught his eye. He snatched his hand down to his side, and tripped on his coat edge, and banged up against the wall. His face was not mammish anymore, and not at all playful; he was the littlest of us, and the most frightened. He and Jakes had the most to lose, after all, with Baker's dad there at the back of us, and Mister Grinny too come soundless from the snug to catch us at whatever.

We shrank into a bunch, back around Kit and Jakes against the wall there, staring at those men. Grinny's dad's face was white and stiff with the surprise, but Baker's trembled, and red rage tided up it—jolly Mister Baker, who at any other time would have twinkled and mussed our hair as soon as look at us. Honest, I thought his head was going to burst, it swelled and stared so.

"What do you think you are up to?" he hissed into the utter silence. Someone gave a little peeping fart, and nobody even snickered, we were *all* so close to shitting ourselves, every lad of us.

Kit Cawdron didn't make a sound. He was *glued* to the wall behind us, trying to melt away into it.

I thought Baker would wade in and belt him. Everyone expected it. Grinny's dad expected it, and decided it must not happen, and put a hand on Baker's arm.

"Take those off, lads," he said, gentle as gentle.

The crowd of us loosened, but only a little. "Here," Raditch muttered, helping Cawdron behind. There was silence except for the fumbling, Cawdron's unsteady breathing, the slither and clop of the coats.

"Come, lads," said Mister Grinny, holding out his hands. I could not tell what he might be thinking—how does anyone else's dad think?—but he was not so frozen-faced now. Good, I thought, they'll not thrash them, then. This is too wicked even for that. "Hang them coats up, lads," he said, "and show some reverence as you do." And he stood there, one freckly hand ensausaging Kit's white slip of a paw, and the other on Baker's sleeve who was steaming and readying to roar and punch something, as we hauled the cursed things into the coatroom, and managed to rehang them. Everybody was shaking like the leaves of the poplars on Watch-Out Hill; everyone was clumsy and needed each other's help. The cupboard was full of our breaths and the coats. Beyond it, I heard Grinny say to Baker, "Fetch Wholeman. And Wholeman's boy."

When we were done we closed the door, whisper-quiet, and turned to face our punishment. Mister Grinny was still there holding Cawdron. "Wholeman?" Baker bellowed in the snug doorway, and the room went silent there. "And where's young Rab?" Bottles clinked, glasses knocked on tables, chairs squeaked under shifting men.

Mister Grinny squatted among us. "You'll not touch them skins again, all right?" he said softly, almost sadly.

"No, sir."

"No, Mister Grinny."

"We won't. Promise."

"Even if you find it unlocked," he said. "Even if the door is swinging wide open, you will not go in. You will not lay a finger on your mams' coats."

"Not a finger, sir." We shook our heads.

"Shan," he said to his boy, "you go on home to your mam. All you boys, go on home. Look to your mams and see if they need aught. Bring in some coal. Make them a tea. Rub their poor feet. Or just sit and talk to them the way they like, about nice things, the spring, mebbe, or the fishing. Go home and do something nice for your mams, each lad of you. You've insulted them so, you must make up for it with them. Though they may not know it—and do not tell them, any of you, not a word—you must make amends for this, the way you made fun of them, Kit and Jakes, and the others of you for laughing—and even if you did none of that, just for going into that room and for touching!"

He stopped there, and raised his eyes, which had been steady on us boys. Until then I had not really thought how bad we'd been, being so caught up in the fun and fear of it. But at the sight of the cupboard door, firmly closed now, and the memory of what he had seen behind it, Mister Grinny's face took on such wonderment, he looked hardly older than Kit beside him. Something of this expression I had seen now and again before, my dad looking to our mam in a quiet moment. But on Mister Grinny, who should control his face in front of boys not his son, the bright eyes and the open mouth made the skin on my head crawl, and his sudden silence sent such a shiver down me, I worried that my bladder might let go.

Then the men's footsteps sounded in the hall, and we all crammed together, and Grinny was a grown-up again.

Baker, still flushed red, led Rab Wholeman and his shrewd-faced dad into our sight. Rab was a big boy, all but a man himself, but when his gaze fell on the latch without its padlock, all his color went and his face sagged ancient; the light went right out of his eyes a moment there; he staggered some, though he did not quite fall.

"Who has it?" said Wholeman in a tight little voice, to all of us, his head swinging like a lighthouse lamp. The hair above my ears lifted under the sweep of his look. "Who has the lock?"

"Me, Mist'r 'Oleman," whimpered Aran, and pushed forward, and held up the padlock in a shaking hand, which looked very small. Wholeman's bigger one swiped the battered thing out of it. Aran flinched and stepped back in among us. Out the corner of my eye I saw Raditch touch his back, to tell him we felt for him.

But now, it seemed, we were not the ones so much at fault, for Grinny stood and turned, and Baker turned, and Wholeman's lighthouse beam swept around upon his son. Rab met all their attentions one by one, quaking smaller with each face. "I don't . . . I can't . . . how did this *happen*?" he finished on a little wail. "I *always* lock after I put away the boxes! Always!" And he began working up to sobbing.

Wholeman waved the padlock full in Rab's face, struck him hard up the back of the head. Rab swayed there blinking and absorbing the blow. "I'm *sorry*," he said eventually. "It's a terrible thing to have done."

"It is," said Wholeman tightly, as if he must almost close off his throat if he were not to break out wildly shouting, if he were not to go *mad* with anger. He smacked the lock into Rab's chest—the hook was askew on it, and would have dug in nastily. "Put it on," he said. "Make *sure* it's clapped closed."

Us lads shrank aside either way, and poor Rab walked through us, alone in his shame, bright red with it, his eyes swimming. His hands shook as he put the hasp over the loop, put the hook through it. A tear splashed on his wrist, silver in the window light. We all heard the chink of the lock, and felt the relief the sound brought us, everything returned to the way it should be.

Wholeman sighed with it too, but then gathered himself up again as Rab faced him. He put out a finger and shook it slowly, glaring through his eyebrows at his son. "If ever, *ever*—" And Baker at his elbow silently raged the same.

But Mister Grinny waved the finger down. "I think the lad realizes."

Rab pushed past the older men, slammed out the back door.

"There's bottles need washing!" Wholeman roared after him.

"Let him collect himself, Storn," said Grinny.

They remembered us then, Baker and Wholeman looking us over with dislike.

"But do *these* lads realize?" said Wholeman.

"I'm sure they do," said Grinny, and I loved him in that moment for his calm voice and his uncongested face. "They'll all go each to his mam now and please her somehow, and not let a word slip of this what's happened today. Won't you?"

"Yes, Mister Grinny," we said, subdued.

He opened the back door. We flowed out into the wind, each of us, like Rab, marooned in his own part of the guilt. We said no goodbyes, only cut one way or the other, some of us having to hurry past poor red-eyed Rab, his back to the wall out there, clutching his elbows and staring out stonily as if he saw none of us. Thinking of Grinny, thinking of Raditch, I reached up and touched Rab's arm in passing. He did not lower his gaze; his chin crimped as if more tears were coming, and I scurried on past to save him more embarrassment.

That morning I had raced up to school and played footer to keep warm till the bell rang. Now we lined up in the cold spring wind.

"Where are the Wright boys?" said Mister Paste with a frown.

"They are cousins, sir," someone called.

"Oh." He turned away to take up his position at the door.

"Cousins?" I said blankly to Eric Cartney next to me, who was stamping and rubbing his arms against the cold.

"Cousins of Tom Dressler."

"Why, what's happened to him?"

"Lost his wife. Don't you know anything? All of Potshead knows."

Lost his wife. I pictured Tom Dressler wandering the hills and beaches, calling, weeping. "Have they gone to help look?"

Eric screwed up his eyes and twitched his head at my stupidity.

"You said he lost her," I protested.

Eric pushed his face at mine, so hard and pop-eyed I had to lean back. "She died!" he said in a shouting whisper. "She hung herself from a kitchen beam!"

"Everyone *knows*, Eric," Raditch said wearily over his shoulder.

"Daniel here doesn't," said Eric. "It has somehow managed to escape Daniel's attention," he added hoity-toitily—but very quietly, because we were approaching Mister Paste, and it was Mister Paste whose accent he was imitating.

"And it's 'hanged,' my dad says," said Jakes Trumbell behind us. "Not 'hung.' "

Eric rounded on him. "Hanged or hung, don't make her any less dead!" But now we were right in front of Paste, who reached in and neatly clipped Eric's ear.

Eric veered away scowling to his desk, and I went to mine, moving out of habit. *Hung* herself, *hanged* herself—neither made better sense. Hanging was for robbers and murderers; you had to have a scaffold and a priest and a man to put the hood on, didn't you? How did you hang *yourself*? I didn't see how that could be done, the mechanics of it. The question of why, I didn't even know how to ask.

I had sat on the church fence just last summer and watched Amy Dressler walk out smiling on her new husband's arm, in the beautiful wedding dress that Mam had worn, that all our mams had worn. And I had seen dead things—fish by the millions, seagulls going to pieces in the tide wrack, Jodper's cows and sheep freshly slaughtered, and one memorable time fourteen whales beached on the Six-Mile sands. I could put the bride next to the dead whale right enough, but I could not seem to combine them into the one thing. A live person become a dead thing, and by her own choice? It went against all the sense that I knew.

I went through the day unmoored from what I had known and believed, pushed to and fro by bewildered thoughts. I had not known that people could choose to end themselves. A new danger was abroad—who might take into their heads this senseless idea, if smiling Amy Dressler had been able to? Which other mam, weeping or only quietly enduring under her weed-blanket, might remove herself from us? Why should not, indeed, my own mam do it? For we had beams across our kitchen ceiling too, if that was all that was needed.

The boats were in when school finished that day. Mam was not about when I reached home, but my dad was in his garden, digging over the beds for his spring planting. "Hup, day-up!" he said when I came out the back door.

"Missus Dressler," I said.

The near smile fled his face. "It's a very sad thing." He went back to slowly digging.

I ambled across the yard to him. "How would you do that, hang yourself?"

He looked me up and down. "Never you mind," he said eventually. "If you ever need to know, you will find a way. Your mam, though, she's upset about it. They all are. All gone down commiserating." The spade huffed into the packed dirt; the lifted dirt broke up most satisfyingly. "And when she comes back, we won't talk of this, do you hear me? We'll not mention Dresslers, living or dead."

I nodded and watched him work, and after a while I began to help, picking stones out of the turned earth and piling them up to one side. It seemed as good a way as any to hold my mind in place, just to move from stone to stone, and think about seeds and sprouts and growing things.

Mam came home while we were out there; we saw her at the kitchen window, but she did not wave to us or come out to greet us. When we went in for tea she was quieter than her usual quiet self, and around her eyes was puffy, but not red; she had wept today, but quite some hours ago. Dad was perhaps the tiniest bit fonder in his touches of her as he passed, but no one but me would have seen the difference from their usual evenings, except perhaps in the strength of wide-eyed watchfulness with which their son regarded them, fearful with what had happened outside their home this day, and itchily uncertain what it might bring about tomorrow.

In the days when we ran about among our mams' skirts, they took us with them when they gathered in this house and that. At first there would be greetings and tea and sitting upright and eyes everywhere. They would talk of their men and their men's tempers; they would talk of us, and how we were coming on, how we ate and grew.

Then one of them would sigh and cross from table to armchair or settee or fireside stool, or even settle to the floor. All the mams' movements would suddenly change, slowing and swaying, and their voices would lower from so bright and brittle, and someone might laugh low, too. As we ran in and out we would see more of them gather at the seated one, leaning on her or pulling her to lean on them. Hairs would be unpinned and fall, and combs brought out and combing begun, and there is nothing nicer than a mam's face so free of care while her hair is being combed. When we were littler we would run in from our play and lie among them, patted and tutted over and our own hairs combed and compared, the differences in wave and redness. Sometimes we were allowed to comb theirs, but our arms were never long enough to do it as well as they did for each other, long slow silky sweeps from scalp to tips, comber and combed both dreamy.

Their talk would grow less proper, and have more sighs in it, and more seal: the high crooning, whistles and coughs of their attempts were always followed by laughter, or a shaking of the head. They loved when the littlest boys, learning to speak, would try these noises; nothing amused them better than a tiny trying to loose a bit of seal-song, and a mam singing back to him.

These gatherings were the only times we heard these songs, these attempts at seal-talk among the mams. When I was still quite small it occurred to me that as we grew into men, it must happen that we grew to not like the sounds, that men did not want to learn the sense behind them, and did not want to hear them senseless.

I remember lying with my mam in the sun on a rug on the sand at Six-Mile, and the thought coming out my mouth: "When I have a wife, I will let her speak seal in our house."

"Oh yes?" she said, surprised. "Why will you do that, my Daniel?"

"Because when wives talk seal they are happy, and I want my wife to be happy."

I lay there pleased with myself for this wish, pleased with my own kindness uttering it to my mam, pleased with my plan for my future self, who would become a kind and admirable man. All was well with that day, the warmth of the sun and my mam and me on our island of blanket, other mams at a distance, other boys running and kicking up the water.

Mam turned toward me, propped her head on her hand. "My darling," she said softly, "if you want your wife to be happy, and to speak the seal-tongue truly, you will not take her as your wife."

For a moment our conversation ceased to make sense. I frowned up at Mam, hands behind my head still, the little leisurely gentleman.

Then, "Oh," I said. "I should leave her as a seal?"

She nodded. "Leave her as a seal," she almost whispered, as if testing the words in her own mouth.

I laughed at her solemn face with the sky behind it. "But who will cook my dinners and do my laundry? Who will sweep my house?"

She poked my middle. "Why, you could do all that your own self. You are a good little sweeper, very thorough."

"But who will be mam to my boys?"

"A woman," she said. "A woman of the land, your own kind. She could give you girls as well, that woman. I hear they are a great comfort, daughters."

I pitched myself at her, instantly jealous of those daughters she did not have, the comfort they did not bring. "*Sons* are a great comfort!" I clung on and kissed her bossily, kissed away that solemn look and made her laugh at me, pushed all that talk of the future *into* the future, where it belonged.

"It's true. They're a great comfort!" And looking in my urgent face she laughed some more. "My son particularly, my Daniel!"

And I was so occupied with obtaining these assurances, and pressing my need for them upon her, that it did not occur to me even to wonder, let alone to ask her, why at all, in the first place, she might require comforting.

I was idling outside Grinny's place. He was ill in the armchair inside, and we were talking through his cracked-open window. It was the grayest darkest cold day, with lamps lit in most houses, though it was barely past midday.

A white ghost went by down the hill, but running harder than any ghost would run—its feet slapped and its breath sobbed. By the time I looked there was only the back of her to see.

"What!" said Grinny and pushed the window wider, though his mam had forbidden it.

Her hair spilled down her back like black paint, her poor feet ran, all warped and bunioned from shoe wearing, their soles gray with dirt.

"That was Aggie Bannister," Grinny said in flat wonder.

"Aggie Bannister?" I said stupidly.

She floated away down the town, as pale in the dimness as a falling flare. She had been shut away from us for some time. Aran had hardly come out to play since that day up at Wholeman's—or Timmy or Cornelius either, any Bannister boy. Bannister himself we'd barely seen since last spring when they'd had to put their girl-bab in the sea. He'd been mourning so hard, it was all he could do to fetch himself to the boats and back.

"Follow! Go after her!" said Grinny. "Come back and tell me!" He waved me away and brought down the window, nodding, bright-eyed.

So down I ran, and other boys ran too. There were enough people out, coated and hatted and pinch-faced with cold, to make noise to bring out others—our running left a path of opened doors behind us, a path of *What's up?* and *Where are you lads off?*

I didn't slow to answer. Aggie ran around Low Corner. I thought she would slip and fall there, and I picked up speed. We slid into the corner ourselves; she had fallen just beyond. Men started toward her to help her, then did not know what to do because she was naked—one began to take off his coat. Their wives had hardly time to cry "Aggie! Oh!" before Aggie blundered up, and ran off again, shaken off course by the fall, nearly smacking into a house front, like someone's cow got out, not knowing about towns and how to pass through them.

She steadied and ran off. Some mams went to go after her, but their men stopped them. "It's clear enough where she's headed," said Robert Dunkling, pulling his wife by the hand to the head of Totting Lane. All the others, realizing his sense, went too—our little clump of boys poured ahead of them down Totting and Fishhead with windows opening and people crying out above, reached the cross lane and slipped down to the seafront under the rail of it, staggered out staring to the south where Aggie had not yet appeared.

And then she had, a shining slim streak of person, determined, churning into the beginning rain. Several mams ran for her, never minding their husbands.

"They're not fast enough," said some man up on the ramp.

"Aye, she'll give 'em the slip easily."

She was already across the front. She saw the mams, decided she would not make for the steps or they would catch her, began to clamber down among the boulders of the south mole.

"Oh, ho!"

"She'll hurt herself in there. She'll break herself— Oh!" as Aggie slipped and fell among the rocks.

"But up she is again. She's bleeding."

We boys were down at the sea-rail now, grown-ups hurrying to lean along beside us, the whole town lining up to see. Younger men turned their faces aside, hiding embarrassed grins from each other. Older men watched, composed. The mams held their hands to their fraught faces; they spoke not a word, to the men or to each other, and their eyes didn't leave Aggie for a moment.

Somehow she had reached the beach. Bloodied at knee and hip and elbow, she went at a limping run out across the stones. Now some men, my dad among them, took it into their heads to start down the stairs and catch her that way, but when she saw them she turned straight for the water, staggering, clumsy, as if she were transforming to seal right there, and might have to heave herself legless and armless the rest of the way.

"Where's her man?" said someone. "Is he so gone in his grief he is *letting* her swim away?"

And then Aggie was a naked back and bottom in the middle

of a white fan of water. The green-white froth passed over her, streaking and swallowing her blood, pasting her hair flat to her head. "So cold!" moaned a woman behind me, but Aggie embraced the waves, swimming strongly; she was not clumsy there, and the cold did not bother her.

"She wants to stay in the lee of the mole," said Prentice Meehan above me. "It's dirty farther out."

"She is not out swimming for her *health*," said his wife. "She doesn't want to *stay* anywhere."

The mams in pursuit were stranded along the south mole, begging, waving their arms. The men had strung themselves out along the shifting brink of the water, trying to see her, seeing and calling out uselessly. I remembered Rab Wholeman that day at the inn, alone in his guilt, us shrinking away as if the very touch of him were poison. Here was a very different thing, everyone forcing forward, crying out help and worry, and still Aggie went, striking out as if none of us were here, laboring away through the cold sea.

"She would rather drown," said Missus Meehan, with a mix of certainty and disbelief, into the little silence that had fallen on us. We could only watch Aggie's smallness in the edge of the sea, beyond the waves now and crawling forth across the great wind-plowed field of it, waking the green from its grayness with her splashings, drawing her messy white line out and out.

"She'll tire fast in that cold," a man whispered.

A howl of the wind turned into the howl of a man—"Aggie!"—and Bannister ran out at the far end of the house row.

"He has her coat!" It flapped around him; it looked as if it had blown against him by accident, and he was trying to fight free.

"He's too late wi' that," said Whisky Jock.

Bannister lumbered on, woeful; Aggie was a dot in the water, a white haunch shining for a moment, a white foot splashing, and then nothing, hidden behind the glassy green upshelving of a wave.

Along the mole ran Bannister, quite thrown out of himself and his usual miseries, his mouth wide in his face like a bawling bab's, his arms reaching. The wind and waves tore up his bellow and threw it at us in shreds, some strange animal's cry, not a person's, not a grown man's.

Right out to the end he got, and still he yearned farther. He made to clamber down the end point.

"Don't be daft, man!" said some man.

"It'll sweep him away!" a woman said dreamily.

The sea jumped up and smacked the mole end, a great fanfare of spray. Bannister staggered back, soaked. And there he stood a moment, clutching the coat and staring out to where Aggie came and went, came and went, bobbing and struggling now among the wilder waves that came at her irregularly, and from every direction.

The sun poked a hole in the clouds, sent a bar through the spume and beginning rain, flung down a patch of light on the sea near the mole end. Bannister threw the coat. It did not fly far, for it was heavy, and the wind was against him. It lumped out into the air and splatted on the water and was gone. Then it was there again, struggling, just as Aggie was, to stay afloat.

Our silence tightened at the rail—the coat and Aggie were far apart, and neither was swimming toward the other. The coat's edge broke the surface; its whole shadow hung within a big sunlit wave like a hovering hawk. Aggie's face showed, her mouth, her arm and breast, and then a wave crashed down, folding her into the sea. Even mad with grief, Bannister did not dive in. He stood a little way down from the mole top, his legs bent and his hands red claws upon his knees, bellowing out to Aggie not to die.

She did not obey him. She lay slumped in the water when next we saw her; only her back showed, the water moving her black hair on it. The sun went away. Some of the mams wept, in their quiet way, not much more than a gasp and a sniff now and then. Men's and mams' and boys' faces alike fixed on Aggie, unspeaking, unblinking.

The sea brought her in between the moles again. Through the gray rain-beginning, through the curling rows of green-gray waters, up and down it brought her, slowly. Mams ushered some of the littler boys away—*Come, Dav. Come, Phillip.* We stood at the rail unable to tear our eyes for more than a moment or two from the dead woman floating in.

"She looks so calm now," whispered a mam. "Now she is not fighting."

"Free of suffering," said another.

"Which is grand for her," some husband rumbled. "And for her lads?" And the awfulness of that hit me. Yes, how could she have been so cruel? How could she be so *sad,* that she could be so cruel?

"And look at Bannister." The man was folded around himself among the mole-rocks—we could see his shaking from here. Several of the mams were making their halting way up toward him, pausing to throw up their arms or embrace each other.

"If only they could have kept that girl," breathed a mam.

"It's no good thinking like that," said Trotter Trumbell. "We've all of us given up daughters; that is just the way things are."

"It is not as if the girl-babs are *dead*," agreed Martin Dashwell.

Some of the mams lowered their heads and pulled their shawls down. Others only faced the sea and Aggie, their sorrow wearier, beyond the freshness of tears. Missus Cawdron saw me looking, and worrying for them; she sent me half a smile, warm and sad, her head tipped to one side.

"Even with that girl she would have been miserable," said Garvis Marten boldly, and we all tightened away from him. "It's their natural set of mind. And it's only made worse by lads getting in where they shouldn't, and coming home smelling of—"

"Enough, Marten," said Trotter sharply. "It doesn't help anyone to belabor that."

The waves brought Aggie back to almost exactly where she had gone in, and not three yards from where they had thrown up the coat. The men were all over the beach, the stones clacking and scraping under their feet like dogs mouthing bones. The mams broke away from us in pairs and groups along the seafront; the ones who had run to stop Aggie now met and milled in with them; three women, out at the mole end, were trying to persuade broken Bannister to come in. Someone had gone for Misskaella, and here she came hurrying along the far beach with one of her blankets in her arms, its corners trailing. Only boys were left along the rail.

"It is his own fault," said James Starr offhandedly, "being so miserable about the daughter. Timmy told me, he'd sit to dinner and go to tears and mawk there while they ate around him. That's no way for a man to behave."

"It is *all* their faults," said Raditch's big brother Edward savagely, kicking at a rail post. "Stealing our mams out of the sea in the first place."

"Oh, you cannot blame them for that," piped up little Thomas Davven beside me. He clutched himself and bowed and bent in the cold wind, without the shelter of the crowd anymore. He nodded at Misskaella struggling up the dune onto the seafront. "If you had to choose between women like *her* and our beautiful mams, which would *you* choose?"

"It's true, Ed, that is no fair choice," said Gordon Crockett.

Edward eyed Misskaella too. "Still," he said, through teeth clamped tight against chattering. "Still, they never ought to've done it. They didn't belong here. They belonged under the waves, and they still do."

"They belong with *us*, their *lads*," said Kit Cawdron hotly, and ran off to his mam so as not to hear more. I could feel my fellows around me wishing we were young enough to do that; instead we must stay near the bigger lads and pretend that their remarks did not upset us.

Against the green-gray of the sea and the mottle-gray of the stony beach, white Aggie glowed. So did the pale feet of the men preparing to pull her from the shallows. The water nosed and nudged her where she lay, as if it were proud of what it had done and wanted us to praise it. At its little distance, the coat lay, glossy and almost black, like a shadow that had fallen off her, curling and useless without her, kicked by the wavelets. The men and some of the mams now picked their ways across the beach, all caps and coats, boots and dark skirts, with a brighter shawl here and there. All were well protected except Aggie; her nakedness lay at the center of them, unembarrassed, the men now turning to it, now turning away.

Misskaella hurried across, a snarl of red and white hair above a filthy black coat, ashy handprints about the hips. The blanket draggled out either side of her, until she reached the sea-edge, and threw it out. It fell and covered Aggie, making her decent for the men to rescue her.

And now it ceased to bother me what the big boys or my fellows thought of me—I must see my mam, and she was not among these mams flowed down from the town to spectate. She was under her blanket in bed, and no cries from the street would have stirred her out of it.

I hurried up the hill, away from the crowd and the witch and the disaster. I did not care if Mam talked or wept or slept or hid from me under her seaweed; I wanted only to be in the room with her, to see the mound of her and know she was not drowned and naked, with all of Potshead looking on.

I let myself into the house, went in and sat by her window. My breath, which as I walked had turned ragged and sobbing, before long was soothed quiet, quieter than the wind outside, than the sea, rushing, pausing, falling on itself. Mam's breathing was quieter still—I could not hear it, only see its rise and fall.

Now and again the sun broke through and lit the sea, and the ceiling swam with silver reflections. The furniture sat plain and solid in its places; the rug that I remembered Mam making—her twisting fingers with her singing face above—lay by the bed as it had always lain, as it always would. The table bore up her shells, and her stones that meant something to her, and her pieces of sea-glass, red and blue and powdery white, smoothed harmless, beaten to beautifulness by the sea. Looking on these things I ceased to think about the Bannisters, about the mams generally, and the men.

Mam woke, or became aware of me, and she turned to me suddenly out of her hair and blanket. One cheek was printed with hair swirls and weed weave and pillow creases. She had not put on a face for me; there was a moment when she seemed not to even recognize me. And then she did. My mam was there again behind her eyes, although a long way in.

"Is there anything I can do for you, Mam?" I said—and I heard myself speak lightly, as if I were much younger and more innocent. I always spoke this way, I realized, in this room, to this blanketed Mam. "Can I make you some tea, nice and sweet? There are still some of those biscuits there, that Dad and I baked, remember?" I could not seem to stop talking, offering, and in this silly voice.

She shook her head. "I am not hungry or thirsty, Daniel."

"I can rub your feet, perhaps. I could comb your hair—look at the mess of it."

She shook her head again amid that mess, the black wild hair that I could not tell apart from the green-black woven weed. She smiled at me. "No, sweet," she said. "There is nothing I need, right now. I am quite comfortable."

With a great sigh she sent herself back to sleep. I watched her, her words echoing gently in my head. She had lied to me;

she had lied herself free of me. She was not comfortable—she was miserable. Like Aggie, like Amy Dressler, like all the mams, all the wives, she was more unhappy than I had ever been; they were unhappy beyond any unhappiness that a boy like me could imagine or fathom. And Dad was miserable too; all the dads were—for who could be happy with his wife in such a state?

The reason for all this distress about me was equally slippery and outsized to my mind. *They belonged under the waves, and they still do,* Edward had said. It had stung me, as it had stung Kit. How could my mam belong anywhere other than in our house, or at my back as I stepped out into the town, into the world? But of course it was true—she had told me often enough, hadn't she? *I come from the sea.*

I could not mind Mam's lying to me now. Indeed, I was grateful that unlike Aggie or Amy she strove to keep her sorrow from burdening me. My own lightness, my own cheer, was something of a lie too, was it not? My voice might take on that high, sweet, helpful tone easily, but that made it no less a pretense. Who did I hope to fool by it? I was unhappy too—all of us boys were, seeing our mams so miserable. And though we combed our mams' hairs and pointed out finches and brought cats and cups of tea, how could such tiny activities lift the weight of misery from our parents' backs, and from our own? *There is nothing you can do,* Mam had said, often enough, to me and to Dad and to both of us embracing her together.

Who *could* do something, then? I sat back in the chair, my eyes on the sun-blotched sea, resting from the sight of my sad mam. The smell of the damp weed-blanket was warmer, cozier than the powerful sea-smell of the coats we lads had pushed among in Wholeman's cupboard. It was the same smell, though, sure enough, and when I smelt it I could not help but think of them. Oh, it was a terrible thing we boys had done, was it not, in the light of Amy, in the light, now, of Aggie? How had we been so brave and frivolous as even to enter the same room as those coats, let alone take them down and put them on? They were not *costumes*, they were peeled-off parts of our mothers; without them, how could our mams be themselves, their *real* selves, their undersea selves, the selves they were born into? They walked about on land with no protection, from the cold or from our dads falling in love with them, or from us boys needing them morning and night.

I remembered Aran standing shocked at the cupboard door, the padlock in his hand, and all of us staring at it. But it was not the padlock keeping the skins in that cupboard, it was what had hooked and locked it there in the first place: the whole island's agreement. *Let us take these coats, by force or by trickery, from their rightful owners,* Rollrock men had decided, *and forever keep them apart.* They may have thought this would gain them their own happiness, but they might as well have vowed, *Let us all stay miserable together—dads, mams and lads alike—to the ends of our days!*

And *all* the men had agreed this—even a man as kind as my own dad. Against so many grown men and what they wanted, what hope did one boy have of bringing relief—of bringing maybe happiness, even!—to our poor mams, to our poor dads?

From the black tangle on the pillow came another sigh, and Mam's voice: "Well, perhaps a cup of tea."

I knew she did not want one, that she was saying so only to

make me feel useful. Still, I rose from my chair, ready to do her bidding, as eagerly as I'd always done. But when I spoke—"I will fetch it"—my voice was my own, not at all forced or sweetened.

Next day after school, with the boats gone out, I decided I would not head for home just yet, to sit oppressed by my mam's sorrows another afternoon, with no Dad to busy about and keep cheerful for. I strolled instead down to the seafront. It was quite sunless, and a raw wind gusted, strongly enough to knock me off balance now and then. I hardly met a soul along the way, and those I did were scurrying between one shelter and another. My town had become an entirely charmless and cheerless place, and the shadow of Aggie's death hung like a low cloud over it, or like sea-fog rolled into the streets.

I reached the harbor beach and leaned on the rail, watching the far waters heaped up gray. They seemed higher than my head, yet by some miracle they did not tumble forward and drown me. Here, closer, the water threw itself onto the stones as if cross with them, and it was hard not to see again white Aggie and her black coat caught near her in the edge there. *Free of suffering*, that mam had said in the crowd of us, as if there were nothing else for Aggie on this island, no man who loved her and no boys depending on her, no beautiful birds, no laughter with her sisters, nothing that could make up for the pain of living out of the sea.

The wind made my ear ache, so I turned my face into it and plodded past the northern mole to where the larger sea stretched away, and the proper sandy beach, the dunes' fine hairs blown back from their foreheads, opposite the lumpy water. The witches' house was buried in among them somewhere, with Misskaella in it, and Trudle hardly less fearsome, and Trudle's two wild daughters, who did not come to school and were not made to. I shivered at the thought of them, wild in that weird cottage. *They* could put an end to all our sorrows, those witches. They could refuse to bring wives out of the sea. They might terrify the men into agreeing that the coats be unlocked. Or could they magic them some way? I hardly knew what they were capable of. But if anyone could change the way marriage was done on Rollrock, those two women could.

But why would they? For it suited them, all the money they made from the bringing out and the blanket knitting. Why would they be moved by a boy's plea for his mother, to restore her to her home and happiness, to set things right for her? Misskaella had no heart at all, and was training Trudle up to have none either. She had not yet managed to shift Trudle's interest from any full-grown man who wandered by, but sea-wives and children they were both pleased largely to ignore.

I stared again out to sea, to the horizon, and the sky bleached of all promise above it. But then in among the mole-rocks an arm lifted and dropped. I worked out a bit of black, which was hair flopping in the wind, and a pale spot that was boy-face. I didn't care who it was; it was not a mam or a dad or a witch, and greeting this someone would bring me out of my downcast mood. I slithered down the sand to the beach, and walked along beside the mole-rocks to below him. It was Toddy Marten, seated in there where he could see forever and not be seen unless he chose. He swayed and he sang, wandering in his own head, swimming his own private ocean. Then he lifted something up from between his feet—ah, it was a spirit flask—and drank from it.

"Dan'l Mallett!" he cried as he distinguished me from the other rocks climbing toward him. "What brings you here this fine day, sirrah?" And he put out his hand like an old gaffer from a village seat.

I shook it, cold frog that it was. "What are you up to out here?" I sat my bottom to the wet sand in the cavity next to him and saw the attraction of the place. Potshead might not exist, the mole hid it so well behind us.

"What am I up to? Why, I am drinking."

"So I see. Won't your dad thrash you, taking his spirit?"

"Maybe he will," said Toddy cheerily. "Maybe I will thrash him back—and maybe my granddad too—and maybe my *great*-granddad, for having made the mess we're all in. Here, Daniel, have a slosh of it. It is like carrying hot coals in your stomach. It warms all of you, right out to the toenails." He twisted out the cork and offered me the flask.

I lifted and tipped. The air off the stuff rushed out the neck and nipped my nose; the spirit itself ran cold and stinging across my tongue; a little spilled out the side and dripped to my collar, leaving a line of cold burning down from the corner of my mouth. "Wo-hoah." I gave it back to him, and wiped my chin.

He swigged again. "And it makes you forget. It blurries out your brain. You can just sit here and sing. And then a friend comes along!" He flung his arm about my shoulders and growled with satisfaction, and we both laughed at his pretending. "And everything is just fine and champion! Look at the lovely—the water, Daniel. And is that an albatross I see? Isn't that good luck?"

"An albatross is, but that is a gannet." I was still negotiating the spirit into myself; it felt as if it were eating holes in my gullet, making lacework of it.

"'Tis a fine bird, your gannet, no?"

"It is a very fine bird."

"'T's a *very* fine bird." He took his arm away, so as to smack the cork back into the neck. Then he collapsed somewhat. "How is this, Dan'l? It is in-*suff*'rable the way things are, do you not think?"

"With the mams, you mean?"

"With the mams, with the dads, with *everyone*." He spread his arms, as if those people were out there seaward, not behind us, and as if he would embrace them all.

"None of us is happy anymore," I conceded.

"Was any of us *ever* happy, I'd like to know? It seems to me that Rollrock lads are only happy for as long as we're too little to see that we *oughtn't* to be happy. Soon as we find that we might have sisters, *but don't*, as soon as we see that our mams and grandmams are only our mams and grandmams by witch-work, why—" He shook his head at me impatiently, then waited for his eyes to catch up. "I don't see why everyone's fussing so," he said more pettishly. "Who wants girls anyway? What are they good for?"

"I don't know," I said. "I haven't ever known any besides Trudle's." Well, there was that red girl at Knocknee, her hair fizzing and flaming, her inquisitive eyes looking me up and down. But I could not be said to *know* her, exactly.

"And as babs? Gawd, that last one! Yawped all day and night until Mam took her down. Dad was glad to be rid of her as much as I was, the racketing. We could all get some sleep."

We listened to his cruel words in our shelter there. Then—*doik!*—he pulled out the cork again and thrust the bottle at me, as much apologizing as daring me to drink more.

The second pull of spirit was gentler; it soothed the damages caused by the first. Watching Toddy's throat jump around his next swallow, I told myself I must not do this again too soon. It was far too pleasant, too warming against the weather. Enough of it, and I should be agreeing with Toddy Marten; I should be agreeing with every Toddy Marten of this town; I should be blabbing out everything about my own mam and how she lived alone in her room under her weed, how we were helpless to help her though we had tried every remedy we knew of, and how *hard* it all was and oh the great *burdens* women were, were they not?

After the third pull I found it in me to take no more; I only kept Toddy company while he overdrank, and stopped him making too bad a mess of himself. When next he could in any way stand, I helped him up and wheedled and carried him home.

When we reached his door, "Just go in," he said from his hung head. "There's no point trying to get my mam up."

I left him in his front room curled up in an armchair with a cup of water by him and a bowl to be sick in if he needed. The house smelt as ours did, as if a sea-fog had got into its bones, sour and cold. I was glad to leave it, as I'd been glad to avoid my own.

I took myself hill-walking, not wanting to present myself at home with spirit on my breath. Up over the top of Watch-Out I went and down, and right the way across the Spine and to Windaway Peak, as far as that. I stood in the rain there and listened to the chattering of my teeth. Did my head ache from the drink, or from the cold rain's drumming? Should I go back to my home, to my town, to those unhappy people, or should I stay here in the weather, the size of it and the cruelty, and the lessening light? The one choice seemed as unpleasant as the other.

In the end I turned without deciding to, and reminded my legs how to walk. It was a trudge home, and more of a trudge, and more. I thought I would never get there. But of course I did, and of course it was no better than outside in the wild, only a little warmer, and without the promise, at the end, of death by freezing.

I woke in the morning knowing what I must do. I ached all over, from my hair ends in to my heart. I sat up and regarded the different ordinarinesses of my room and its furnishings, the spills of light on the wall around my window curtain, as I moved around my idea, considering it from all sides. It held good—as far as anything could be thought good on Rollrock, in Potshead. At the very least, it would move us on into a *different* dreadfulness.

That afternoon I walked home from Wholeman's hearth with the first part accomplished. Dad had stayed behind with his pipe and pals awhile, to talk that special dreary eldermen's talk that I could not bear, but that gratified dads so.

Into our little house I broke, the seaweedy silence of it. I hummed part of a twiddling tune that Jerrolt Harding had been whistling up in the snug.

I went in to Mam. She was a low dark dune there. She was awake, though; her breathing was full of thoughts and pauses.

There was not much light; she still had the curtains across. I sat at her pillow edge beside her tear-salty hair. A scooped sea-heart lay in a saucer on the farther pillow, beginning to go rancid; the spoon was licked so clean, you'd mistake it for new-polished.

"Mam," I said, and not lightly or cheeringly, "I have some news for you."

She burrowed a little deeper into the blanket.

"Your son," I said, "has got himself a position, as bottlewash at Wholeman's."

I had thought her still before, but now she was properly listening; not a leaf of seaweed moved.

"I'm a good lad, says Mister Wholeman. He says they can trust me. Can't they."

The dune quaked and her white face rolled up from under. "Did he take you to task," she said, "for last winter and that business with the coats?"

"You heard about that?" Which of the boys had spread it among the mams? "He mentioned it," I said. "I told him I would always show that room the proper respect."

She crawled up to me. Powerful from under the blanket came her warmth and the smell of the warmed weed. I remembered that sea-smell on me, in the coatroom. Perhaps no boy had blabbed; perhaps the mams had smelt on all of us what we had done.

"Do you have a plan, Daniel?" she whispered. "Are you *scheming* something?"

"I am," I said. The sight of her so close, so alert, so present with me, made me breathless. I was frightened of the hope I had woken in her. "But I don't know yet. I must work and show myself trustworthy, and watch and learn the habits and timings of things up there, and then scheme some more."

She nodded. "Where is your dad?" she hissed.

"Still up there," I said.

Mam swayed on her hands and knees. Even with the slight window shine in them, her eyes were unclear, hardly more than holes in her floating pale face. Out of them, her attention poured and poured at me.

"I know I don't need to tell you," she said low. And then she whispered, half strangled, "You must not say a word."

"Not to anyone," I said to her, as earnest as she could wish. "Don't you worry. Not even to *myself*."

She laughed suddenly, and knocked me to the bed, and squashed the breath out of me the way we had always liked to fight. She was still the stronger, but I was grown-up enough to be bottle boy, and I was beginning to see that I might soon have a chance against her. It was all darkness and strain and struggle a little while, and stifled laughter and threats. "You cannot hold me!" "Oh, I can!" "Weakling!" "Land-lad!"

She pinned and then released me, sprang back onto her haunches and the fight was over. "They will punish you, Daniel," she said. "Not for freeing me, but for showing other lads that it can be done."

"I don't care," I said, panting. "You will be home by then."

"Foolish boy," she said fondly, and her thin hand reached through the dimness, pushed my hair behind my ear, tickled down my neck and along my collarbone. Then she slapped my cheek twice, lightly. "Let me think on this. Out of here, laddie-lad, before your dad comes. Just a glance at us and he'll know we're up to something. Go."

Things fast went out of my control, as they will when a boy lets slip his secret, even to one other. First Mam confided to me that Kit's mam too must go to sea. And then all the mams must come, she said. Then Kit's mam must bring Kit, and then, yes, all the other mams must bring their boys too. "Especially you, Daniel," said Mam, "who are up for the greatest punishment. The only way I can protect you is to have you with me."

"You can do that? You can take me?" A mad hope lit me. "How? I have no coat."

"Oh, any coat will do for you: fish, sheep, bird, rabbit, sewn together with seaweed."

"Will Misskaella magic it onto me?"

"Misskaella?" She laughed. "Oh no! We've no need of her. I'll do the same as I'd have done if you were a girl-child—sew you up in skin and weed, take you down to the water, sing you across, land-child to sea. You are seal enough in yourself; the moon and the song will bond it to you. We all know how to bring that about."

She put me in charge of the boy-skins, of collecting enough to cover each boy, without telling them what we were about. The only way to accomplish it was to pretend to be preparing a secret costume play for the dads, in which each lad large or small had a part, for which he must be costumed. The crafting of this play to the point where it convinced the players, the devising of song-and-dances, the deputizing of the littler boys to gather sewing-weed, the fighting off of propositions to costume us in cloth or crepe paper—all this nearly broke me, especially in the face of scorn and resistance from some of the big lads. But our skin hoards grew, and the knowledge of our project spread so that even dads sometimes offered bits of leather that they had about, for use in our entertainment.

"Stand still, Daniel." Mam's hands were at my face, pinching, pinning. "Or I'll have your eye out."

"It's tight as tight," I said. "A boy cannot breathe in it."

"Not here," she agreed. "But once you touch water, it will soften, and you'll grow great underwater lungs, so as to swim full minutes on a single breath. You've seen us."

"I have. And will my nose work the same, and close and open on top of my snout?"

"It will, my sweet."

I tried to make my boy-nose do it within the hood, twitching and snuffling.

"Tsk, wretched lad . . . There," she said. "Now, don't dislodge my pins, taking it off. It must be sewn right if it's to fit and form you."

I did not believe, particularly once the mams were consulted, that they would ever all agree on a plan. Once they had, I could not see how we would do everything that needed to be done to carry it out. Someone, surely, would betray our intentions to the dads, by accident or out of sympathy for them? I had come close to spilling everything to my own dad several times, so much did I pity him.

But the time came. The moon entered the right phase for the thefts from the coatroom—and for our flight straight afterward, for once the mams had their coats in hand they could only go straight to the sea. And still, somehow, we remained undiscovered.

My other main task had been to engineer for the cupboard door to be left unlocked. This must be done early in the morning, when Mister Wholeman was doing the books, when he would not be tempted to follow his son around, nagging and chivying him and faultfinding every job he did. Then, as Rab put away stores, I must manufacture some small emergency for him to deal with, and finish the job for him, and hand him back the key just carelessly enough. This was not difficult; Rab was never good for much in the mornings, let alone spotting the sneak-thieving of a blameless boy like me. Still, I felt relief when it was done, and neither Wholeman's suspicions had been roused.

At the same time, I was sick with terror of what was to come. I signaled that I had done my part, by hanging the rinsed bar mats out along Wholeman's wall in the sun in a particular order. I didn't know half of what the mams had planned to follow on from this signal; some things they had kept from me, so that I could not confess them if pressed by the men. There would be all the little businesses of making the day run along not too noticeably differently from other days, which was more difficult playacting than anything we lads had done. And neither must Trudle or Misskaella suspect anything, or they would alert the men to our plan, or thwart it themselves.

I went from Wholeman's to school, and labored there over my

numbers and letters. Little rushes of gooseflesh ran over me, and I must remind myself to be calm and ordinary about things. The mams' quiet work went on about me. Although it could not be seen or heard, I was astounded that no one else could sense the itch of it, the suppressed excitement. None of my fellows gave sign or word that the day had been signaled, that this night our lives would change—could it be that I'd devised and executed this whole marvelous scheme in an elaborate dream the night before?

Mam gave me lunch, and likewise we barely met each other's eye, let alone spoke of what was to happen so very soon. I walked up to Wholeman's again. As I passed Cartwrights', out of their window issued a stream of seal-woman song, and the way the mam held some notes and ran others together made me shiver and flee, stamping hard on the cobbles of my childhood, hurrying past the sunlit cottages of my friends, and their dads, and their lives that I knew so well, every one.

That afternoon I was sure someone would notice the difference in me, put it together with other odd happenings in the town and be wise to us. Every time a man glanced at or greeted me in the snug, or bid me bring him this or take away that, I must control a startled movement and swallow a gobbet of fear. Had he seen that I was not the boy Wholeman thought me, the one that could be trusted, the one in league with them against their wives, our mothers?

Grinny and Batton met me out the back as arranged, and I shut them in the coatroom, hooking the padlock on the hasp as before, but not quite snapping it closed. With only a pair of candles for light, they were to take down the coats and tie them, so that boys could more easily carry them away after dark. I was sure that they would set themselves on fire in there, or stack the tied coats poorly so that they tumbled from their stack and made a noise, but I heard not a sound all afternoon.

As night fell I found a moment to tap the cupboard door in the agreed pattern. The response tapped back through, softly but clearly, and I hurried away, out to the yard beyond the pisser, where Angast was posted, both to give him the nod and to tell him who had turned up for drinking tonight, who was likely to stay and who might leave and be wandering the lanes at the hour appointed for running all the skins to their respective mams.

The snug clock had a chime that could be heard in the hall. The plan hung now on my keeping any man from going to the pisser between ten-fifteen and ten-thirty. In this I was aided by the fiddler Jerrolt, of whom I requested all the songs that were slow and funereal, and that it would be rude to get up and piss through: "The Night My Mother Died" and "Low Lay the Boat in the Harbor" and "The Fiercest Storm." While he held the men perfectly steady and somnolent there, some of them joining in singing, some of them weeping, I hovered behind the bar where I could deliver the signal knock through the cupboard wall, if any man sprang from his seat between songs. But Jerrolt outdid himself that night with the emotion of his playing, and all of them controlled their bladders as if they were fully aware of, and determined not to disrupt, the game of fire buckets going on out the back, the tied skins passing along a chain of lads to Lonna Trumbell, who sniffed each one and told the next runner whose it was.

Ten-thirty struck during the storm song. At the end of

it, Nerdnor Prout sprang up and made for the hall door, and I knocked out the signal, just in case Grinny and Batton had run overtime in their emptying of the cupboard. Surely fifteen minutes had not been enough time. All those mams! All those coats!

"Give us a cheerful one now, Jerrolt!" cried someone. "A jig or something—'Frugal's Ball' or 'The Elf-King's Daughter,' one of those!"

I all but held my breath waiting. Nerdnor reappeared, and came up to the bar, and in a terrible fright I waited for him to deliver the news to Wholeman that the back hall stank of sealskins and the yard was full of shrieking children carrying mysterious bundles.

But all he said was "Another nip o' the Gorgon, Storn," and began to search about himself for the coins for it.

Was it done, then? Had we managed it? Were mams even now hurrying down to the waterside, singing and sewing their boys into patch-skins and swimming away with them? And what was the more terrifying, that our plan had run up against some unforeseen nosy-bones or circumstance, or that it was carried out faultlessly, that the wish I had had for my mam's happiness had now emptied Potshead of every wife and son?

I went around the snug and gathered, then hurried to the scullery and washed and washed, wishing I had never begun this plan, wishing that the coats were still in their rows behind their padlocked door. I stacked the bottles and pushed the rack of glasses through to the bar, and then I ducked out into the hall myself—and to everyone in the snug it would have looked as if I were only going to relieve myself, but in truth I was abandoning my post, abandoning my job, abandoning my dad chatting there with Fernly Ashman and Michael Clift, leaving behind the only life I knew.

It was quiet once I shut away the noise of Jerrolt tuning up again, the tide of talk rising again. The hall was empty, and smelt only slightly more sea-ish than usual. I hurried along to the cupboard, with the padlock closed in the hasp as it ought to be. I lifted the lid of the chest by the door, and there as promised was my mam's bundled skin, which they had not conveyed to her in case she went straight into the sea without me. I pulled off my apron, snatched up the skin, closed the chest lid and left by the rear door, wrapping the bundle in the apron as I went.

It was uneasy weather. The secrets gusted about the streets with the leaves and litter, thick enough in the air to choke me. I tried to walk and look calm, but there was no one about, and before long I was running. House after house that I passed, that should have had a light in the window, was dark, and I heard no noise of movement or conversation within any of them, and this terrified me. I became possessed of the senseless fear that my own house would be as empty and dead, my mam gone never to return, that not only had all the mams and lads gone, but all the fathers too, so that I was the last person on the island, running from no one to no one, never to find companion or family again.

But our house was lit, and I burst into our front room, and there was Mam pacing. She scooped me up and squeezed me, tightly and for a long time. "While I have arms to do this," she said.

She put me down and I thrust the aproned bundle at her. "Ah!" She hugged it to herself, pressing her lips and nose to the edge to draw off the scent.

"Do you remember it, then, from when you jumped out of it?" I patted the slithery skin with my bottle-washed hands.

"No," she said. "But it is me and mine, very distinctly, by look and by smell. Let's get on, then." She fell to whispering. "Everyone else is gone, Daniel. Let us shut up house and follow."

I had left my coat up at Wholeman's. Mam took hers down from the peg, put it on, but did not button it. She picked up the tied skin, and the patch-skin she had made for me, and I put my hands on the latch and doorknob. We looked at each other, my dad's absence thunderous around us. So as not to hear it, I lifted the latch and pulled open the door. We went out, the two of us, into the night, and I closed the house behind us.

She took my hand as we started walking, and hers was cold and tight. I thought she smiled down on me out of the stars, but the light was not good and her hair shadowed her face; she might just as easily have been wincing.

Down slippy-slap we went, the wind skirling and twiddling around us, caught in the narrow ways. Every now and again a strong breath from the sea would push at our faces, green and alive and massive. When that happened, Mam would almost run a few steps, as if being summoned more sharply.

The water was rucked up and difficult-looking between the moles. I thought I saw seal heads out there, two or three, but when I looked again I could not find them. I thought, then, that seals were strewn along the stony beach, all shades of them—but no, those were clothes: coats and dresses, trousers and jackets. "Oh!" It was as frightening as if they had been bodies there, of all the boys and mams I knew.

Mam squeezed my hand. "Let's go along," she said. "I don't want to leave from here. I want wilder sea."

"Wilder than that?" I stumbled after her, eyeing the crisscrossing foam between the moles. I hoped this was a dream; certainly I had never felt such terror except in dreams.

Mam was entirely sure of herself, though; if I stayed right with her, perhaps I would catch some of her confidence. I waded down the sand dune at the end of the harbor front, and ran out after her across the sand of the northern beach. The town's windows, its eyes, rose behind us, tightening the skin of my back; I glanced up, and there were the two orange squares that were Wholeman's against the hill. The wind blew strongly with no more buildings in its way; the water shouldered up and smashed itself on the sand before us.

Let us run home, I wished I could say, *and all go on as before*. But clothes were scattered about here too, half in and half out of the shallows, and lengths of twine from Grinny's and Batton's bundles. So many mams and boys had already gone! And Mam knelt before me, humming, unbuttoning my shirt, and her face in the moonlight was clear—alight as the moon, it was—and I was at first too cheered by her happiness to voice my doubts, and then I was too shocked by the sea-wind and the floating spume on my naked skin.

Last of all she took off my boots and trousers. I steadied myself with my hands on her shoulders, steadied myself against the thought that she would not *have* shoulders much longer, we would neither of us have shoulders or hands. Now I was clothed only in the night cold and my terror of the water, shivering and goose-fleshed top to toe.

"Step in," she said and then I was preoccupied, wasn't I, with fitting myself into the sheepskin suit with its scratchy seaweed seams, trying to keep my balance with my feet thrust into the narrow tail of the thing. I had grown by the tiniest amount since she made it; I gasped but did not complain as she laced me in, for she sang as she did so, and in a particular way, building and building on the same repeated pieces of tune, and I feared that if I interrupted, she would have to begin again. Then I would be trapped even longer in this cramped stiff suit that stank of mutton and sea-rot. Both of us would be further delayed on this nightmare-strewn beach.

She checked that my toes and then my fingers were pushed fully into the suit's tied sleeve ends. She pulled the ragged hood mask down over my face and set to fixing it at the neck. It was as if she stitched my mouth shut and my chin to my chest—she had never been so brisk and firm about her sewing before. I stood there with my neck pulled into an ache behind, my little whimpers nothing against her singing, determined now and perhaps a little mad, louder to me and more frightening than the sea's snorts and crashes.

Through the eyeholes I watched her as well as I could, so as not to look at the waves, so as not to think too clearly about what we were doing. She flung down her dress among the others, took off her underthings and held them up and with a joyful laugh let the wind snatch them out of her hand, and then she was just flesh and fur and flying hair, unworried by the cold, uncluttered by the trappings of land-clothing.

She pulled the knot of the coat bundle undone in a single joyful movement. The skin fell open on the stones, and with a shriek to myself inside my mask I jumped back from it, so lively did it settle and so blackly shine there, fattening and smoothing out as I watched. I gasped inside my dry leather mask, and my flattened hair crawled with sweat and fear.

She lunged at me and kissed the mask of me, and shouted something—perhaps in seal-language, for I could not hear sense in it. Then she lifted the swelling coat high, and it sank upon and encompassed her, clung on close, clung to its own edges around her. *Clap* and *clop* and *zlip*, it went, and *snick*, until she was disappeared within. And then she fell, from standing, foot-fins together, straight into the wavelets, where she was now seal, and she flung herself down toward the deeper water.

She turned and there was enough of my mam left in the seal that I as her boy could not refuse to follow, so I too fell and floundered through the curdled air and into the foamy edge of the sea. There the water, and the magic, overtook me, and what was seal of me supplanted what was boy. I ceased to think and to intend or decide, in any way that makes sense in a story, but only followed my mam, crying after her into our dark world, alive to the tides now and the temperatures. I sought the bubbling trail of her with my whiskers and went after it, to the depths and wonders and fellows and foes disposed on all sides of us, and before us, and below.

During the time I lived in the sea, nothing happened in the sense that humans know happening. Seals do not sit about and tell, the way people do, and their lives are not eventful in the way that people's are, lines of story combed out again and again, in the hope that they will yield more sense with every stroke. Seal life already makes perfect sense, and needs no explanation. At the approach of my man-mind, my seal life slips apart into glimpses and half memories: sunlight shafts into the green; the mirror roof crinkles above; the mams race ahead through the halls and cathedrals and along the high roads of the sea; boat bellies rock against the light, and men mumble and splash at their business above; the seal-men spin their big bodies by their delicate tails as lightly as land-lads spin wooden tops, shooting forward, upward, outward. Movement in the sea is very much like flying, through a green air flocking with tiny lives, and massier ones more slowly coasting by.

Seal-men I found to be very like our land-dads, possessive and anxious, patrolling the borders of the clan. When we went up on a beach, they must always be seeing other seal-men off, coming back blown and bloodied. Sometimes my fellows and I played at this man-work, but for us it was two rubber heads bouncing off each other, no teeth and no purpose, and the mams laughed lounging around us.

And then there were those sister-seals, our size, but not fighters. Those whiskery sea-maids, some part human, most entirely seal, they slipped with us among the columns of sunlight. They blinked beside us through the roof of the world into the windy air, the new breath rasping in our nostrils. Like flung seeds or stones they moved, like arrows or bullets through the water, and like weed undulating away along the tide or teasing your face with a leaf end.

I don't know how to tell it all. Seal feelings are different from human ones, seal affections, seal ties with other seals. The best I can do is overlay a skin of man-words on the grunt and urge and song and flight and slump of seal-being.

Our mams belonged better underwater than they ever had belonged above. Our mams found their wings, is how you might put it. They did not glory or revel or make any particular celebration, but only slipped back to rightness, went back about their business. The bulk of our mams was not beautiful as a man sees beautiful, but to seal-eyes, as their black teardrops fell fast, flew fast, twisted through the home depths, they were lovely in their solidity and their speed. Each had her own self, with her own pattern of blotch and freckle, her own manner and song—each seal was clear-marked friend or stranger.

The days were long and unformed; the seasons beckoned us, then pushed us away behind them; stars rode over us, as did the moons in their boatishness or bulbousness; towns were a crust on the edge of our world's eye and people were mites that crawled there. If I saw my father in that time, I don't recall it, or recognizing any man of Potshead—or Potshead itself! I would be hard-pressed to know that it was Crescent Corner where I lounged or fought; recognition of a place, for a seal, takes count not of the landscape above but of the sea surrounding, the rocks and depths and kelp beds nearby, the approach and escape, the presence already of friends and rivals. As the sea, beyond the point where men can see bottom, becomes to them only depths that hold their loves and livelihoods, so do the heights become to seals only wastes of dry blaring light from which weather and occasional dangers descend.

I felt no pull to the land. I barely knew that I *knew* the land; land thoughts deserted me and I neither reflected on the past nor anguished about the future. I only was; I only knew—or I learned by following and doing—where to go, how to behave; I only followed flurries of friends and of fish, took flight from enemies, sang what songs seemed to require to emerge. I came ashore and basked in the sun; I slipped back away from the lumberous, slumberous earth-life, and took flight again, took life, in the undersea.

"Sealers found it out," says my dad when he has relit his pipe. "As you've probably heard."

"Well . . ."

"Or sealers knew already—sealers' grandpas and great-grandpas had all told them. I daresay stories last better on those boats, they are so long off land and must amuse themselves." The room brightens as the window light catches in his puffs of pipe smoke. "At any rate, the first seal they saw for what he was was Will Canker. You could not mistake him, they said—he was all-over stitches, stretched out, where his mam had made them in the rabbit or the lambskin. So they did what they do: they cut along those lines, but not deeply, and they let the seal bleed out. And then when the skin clung close and Canker inside started to kick, they cut him free and put him on the boat. The skin went back to . . . to lambskins, it was, with Will. He had it with him when he stepped onto the dock here at Potshead six weeks later. So they didn't need a witch with them for that, we learned from sealers; all it is is knives and the beast itself, its double nature coming out."

The pipe smoke has spread into a cloud around Dad's head. Evening is coming. I am glad we have the fire going, to counter the cheerless gray-blue light.

"So you didn't know this before Willem Canker came back," I say, "that lads could be cut out of seals?"

"We hadn't even known that lads could be put in!" he says with a bitter laugh. "If we had, we might have kept our wits closer about us. No, when you went, we had no hope, Daniel, ever, of getting any of you back. Willem stepping off that boat was like the world starting to spin again. Men came back to life, put away the drink and the weeping, smartened themselves up thinking their sons might arrive from the sea and find them in this shameful state. There were men went down spring and summer to Crescent Corner with their knives, eye out for young bulls with the seams all over them, but only your friend Raditch and Feenly Cooper ever came up there."

Dad lays aside the pipe, clears his throat. "We went to Miss-kaella, a crowd of us, to ask if she could bring you up—only as seals, mind. We didn't want any strenuous magic of her; we would do the cutting ourselves. Well, I don't know, maybe the bringing *is* the wearisome part, but she would have none of it. Any more than she would consent, right after you left us, to bringing up new wives, for those few men who could afford them. We lost our younger men at that time, all our marriageables, as well as our boys. All off to mainland they went, the bachelors, and the ones that found wives did not bring them back to Rollrock, but found occupation there, with Cordlin's fleet or on Knocknee farms. And I am glad to say, neither would Misskaella bring up one single sea-maid, contributed for with pooled bits of money from low sorts in the town, with the idea that they would all use her, pass her from man to man. She had had her fill of us, the witch said. We were not to come moaning to her. She was done with seals and seal magic.

"You cannot blame her; she was already quite old and ill. She was owed money too, by some of the men; they had gone back on their agreements once the wives were lost to the sea; they drank away their wage and she saw none of it. Not that she was in need, her nor Trudle nor Trudle's girls. Misskaella has made her fortune out of us—you've seen her house on the hill, haven't you, so stuffed with treasures a person can hardly step inside? And Trudle had wanted for nothing once she birthed that first bab. So *she* had no reason, did she, to put herself out for us? All that we found of you we had to find on our own. So some, as I say, kept an eye on Crescent, and others, as you well know, went by the Skittles every chance they had when the seals were there, and other dads went farther a-sea and searched the other islands. And every season since, some of you have come back, skins in your arms to show what you were, from wherever the sealing boats docked once they took you off the ice."

I shudder. "Toddy Marten still has nightmares of those boats. Though they locked him up belowdecks, he said, still there was the smell." *Mams being rendered down*, he said to me, and the words toll in my head, but I cannot speak them, just as Toddy could hardly get them out.

"We could as well stop the seal-trade as hold the sun down in the morning," says Dad. "And some of us it tortured, the thought of what they did, and some were glad, I am ashamed to say, that mams and colonies should suffer as we suffered. But all of us went down to meet the boats each day, in hope of some word, or of some actual boy, our own boy, stepping off the gangplank to us. I did go there, every day, until you came, and if a sealer had brought you, Daniel, instead of our own fellows, even if that sealer were slathered all up and down with sea-wives' blood, with a bloodied pick at his belt and a seal-tooth necklace on him, still I would have embraced him, and called him my brother forever."

There's a glint in his eye, and he lets me see it a good long minute before it passes into a twisted smile. "We never really owned those women," he says, "however much we married them and called them wives to the death. But our lads, well, you were at least half ours. I suppose we thought we had a right to claim you back. Otherwise"—he leans toward me, pipe in hand—"who would we have to fill our pipes for us, and bring us grandchildren to brighten our old age? Oh, there's plenty have no one," he continues, watching me knock out the bowl against the fireplace and pick up the pouch. "But they're still hoping, mark my words. The ones who gave up hope, they went, off Chisel Top or swimming out Six-Mile in the winter storms. The others, though they might not go out and search themselves, still meet the boat each day, never knowing when their lad might show."

I was born again and I came out crying—a lot of us did, they say. There never was such a race as the seals for mawking and moping. Out into a driving rain I was brought, part bound tight and part bursting from the lambskin Mam had made for me. All sounds hurt my ears, the rain-hiss on the rocks and the men's voices: "Daniel Mallett! Welcome home, boy!"

"Mallett? That's the boy that worked up Wholeman's, no? That stole the coatroom key the night they left? We should throw that one back, and without his skin too."

"Shall you take the skin to Dominic Mallett, then, Clift, and tell him his son fell over the side?"

"Hush you both! The lad has ears, you know."

"Oh, paff. They lose their language under there; you've heard them."

"Don't mind him, lad. Your dad will be right glad to see you."

They cut and cleared the skin off me. The weight of me fell out, onto a sloping rock that was wet with blood; it had run and run, right off the edge down there and into the sea. Legs rose all around me and faraway faces leered; here, closer, the man with the knife crouched, and slapped my face, and beamed, and wiped his eyes. Behind them one of the Skittles rocks towered, and I mistook it for a huger person yet, all shoulders and no face. I tried to bring my arms up to protect myself, but I had no strength in them; I had forgotten how to use them.

Amid the brute noise then and the confusion, I recognized the blurred uppers of a fishing boat. They carried me onto it, and laid me raw-skinned and bony-shouldered on the deck. Some man put a rope coil under my head, which pressed into me painfully. I was trying to accustom myself to my man-eyes and what they showed me through the air. All the bulk had gone off me; how was it that I felt so much heavier? And everything was heavier around me, glued to the deck. The men shuffled stuck there to the boards; none of them could fly, and neither could I anymore.

Around me the air racketed; every movement was quick and startling, every contact sudden and loud, throwing out more noise. To no rhythm, the land-men moved and swore and fumbled, the men of my town, of my land-life, and the seabirds stuttered in the sky. And I was crushed flat to these remnants of my coat, pressed to the damp wood by this sea-grass blanket, that held in what little warmth I had. The only thing the wind could do was push the damp hair back and forth on my brow; it could not lift and return me to the water; it could not lift even this knotted knitted thing off me.

It was an ill-making dream, and the men came by, smiling and patting and consoling me, all the way home.

"Nobody holds what you did against you, Daniel, don't you worry."

"Well, only men like Clift, and their good opinion's not one you need hanker after."

"A lad that loves his mother above all, well, didn't we love them above all too?"

They required nothing of me; they did not expect me to speak with this strangely packed mouth, out of this flat face with its new framework of jaw, using this new voice all strings and hollows. The sky lingered, never to be veiled by seawater as I took my breath and dived with it below. The illness went on, and through it, the men's mutter-and-crooning slipped together, interlocked into items of sense. ("Didn't we want them happy, in the end?" "Only none of us could put ourselves aside enough, and our own convenience." "It's true, the lads only did what we should have done ourselves.") They welcomed me; they were welcoming me back. They spoke of their gladness, and of the preciousness and rarity of sons. I was one among their sons, it seemed. These were changed men from the ones I was beginning, *just* beginning, to remember.

"You'll be heavy to yourself awhile," said one, over the grinding of the boatside into the jetty, over the hard explosions of sound in my back and skull. He lifted the weed-blanket off me, and I waited to fly up into the air. But I did not. I lay helpless.

They hooked my arms over two men's necks and tried to teach me walking on my new, long legs, across the deck cluttered with box and bolt and reel; when I was steady enough they took me across the frail plank that was all that kept me from dropping into a dirty corner of water, some ignored, avoided corner of my home below. They walk-lifted me to the land, which had no give or movement; the jetty stood firm as the water slapped and fought it below. My feet dragged and my legs tried to rescue them—how was I to support myself and balance, on these two stalkish things?

The men had put a shirt on me and trousers, but still the foreign knees swung and braced below my blurring eyes, my heavy head. I knew that they belonged to me, but I could not see how ever I was to control them.

My father was brought down the street to me, but I did not see him, only heard clomping boots and men saying, "See, Dominic? There he is!" And then a voice spoke out of years ago, out of my bones, saying, "Is that him? Is that my Daniel? Are you sure?"

A space opened before me. I heaved up my head. Some boots swam there and his familiar belt buckle, and then the rest of him leaped into view, sharp-edged and astounding, his big hands out wide at me and in between them his awakening face.

"Daniel," he said, and "Dad," I managed to say; even words were heavy here, all burdened with the years and the mess of my new voice. My head sagged again with the weight of everything, and I saw nothing but wet greeny-black-blue cobbles ringed by boot toes and the legs of marveling men.

"Here, let me take him," said my dad to the man at my right, and they unhooked and rehooked me and I seemed to walk worse than ever, leaning onto my dad with my head swung fast into his shoulder.

"You will be fine, my boy," he said. "Fine and good." And he held me up and walked me. A splash appeared a brighter blue on his shirt; I had not known it was raining, or that he was crying. I tried to speak, to tell him that I knew him, that I was surprised, that I was sorry, that I had found my way somehow into this strange, long, wrong-grown body. But all I could manage for the moment was cries very like a seal's, that said nothing, that had to say everything, to the man beside me.

"I remember the day the boy came among us again," says my dad by the fire. "It was a whole new weather and season, bright and blowy. Suddenly there was color in the sky and flowers on the hills. I opened my curtains and there he was walking up the town good as gold, long and limber like a proper man—just as you do, Daniel, only of course I'd not seen you then. Had no surety of ever seeing you, always I reminded myself. I remember he lifted his face—not to see me, not to see anyone, but to look at the town, at walls, and maybe at hill and sky above—and the sight of him, of all our boys and our wives and ourselves rolled into the one face, it near split me down the middle. The last five years along at Wholeman's, every word any of you had ever spoken we had turned over and wet with our tears and polished with our examinations and memories.

"And Canker out ahead—he did not need to sing, just his face was singing, the joy of it. They say it is a sin, envy. You must not covet, they say. Well, your old man, Daniel, he's a sinner. I hope you don't mind. I was cloven by envy, *hating* Joel Canker for having what I had not. Not yet, anyway, and who knew I was to get it?"

He beams around his pipe, takes the thing from between his teeth with one hand, reaches out the other and bats my cheek softly.

Then a thought scoops his smile away. "Of course, there's many that only ever got that envy and no more. Corris Snow, bless his soul, and the Green brothers—none o' theirs came back." He feasts on the sight of me, and guilts about it.

Some of the lads could not bear it on Rollrock, not with the mams gone and half the dads still mourning sons as well. Several fled to the mainland in search of cheer and distraction, and many more talked of going, but never got up the courage to take the boat.

Those who stayed were put to fishing. Gratefully the older boatmen passed us their places on the boats, while the not-so-old found some fire in themselves to command and instruct us.

It was good work for us, better than sitting on land with the sadder dads. It felt fitting to be on the sea, halfway between our two homes, and much of the time we were too well occupied with the work to think ourselves miserable. There were times when the difference between a fine catch in the hold and our memories of a fine school of fish undersea was hard to endure; sometimes some creature would come up squirming in the net that had once moved with grace or speed or fascination in the water, and to see it flop and struggle on the deck was like my own heart removing from me, and expiring before my eyes for want of the larger system that sustained it. But these were moments only in long days of earning our keep; the best feature of this work was that it properly wore us out—we grew stronger by day with it, and we slept better by night.

Still some boys stayed distressed, particularly those whose fathers had not welcomed them home, or had not ever known how to treat them, or had found them to be strangers since their time in the sea. The worst-distressed paced the shoreline certain nights of the moon at Forward Head or Crescent or Six-Mile, raging and seal-calling fit to break everyone's hearts. And the unhappiest of these swam out, calling offshore. My friend from childhood James was one of these; he went out one night with a measure of drink inside him, and rolled up whitened on Forward Beach next morning. His dad anguished with the idea of wrapping and weighting him and delivering him to the sea again, but in the end he could not bear to, and had him buried in the churchyard, so as to know his son's whereabouts forever.

I came home early from helping at Fisher's store. The smell was all through the house: wild salt sweat of mams, caverns of ocean. It turned the air blue-green to me, with bars of sunlight shifting in it; I walked in with my arms spread, and it all but swirled about them.

In the kitchen, at the heart of the smell, at the heart of the home, Dad sat at the table with his white plate and spoon. He tried to seem everyday, but "What brings you so early?" he accused me.

"Done all I had to do."

His chin was tilted up, his eyes were obstinate and a flush was traveling up his face. And then there was the sea-heart on the plate—hairy, lined with rubbery orange, a bead of orange curd on its lip. The spoon hovered.

"Here," he said. "There's another." He pointed with his thumb to the pot on the stove. As if this were an ordinary dinner.

I tried for both our sakes to pretend it was. I crossed and lifted the pot lid.

"But were you wanting both of these?"

"I thought I was," he said throat-clearingly. "But I'm discovering that one of them is . . . quite enough."

I pulled the sea-heart out by a hank of its grown-on weed and put it in a bowl, fetched a spoon, sat to table. I took Dad's orange-smeared knife and cut the top off with my big capable hands. I tried the remark in my head, but did not say it aloud: *The last time I ate one of these, Mam had to open it for me, that tough skin.*

The steam flooded up and the smell: bodies, wet hair, boiled shellfish, sour seawater, the coziest of winter nights, her clear pale skin with a hint of green, her hair like a stilled flow of black water.

I spooned up a bit of the curd, and now I held my whole childhood in my mouth, warm and free of worry. The mams laughed together; Mam and Dad laughed too, looking to each other, leaning arm to arm. I would do things to stop them; I would perform; I would stand on my hands against the wall so that they would look at me again, include me with them. That was always my aim when Dad was there, to return Mam's eyes and mind to me.

Well, I succeeded, did I not? The curd cooled on my tongue; it slid down my throat, soaking my head with the sweet-saltness. Up sprang tears, but not so far as to fall.

I raised my eyes and found Dad's fixed on me, a spoonful of curd in his hand. "How is she, then, my Neme?" he said. "How *was* she, the last you saw of her?" He ate the curd, but he did not move his eyes, did not free me from answering.

"I don't know," I realized. "She was there. She was well. It is different there; it is not like here." I was embarrassed, the obviousness of this, but Dad did not laugh at me, or look impatient. He moved the curd in his mouth, as if by careful tasting and careful watching of me he might have knowledge of that place, of those five and more years that he lost of us.

"That was not even her name, Neme," I said with a helpless shrug.

"What was her name, then? What was she properly called?"

I tried to say it, but it was as slippery as water in my mouth, as a piece of wind, and it had a high part that my man-voice would not reach, and a croaking that came out crude in a human room, came out animal only, carried not half its proper meaning. Seal-language, seal-song, were fading from my memory. If only I submerged myself, went down to the sea and put my head under, it might all come back to me, but while I stayed above, I could not keep hold of it.

I tried again. "No," I said, "it is more like this."

He listened to me try several times; he did not laugh.

"It sounds like nothing," I said. "It sounds nothing like— But perhaps more shrill at the end, more trailing . . ."

He copied my next attempt; it was a good effort, and yet . . . I shook my head.

"Nothing like that?" he said sadly.

"Oh, something like it." I scraped the curd out of the bottom of the sea-heart rind. "But only a very little."

He made the sounds again, his only-human approximation. "What does it mean, then? How does it describe her, or set her apart from all the other . . . all the others down there?"

Again I thought, If only I were under there, if only I had a moment's swimming. With the taste of curd in my mouth, I pressed my eyes closed with the heels of my hands and tried to imagine. A twitch of seal-muscle, a tail I no longer had. "I think it is about . . . how fine it is to move. How wonderful is smooth swimming, high in the sea, where there is light. I think it—" I dropped my hands. Here I was in this man-box with another man, both of us with our gangly, long-limbed bodies that never could do such swimming. "I think that is it," I apologized. I licked the spoon clean of curd and laid it on my plate beside the hairy heart.

"That's good!" he said. "That's better than no idea at all." He dug with his spoon in the corners of his own sea-heart. "And strangely like the name I gave her, which is brightness, and shiningness. I would like to think I knew that." He sent me a bashful smile, and spooned up the last.

I smiled back at him, but he was already serious again. "How did she seem, under there?" he asked. "Was she glad to be rid of me? Did she even remember me, Daniel?" He covered his mouth then, to stop any further fears pouring forth.

I could not speak to those begging eyes. I turned side-on in my chair, made as if to take my plate from the table, slumped there, trying to recall. "Oh, Dad, who can say? They don't feel the same things. Or think the way we think up here. Or talk the way—the way we do now." I could not look at him; he would be so crestfallen. "You want me to say she missed you. But do you want me to lie? I did not see it. But did that mean she *didn't* grieve after you?"

His face confused my thoughts, and I hunted for something more consoling to tell him. "But as for how was she? She was her own self in the sea, that's all." I tried to find a way to explain it. "She was not in pain, you know, from her feet, and she could move, so well and so easily, not like under the blankets here, all weighed down—"

"She was happy, then," he said.

I shook my head. "Not even that. But she was freed of . . . she didn't have the sadness that she carried around up here. So I suppose, yes, she was happy. But, no—"

"It's all right, Daniel—it's *good* that she's free of her misery." He smiled me a painful smile. "I'd like to be remembered fondly, but I don't want just a new misery to take over from the old. Otherwise, it would make no sense, what you did."

"*Does* it make sense?" I looked to the window, as if the answer might fly in there.

"Oh yes, a perfect sense. It needed to be done, and none of us charmed men would ever have done it."

I shook my head again, not in agreement or otherwise at what he said, but only at how, whosoever's pain I thought of, it could not be resolved without paining someone else.

"What of you, then, lad?" he said softly.

"Me?" I seemed, to myself, to be nothing, beside Mam's being gone.

"What of you—and the other lads, if you know, if you've spoken together? Now that you have been there, lived under that sea, are you always yearning, as your mams were, to go back?"

"I don't know." I lifted my shoulder to fend him off.

"Come, now—if you had the chance, if you had the right-sized suit made, and the magic?"

I all but hid behind the table. I put my elbows on my knees and my face in my hands and suffered there awhile. "Yes, but only because . . . Down there, you see, I did not *care* and I did not *feel*. Whereas here—" I laid my head on my arms; he would only have been able to see the rounded-over back of me beyond the table now. "Here it is *all* feeling and caring, and it makes me so *tired*," I said muffledly into my lap.

His chair scraped back. He came around to me, crouched at my head, rubbed my hair. He did not trouble me with more words, only rubbed and scratched my head as you would a cat's awhile, and then he kissed it, and carried our plates away to the scullery.

When the wind was a particular strength of nor'easter, Toddy and I would run up toward Windaway Peak. There was a blade of land there, up which funneled all the airs from Gambrel Wood to Oaten Share, and we stood on it with our toes curled over the rock like eagle claws, and spread our arms and were held up by the wind. It would push and sluice around us, and overbalance us back down toward the path, or desert us so that we fell forward into a shallow little tumble room on the south side, and make us laugh. Toddy was a long stringbean like me; neither of us took much holding up. He was not glad to have been brought back to land, for he and his dad never got on, but he had emptied one of Wholeman's junk rooms and installed himself there, earning it with the kind of work I used to do.

"You can almost imagine, can't you?" Toddy would cry when

we had it right for several moments, when we were balanced in the streaming air.

And you almost could, though the wind was so much lighter and more fickle than tide and swell, and the bodies we put up to it were such different shapes and felt so differently from inside, so raw and rangy. They were right enough that we could convince ourselves that we were carving paths up and down the watermass, that that flap of coat was the touch of some sister, that others, large and small, sang and shifted their formations all around us. We could almost feel the excitement, the bursting of the family at its edges and the hugger-muggery in the middle, the jostling, the smooth adjustments and reinings-in and spurts of speed.

We would walk home quietened, blown clean of our sorrows.

"When it comes summer," Toddy said, "when we can swim without freezing the nuts off ourselves, we will go down Six-Mile."

"Yes, that will be closer."

"So much more like it."

A few paces of silence. The Spine was like the top of the world, with the sky all around us.

"But never quite, Toddy."

"Oh, no. I know that. But perhaps . . . well, the next best thing. Perhaps close to close enough, what do you think?"

Lory Severner

So I packed myself and set off for Rollrock Isle. There was no one to tell me not to, anymore.

I would not set foot there, said my late mam in my head, *after what they did to the women. What they did to your* own gran.

But that's all over, said that man. Since years ago.

Oh, not so many years. And no doubt that's what they told themselves last time.

But I did not listen to Mam.

An island of nothing but men! my friend Sally had said. *It sounds wonderful, and frightening! I should come and see you off at the bus—but I've to be at the bakery.*

Never mind—I shall see myself off.

You are so brave, Lory. I could never do something like this.

I was not brave, or frightened. I was not even excited as I left Mrs. Mickle's boardinghouse. The key to the house in Potshead, as black and rough-looking as if it had lain in the sea bottom for years, scratched at my hand in my coat pocket. Mam's little case that I had always loved and wanted—it was mine now, and I wished it were hers again—onto the bus it came with me filled with the clothes that I'd taken to Mrs. Mickle's. I put it in the rack and sat below, aware of it like some little cloud above me, blotting out the sun.

Knocknee slid away. I had seen this bus leave before, full of schoolgirls headed for a picnic, or surrounded by well-wishers for a departing honeymoon couple. Today it held only shopmen who had business in Cordlin, and a mam and her daughter who must see the dentist there, and rich Mr. Crowly Hunter, who popped back and forth all the time to show that he had the time and the money—and me, under my cloud, with my heart inside me like the husk of something.

We rolled out across the countryside. I tried to notice every shape of the land and every object on it. It's the last time you'll see this for a while, I told myself. But I could not strongly care. I was only grateful to get away from Knocknee and its four deathbeds, its purse-mouthed landlord, its hard-faced carters who had tried to get the advantage of a girl in mourning eager to escape. I had held my ground with all of them, as Gran and Mam always did; I had nothing to be ashamed of. I was leaving the town cleanly; I could come back whenever I wanted. *Don't burn your bridges*, Gran had said, and I hadn't. And I had the deed in my case for the bridge *she* had not burnt, the house on Rollrock, among those wild, sad men.

The port town reached up out of its valley and drew us down to the water. Why were they called the Heads, those two promontories? They were so much more like arms, shielding the harbor water from any blow or swell. Down the town we went, which any other day of my life would have been exciting in its strangeness: the fine houses, the costumed people, the little milk truck there. But the whole world was strange now, without Mam in it, or Dad, or my brother, Donald. Even the most familiar things—my own hands, my face in the mirror over the washbowl this morning—struck me afresh. I was glad of new sights, for they shook me a little out of my grief, but I was not the excited girl I had been. Or the frightened one—getting from bus to boat, which would have terrified me a year ago, would now be a small thing, after these three recent deaths, three funerals.

The *Fleet Fey*, the boat was called. Even in my hollowed-out state I had to admit she was a romantic sight. Neat-painted, she moved just slightly at the dockside, seeming to ignore us as she gazed toward the Heads, toward the open sea.

"Buy your ticket on board, lass," said the deckhand steadying the gangplank, so up I went with my case, and sat at the rear, where I could see all the cabin and out all the windows. With the rumble of the idling engine in my seat and up my back, I watched the mailbags brought on, and some sacks of potatoes. The clouds were breaking up, and the sunshine came and went, now trying to dazzle me with the color and movements of the waterfront and town, now tiring of the effort and letting all fade to its proper gray again. Here I was, making this journey that I had dreamed of since I was a child, that I had never thought I would have the chance to, or the courage for, and still I felt dull and dogged, just as I had when setting about the rigmarole after Donald died. I knew what to do, all the tasks in their correct order, and grimly I was going about them, preparing myself for each upon the next, for the folk I must deal with and the tricks I ought to be wary of.

The captain came through and shut himself into the wheelhouse. The deckhand pulled up the gangplank, and wound in the wet rope that had been cast off from the shore. The wharf slid away; the other boats glided past at their moorings. There was some relief in that, in the water broadening between me and the mainland with its graves and sorrows.

There were more graves ahead, I knew that. The first chance I had I would visit them: Granddad Odger Winch, and Uncle Naseby, those two scoundrels, objects of Mam's spitting hatred and Grandmam's deepest silences.

We passed between the Heads, the rocks piled like messy gateposts either side of us, the swell making the ship restless. The sun came out like a cheer, and the water was the loveliest color, bright blue-green, and the foam curled like cream on some of the waves. The Heads fell behind, and there was nothing but sky and sea ahead of us, and each one's weather. The towns and farms and all their fuss and clutter of memories, I was shrugging them off like a heavy cloak, and sailing free.

The deckhand came around and fetched fares. "Would you mind telling me when Rollrock comes in sight ahead?" I asked him.

And I sat there in the thrum of the engine, plowing forward into my adventure, watching everything too hard to think, until he did. Then I went and stood in the bows.

The island rose from the horizon. It looked like nothing so much as a giant slumped seal itself, the head toward us and the bulk lumping up behind, trailing out northeast to the tail. Its slopes were greened over, its near side all cliffs and cliff pieces, chewed off but not swallowed by the sea. Every cove and cave looked alike inaccessible to me, most treacherous and unwelcoming.

But we did not head for that rough bit of coast as we drew nearer; instead we bore westward and around the head there, and once beyond that I could see where the land lowered itself more gently, making room for a town, a small town only, on the slopes above the two long moles built out from the shore. Above the houses, field walls ran about, looking as if they should topple down the slope. The fields they outlined were smaller and stonier than I was used to seeing around Knocknee.

Quite suddenly the headland cut between us and the southern swell, and the engine was freed from climbing among the mounds of the sea. We came in at a glide, the horizon settling, and the isle looking less liable to pitch forward in its sleep and crush us. Which house was mine, in that town? I tried to follow with my eyes the path Gran had described to me, putting me to sleep when I was tiny. *A little black house*, she'd said; was it *that* little black house, just sliding behind the church tower?

The ferry slowed, churning water about its haunches. In we bumped against the wharf. All the town, it seemed, was gathered to meet us, and all the town was men, just as that visitor Tom Grease had told Mam and Grandmam—men who idled or mended nets on the seafront, stood in groups near the store, or wandered along from the seafront houses, or down from the town above.

I lifted down my case, put it on the seat and stood by it,

watching the deckhand tie up. Beyond him on the seafront appeared a woman, short and stout and bowlegged, hurrying toward us. She carried a baby and trailed four flame-haired daughters, various sizes, but all dressed the same in flower-printed frocks.

It couldn't be. Misskaella? Gran had told us many a tale of that woman—she'd threatened us with her, even, when we misbehaved as children. The witch would come striding across the sea, she told us, and ladle out our punishment. I felt a stab of annoyance at Donald that he was dead and not able to shiver as I told him I'd seen the actual Misskaella face to face.

But no, it could not be, such a young woman and so lively, and all those children. Ah, this must be that *apprentice* Mister Grease had mentioned to Gran as Mam waved me out the door. A witch, all right, but not the witch of legend; one of those wild Callisher girls, from right near us in Knocknee. Still, she had learned from Misskaella the art of being terrifying; my childhood terrors stabbed in me as she rocked toward the boat, seeming all energy and spite.

Meanwhile the men had greeted the deckhand and helped him place the gangplank, and taken off the potato sacks. The potatoes were for Fisher's store, then, which stood there just as Gran had described it, the solidest building in the town besides the church. It was strange to see it, and to know without ever having entered it exactly how it was arranged inside.

Well, I could only disembark now, couldn't I? I walked past the curious passengers for the farther islands, and out of the deckhouse to the top of the gangplank. The Rollrock men fell quiet, lifting faces mixed of two kinds to me, round or long, pale or darker, framed by red curls or silky black locks; as well, there were more weathered instances of these two types, the hair only streaked with red or black, or whitened completely. Small pale eyes assessed me or large dark ones, some sharply, others shyly—some would not meet my glance at all.

The witch pushed through the crowd of them, and took up a position right at the gangplank end, with her free hand on her hip; her girls caught up to her, first swirling about her and then clumping close.

"What's this," she cried, in a voice like gargled stones, "with a suitcase? What do you think you are about?"

I brought a picture of Gran at her fiercest into my mind, the way she would *take no nonsense*. I was not here because I cared what strangers thought, remember? I trod down the gangplank as if I often had to deal with angry witches. "Who are you?" I said to the little termagant while I was well above her still. I spoke plainly, without sneering or fear. I carried all those deaths in me—Gran's, Mam's, Dad's, Donald's—those four people I now represented, and they gave my voice the right weight. "Who are you, that I should account to you? Are you mayor? Are you police or officialdom?"

"What business have you on Rollrock?"

"Business? I live here. I have property." I stepped off the side of the plank onto the dock, and walked around the witch and the daughters.

"Property? What property?" she said, following.

My, they were tall, some of these boys. "This is the way you welcome women home, then?" I said—not loudly, not angrily, but very clearly, every syllable. "Let them be harassed and harridaned even before they've set foot?"

"Home? What home?" The witch pushed in front of me.

"Quieten, Trudle," said one of the older, bigger men.

Trudle Callisher lifted her chin at him, and drew herself up as much as she could. Her four daughters did the exact same thing, glaring at the man. I might have laughed at the sight, at any other time.

"Who is your family, girl?" the man said to me.

"Winch," I said. "I am Lory Severner, daughter of Bet Winch, daughter of Nance Winch."

"Ah." Nods and glances and mutterings went round among them.

"Odger Winch was your granddad, then, God rest his soul."

"And Naseby Winch my uncle, rest his. I hear you gave them both Christian burials?"

The younger men looked to the older, who nodded, and watched us keenly.

"We did. You've been in Cordlin all this time, you Winch women?"

"Knocknee. As far from the sea and seals as we could get. But I heard there are no more sea-wives left here on Rollrock. Is that true?"

"It is. They all went," said the man. "Took themselves off."

"All of them, and none brought up since? Because if there is even a one, I'm straight back to Knocknee."

"There's none," said the man quickly, into the silence. All of them watched, listened, as if their lives depended on it. Several of the lads might be the one I sought, but of course, he would be very much changed by manhood. They all had such *eyes* on them—had no one ever told them not to stare?—but none of them gave any sign of knowing me.

"Oh no," said a man at the big man's elbow. "There's not a one, anymore. There's not been a seal-woman here for a good seven years."

The big man shifted his feet. "I would not say that they've been *good* years, myself." Into the discomfort after that, he plunged with "Might we carry your case for you, up to the Winch house?"

"Thank you. That would be very kind," I said.

Several of the fathers elbowed forward younger men, and silently they jostled for the case. Then we set off up the sunshiny lanes, and the witch Trudle and six or seven men came with us. Trudle's face was still pinched up with suspicion; her daughters flowed around her; her baby boy stared at us. He looked a little odd, that one; there might be something wrong with him. The girls' piles and flags of red hair flamed in the sunlight—my own hair, plaited close to my head and down my back, felt very contained and obedient by comparison.

The big man introduced himself as Torrens Baker. "Your grandmam would recall my dad, I should think."

"Mister Baker," I said, "I have a feeling there were cousins, from my grandfather's marriage, or my uncle's, who ought to have got this house."

"Oh, there were," he said.

I had *known* it, the way Mam and Grandmam had muttered with Tom Grease when he visited, while I made the tea.

"There were several sons from those marriages," said Baker. "But no Winch lads came back, after the mams took them away. Odger and Nase were both unlucky in that. All these lads you see around you, they are what's returned, from Crescent or the Skittles, or from sealers farther off."

I glanced at one or two boys' profiles, their dark hair or red; what kind of mark would it leave on you, to have lived beneath the sea? These ones seemed to move easily enough on the land; they'd more intelligence in their faces than Trudle's boy had in his and, as far as I could see without being seen to stare, no webs joined their fingers.

"And no daughters?" I said. "But wait—" For the older men had one and all flinched at my words, and the younger's faces had fallen. "There was something terrible about the daughters. Forgive me."

"Many a girl-child was born to Winches," said Baker, and then he paused, in the manner of a man on the point of declaring an unpleasant truth. "But . . ."

"I heard something of it." I rushed on to fill in the awkward silence. "But it was hard to keep Gran talking about some things on Rollrock for longer than a minute; she would up and bustle away, first chance she had."

Baker nodded at the ground. I made myself stay silent. "Well," he went on eventually, and quite softly, "they do not thrive on land, the daughters of a man and a sea-wife. There is more seal in them than there is in lads. They must be put back in the sea if they are not to die. They must be reared by their own people. It caused the wives great grief; many of us remember that."

"Not to mention the other griefs upon them," said a man at my other side.

"Here we are," said Baker over him. "Here is Winches'."

I nearly laughed, the house was such a toy. And it didn't look straight; the slope of the land threw my eyes off so much, the house seemed to lean back into the hill—for a better hold, maybe. Grass and weeds grew thickly to the fence tops, to the windowsills, like a bowl of wild salads. Sea-pinks clumped along the fence, and sea-rocket trailed between the palings into the fields around.

"Any one of our lads can cut that down for you, Miss Severner," said a smaller man into my silence.

"I'm sorry? Oh, the weeds? Yes. Well."

I wrestled the gate part open against the weed sprouts in the path, squeezed through it sideways, leaving behind the several young men who had stepped forward to help me. I pushed past the growth that leaned in either side, up the weed-cracked path. I took out the big black key on its ribbon, slid it into the lock and turned it, grasped the door handle, lifted the latch and pushed wide the door.

Dust curled up from the floor, leading my gaze up the papered walls to the pictures on them, two stormy seascapes, faded to mostly dark brown. Beyond the far hall door a kitchen chair back drew its arch on the shadows; a faded curtain frayed from the kitchen window rail, worn through by years of sunshine.

"Did you want those battens taken off your windows, miss?" said one of the young men as I stared in at all this.

"Maybe in a little while," I said. "For now, I need to look about the place by myself, if you don't mind."

I went back for the case, which the young man passed over the gate to me. "Thank you," I said, and, looking around at them, at Trudle bridling and all her suspicious daughters, "Thank you very much for showing me the way."

An older man cleared his throat. "If you should need anything . . ."

"Oh, I'll be sure to ask."

The men drifted away back down the hill. "Come, Trudle," said Mister Baker, for the little bowlegged woman looked intent on staying and watching, and showing her displeasure some more.

"What does she want here?" I heard her say in her gargling voice as she went off with him. "Who would come to this place, to more than visit and go again in a day?"

I heard the murmur of Mister Baker's voice, but his words were indistinct. I nodded to the departing men, and some touched their cap brims to me as they went.

And then I turned to face the house, the dark shuttered rooms, the thick dust, the achingly plain furniture. It would be like taking up residence in my own sore heart, I thought. And I walked up the path and went in.

I knocked on the sunny door, of the only person in Rollrock I could be said to know in the least degree.

His father opened it, and raised his eyes from my shoes to my face as if he had never seen anything like me before.

"Mister Mallett?"

Mallett nodded, realized he ought to speak, croaked, "Yes."

"My name is Lory Severner. I wonder, might I have a word with your son Daniel?"

Down went his eyes again, his whole face; he made away from me across the wide front room. Plates and water sounded deep in the cottage behind him. The morning sun shone warm on my back, and lounged about golden on everything. I put my cheek up to the warmth.

"Don't you touch them; I'll finish them," came the younger man's voice, and I turned back to see him, much taller than his father, ducking his head to enter the far hallway.

"Good morning," I said while he was still a shadow there.

He emerged into the front room. Sunlight lit him, reflecting up from the step where I stood. "Morning."

He was very tall and lanky, but he was the one, all right. He'd grown into his eyes and his mouth now. He wore work trousers and unlaced boots, a red-checked white shirt with the collar fraying and a worn gray jumper unraveling at one of the elbows. His hair wanted cutting quite badly; it was in his eyes so that he had to twitch it aside. I thought he looked lovely.

He stopped just inside the door, waiting for my face to give him a clue. I folded my arms. "You *don't* remember, then."

He narrowed his eyes, then his mouth dropped open. "Knocknee Market!" he said.

"There you go. First girl you ever saw."

He nodded slowly, looking for signs of the old me that he'd met. "It's many years."

"Have you seen any since?"

"Well," he said. "I saw more that day, though I didn't speak to any. And then there were my sisters." He looked at his feet.

"Your sisters? But I thought—" I felt as if I had strayed into a bog somehow, was about to sink suddenly and wallow and be trapped.

"In the sea."

"Ah," I said. It might be a test, I thought, but he did not have a testing face. He was reddening, and seemed surprised.

"I don't think I saw you yesterday," I said, to move us along. "Did you meet the boat?"

"Yesterday? I did not. But Toddy told me, Toddy Marten. He was there."

I put out my hand. "My name is Lory Severner."

"Daniel Mallett." His hand was very big, and probably very strong, but he handled mine as if afraid of snapping it off my wrist. "Severner? But Toddy said you were Winches."

"My mam was a Winch. Bet Winch. She married a Severner in Knocknee."

He took that in, thought of something else. "But how did you find me? For we didn't tell our names, that day in Knocknee."

"I asked, didn't I, down at the shop there? They said it could only be you and your father, the last fifteen years, gone to Knocknee to do business about a girl. Everyone else from here, their business stops at Cordlin. So says Mister Fisher."

"That's true enough," said Daniel Mallett. "So . . . you're settled in Winches' now?"

"I've begun," I said. "I've begun on settling."

"And no one's got that grass down yet?"

I followed his gaze to the edge of my skirt; grass seeds were scattered all along it. "No, they've not," I said, and laughed up at him. He gave me a small smile, like someone just learning how to do it.

"I'll fetch my knife, shall I?"

I looked up in surprise.

"A scythe, for the grass."

"Oh. Thank you. But I've never scythed grass."

"Neither should you have to. Our mams never did."

The mams hung between us there. It *was* a test, whether he meant it as one or not. I did not look away.

"Leave me finish these dishes," he said, "and then I will come straight over to Winches'."

"All right, then," I said. I nodded in the sunshine, and he nodded in the shady room.

So I crossed the town toward home. I paused once to look back to the sunny doorway where no one stood now, paused again crossing the main street to take in the view of the sun-bright sea there below. Daniel Mallett. I walked on, examining both sides of the hand that he had shaken as if it were a precious relic, or some kind of unknown creature, he did not know how fragile. Yes, Lory Severner, I told myself, my heart steady within me. You have made a very good beginning of things.

Trudle Callisher

We could do it all over again, I said to Miss, many a time, when things annoyed me in the town, when men kept me waiting, or did not sweeten me enough with gifts and favors. *Some of the men are safe against seals, crossed front and back as you suggested, or as history learned them. But not all are. We could fix another sea-maid in the rocks at Crescent—or right here on Forward Head Beach so's we could have a good view of the fun. The men might* say *they are not inclined, or have no money, and such, but could they resist if one of those girlies showed herself?*

She always shook her head. *There's some who'd enjoy that*, she said. *Who are asking me for just that—any maid will do for them. I wouldn't want to please those ones so well. And the others? They're suffering very nicely, thank you, pining after the lost ones, weeping for their sons*. I remember the smile she would give me then, nine parts sympathy, one part pure wickedness. That would always restore my temper.

You dreadful woman, I'd say.

And she'd smile broader. *Let's not change a thing*.

Pennylope helps me lift Misskaella onto the table. Ha'penny and Farthing carry a hand each too. Tuppence is too busy crying—she likes to make dramatics, does Tuppence. Serena, I called her for her proper name, and never was a child so misnamed.

We work the cold sweated nightgown off the body, and Penny brings the wash water. I instruct her in doing the top half, while I deal with below. Then we put the old witch's cleaner nightdress on. For the moment that'll have to do.

I open the door a crack to empty the bowl. There's such a blow, I have to all but lay the lip on the sand so the wind doesn't spray the corpse water up and down me. And it wants to slap the door wide, to throw sleet in; I have quite some work to hold it and to close it.

"Well, *you* can wait, for washing." I leave the bowl by the door. "Nobody touch that."

Penny is watching Miss, her hands all precious under her chin.

"What's your nonsense?"

"It's so cold," she whimpers. "Must we leave her lying in it?"

"Why not? She doesn't feel it. What would you do?"

"I would put a blanket on her. I would wrap her over."

I'm about to laugh, but look at the poor gug's face all turned down, and the little tears, jewels in her pretty eyes! "Daft Penny. Fetch a blanket, then! Keep the poor corpse warm."

The others are all along Tup's bed in a row, looking out boggle-eyed at me and Pen and their dead Kaella. "Now listen," I say in the doorway. "I am going up the town. You're all to stay and look to Bartholomew when he wakes, make sure he does not hurt himself lumbering about."

"Oh, don't leave us!" wails Tup. "I don't want to stay here with *that*! Let us come too!" The other three faces change to glumly begging.

"What a grand idea!" I say. "Let's all wander off and get lost in the storm, shall we? Give Kaella some company on that table."

"We'll stay close to you! We'll hold tight!" Farthing is wobbling most piteously. "We'll all go together!"

"Oh, grand again! So I've to drag the lot of you on my skirts through that deadly cold? No," I say as her next idea starts popping out her mouth. "I'll go alone, and you'll stay here and Kaella will watch you. Oh my goodness, yes, and if you misbehave yourselves or leave your brother crying or a-mess, up she'll get off her table and come at you dead!" And I walk stick-legged, claws out, staring-eyed toward them, and they all scream and weep.

"Oh, Mam," sighs Penny at the door.

I look down on the tremulating mess of them. "I cannot believe the sookenses I've raised," I say. "The lads in Knocknee would have pummeled you flat in a minute. Off I go." I make for my coat on the door.

"Please, oh please!" Farthing smacks into me. She clings on, scrambling sideways as I walk, keeping me between her and Miss, noising like a kicked dog.

"Shush this twaddle," I say. "This is your old Kaella. She

sheltered and fed you since you were born, and showed you every kindness." What? *Showed you every kindness?* That's my mam's lies popping out of me, Mam who's bones in the ground this last five years. That's what happens, I suppose, when someone dies; all the other dead start to mutter as she nudges them aside, pushing down into the grave. "So be properly grateful and sit by her."

"That big Baker boy says it's the men who feed us," Tup wails from her bed. "Every man in the town, he says, puts in his little bit now, to pay for having put his little bit in before."

"What on earth are you talking about, Tup!" says Penny in her sensiblest voice.

"Never you mind." I give Pen a push, and she throws me a puzzled look. A laugh springs from my throat, and I catch it back and glance at Miss on the table. "Just you stay, all of you. There in that room, if you must, and bring the boy in with you if he fusses."

"It's very cold, Mam," says Penny over their noise. "Why don't you wear Miss's coat on top of your own?"

I make a face, ready to retort some rude thing, but none supplies itself. *Because it smells of her and will make me sad?* I'd never say that aloud.

But then when I am dressed and scarfed, coated and booted, I look at Miss's coat on its hook, and at the window with proper snow boiling across it now. "Why don't I?" I take it down and sniff the chest of it. "Poargh! Oh yes, that's a good muddy weed-gathering smell, that is. You don't mind me borrowing your smelly old coat, do you, Miss, to do your last will and wishes?"

Miss lies cleaner and more dignified than I have ever seen her. Nothing can tease her now; nothing can goad her into a rage. Can it *be* that she'll never rage again? Shall I never sit giggling, with my girls close about me like mushrooms in a clump, while she crashes in and out the bothy, shouting against men and women and babs, and the terrible life a witch must lead?

"Don't joke, Mam!" Penny eyes Miss too, to see if she's offended, to wish, like me, that Miss would stir and scowl and swear at us as usual.

I pull on the coat and button it. Ooh, won't I be snug. "Pass me that basket. No, the one with the lid, or everything will blow straight out again."

I strap it on and turn to the eyes from the bedroom. "Not a *step* outside, any of you!"

"They won't, Mam," says Pen, the sober little wife.

The wind tears the door open out of my hand, fights my closing it, then punishes me for succeeding: a blow to the side of my head, a push at Miss's coat and a rattle of my hems about my shins. But there, they're shut in. I've shaken them off me for a while, the little limpets.

I'll go through the dunes, I think; I might not stay upright on the beach, and all that storming surf, oh, it's too much this morning; this wind's quite enough. I set out through blowing snow, and blowing sand—I must all but cover my eyes with the scarf if I'm not to be blinded, and the wind really would like to tear my basket off me, the way it batters and jerks. I cannot tell where the next gust will hit me from, the dunes chop it about so; it surprises and surprises me, and I stagger like a drunk man. "Perhaps I should *have* me a drink!" I shout, one gloved hand sunk in a dune's flank. "Plenty of wine bottles up at the house. I should drink a toast!"

On I stump and struggle. *Showed you every kindness*, I hear myself say, hear my mam say. Well, she took me in, I suppose, old Miss, and she kept me even when I turned into six people. *All the little squallers*, she would say as they fell and tantrumed around us, on the beach or in the bothy. *I don't know how you can stand it. I'm so glad I had none myself.*

Some sand has got in my eye. I would wipe it out if I weren't so well sprinkled with sand the rest of me. One-eyed, I steer myself by the merest glimpses in between blinks.

Well, she stood it, didn't she, along with me? Often enough she'd stride out from us in a temper and stay away awhile. *Plenty* of times she raged against the noise and the mess and the stupidity of children—enough that the girls weren't afraid of her shouting, unless she lashed out suddenly and startled them. But she had that room built on, didn't she, when Farthing was coming along?

And she stayed with us. *You've got that whole big house up there*, I told her once at the fireside, the girls blown silent to the walls by one of her outbursts. *There's no need for you to put up with us if you don't want.*

What would I do up there? she crabbed at me.

Have some peace, that you're always saying you want.

Even as I step out of the dunes into the full force of the snowy wind across McComber's fields, I remember the look she threw me, as if I had cut her to the heart. *Would you rather I went?* she said. *Is that what you want me to do?*

No! And it wasn't. *Not at all. But you complain so much of us.*

The look disappeared. *Complain? That's only noise.* She waved it away. *Up in that house on my own? I've had quite enough of that.*

Up the field I trudge. There's a wall and a road there somewhere, though I can't see either. It's a good thing there's a slope, or I wouldn't know which way to turn. I could lose my bearings in the whitening, and freeze solid in a wall corner, rob five children of their mam.

But "Ha!" Every man in town would come forth, then, wouldn't he, Tuppence, and give them a dad? "Ha!"

There, look—a little part of the world keeping still. That's the wall; that's the stile.

I reach town eventually. The lanes are swept empty by the wind so's I don't have to speak to anyone. All the men are shut in by their fires, some still solitary, many with mainland wives, breeding out the stain of the seal-wives quick as they can. Little redhead boys and girls are springing up all over the town these days, and the odd one darker and finer built, that everyone harrumphs at. Remember how frightened I was, the day the Severner girl came? *It will turn into just like Knocknee*, I said to Miss when I got home from Winches' that day. *Everyone prettier than us and sneering down their nose.*

Don't you fret. I remember her queenly in her sickbed, flushed with the first of those fevers that would eventually take her off. *They know now how to treat a witch on this island. They'll not forget in a hurry.*

And it *is* better, a bit of life in the streets, some tumbling children not my own, some men and lads with smiles on their faces, after all those years of misery. I never thought I would prefer it, but it's improved from the wasteland it was, with no wives at all, no women. And there's still a man or two will have me, now and then, for old times' sake, or who cannot afford a wife, or is beyond the whole notion of husbanding anymore.

And who can blame them, after what the seal-girls did to them?

When Ostler Grinny came running that morning, I remember, I thought it a scheme of Misskaella's. That devious witch, I thought, she's kept it secret even from me, so's I don't leak it to my girls and them to anyone else. We all followed them out, Ostler and Miss, along to the top of the steps to the beach, and there we could see, to the south, all the thrown-down clothes in the distance, all the men staggering about, waving their arms and falling to their knees, weeping on one another, tiny in the distance, their tiny cries floating to us on the wind.

But there are little *clothes, too, that they're flapping!* I said.

Yes, as I said, they've taken the lads with them, said Ostler. *Every last one!* My *Banter and my Toby! I'm begging you, Misskaella, if there's anything you can do to get them back—* And he fell to sobbing.

I don't know how they went, man, let alone how to fetch them up again. What a fine play actor I thought her.

You've schemed and equipped those ladies, haven't you? I said, when Ostler had gone off weeping, to join the weepers on the shore.

But, *No, no, no*, she said. *It's none of my doing, Trudle*.

Oh, you have too, I said, pushing her. *You've put some charm upon the little skins to help them turn when they touch seawater.*

I never have, I tell you. How would I do that? She stared out along the beach. *I never heard a word of this. All of them, and all the land-lads too!*

I remember Penny delivering Misskaella and me one of her Looks. *Are you* glad *of the wives going?*

Glad? I suppose I am, said Miss quite seriously to her. *I never thought those namby-pams would have this in them.*

It will make the mens very *unhappy*, said Pen.

Ha! said I. *That's all to the good, isn't it, Kaella?*

I cannot say it displeases me, she said very sweetly.

I stand in the top street and stare up at the great house. It's mine now, and that takes some thinking. Miss always said she'd leave it to me, but what did that mean? I never believed she'd really go; she was like rocks or great trees, always there, always would be there.

Oh, it's cold. I force on against the wind and open the gate, totter up to the door. It only opens so far against that lump in the hall, the armchair that won't fit anywhere else. I shut myself out of the racket, into the gloom. Practically in the dark, I shrug off my basket, lay it on the chair and put the two coats on top.

This place gives me the shudders, packed so tight with furniture and trinkets. All mine now. What the blazes should I do with it all?

I sidle upstairs, catching on this box corner and that chair leg, picking my way slower and slower as the walking way narrows to the front bedroom. *There is a bed in here*, said Miss, the time she brought me, though she was hazy as to its whereabouts.

She was clear enough on what she wanted to show me, though. *See that big cupboard, with the mirror?*

Oh my, I said, at the mountain between us and the cupboard.

No, no, I have made a path. Here, look. And she showed me the line of boxes I could move. *Into this slot here under the window, all of these will fit. We won't do it now. Sometimes I do, though, come up here and admire it. Right behind the mirror, it is, with the shoes below. You cannot mistake them. And then . . .*

I wanted to be away, I remember, from all this talk of death, all this clutter. I was big with Ha'penny then; the place had made me breathless and sick-feeling. I wanted air. *And then?* I said, panting.

In the top drawer, she said, and her gaze was on it though door and drawer front hid it. *There's something there too. Put it in the ground with me. No one's to know.*

I take the first box and begin the to and fro, slowly excavate the path to the cupboard. The bottom boxes are heavy, and must be slid along the floorboards—what can be in them?

At last I'm through. Look at that scrag-worn witch in the mirror. Doesn't she look flustered, though? Rude too, poking out her tongue. I open the door to hide her ugly face.

The dress hangs inside; the shoes wait empty below.

You will think it old-fashioned.

It's a large dress and dark, high-necked, well made, the most dignified dress I've ever seen. I lift the heavy skirt, the better to see the trim around the hem, flat panels with points folded out of them—no silly ruffles for our Miss. The shoes—I turn one over, admiring the make, the buckle and kinked-in heel, the lace tied in a perky bow—they are almost little animals. *It's all bespoke*, she said, and then she had to tell me what *bespoke* was. She went to Cordlin for these, had a dressmaker measure and sew. A town cobbler, trained in London, shaped the shoes. She chose the leather herself, and the cloth, so heavy and rich—such a shame to bury it!

I take out the dress; it falls beautifully into the folds I choose for it. *There is a parcel of underthings, very nice ones, tied up with twine*. Yes, pushed to the back there is, and I fetch it out.

I open the other door, the one with no mirror, and pull out the drawer. (*Put it in the ground with me*, she said. And then Penny bumbled in and grizzled at my knee, and I never did ask what the something was.)

Whatever it is, it's wrapped in tissue paper, crinkled from being opened and shut many, many times.

"It will be a gift," I whisper, pressing on the soft parcel, "from some unexpected man, someone respectable. Scandal would come of it, if I showed the town."

I untie the faded ribbon and draw apart the tissue.

The tiniest of nightgowns lies there—for a doll, you would think. None of my babs was as small as that, even the boy, even fresh-born. To the chest, pinned with a silver pin, is a scrap of paper: *Ean*.

"Ean?" I breathe. Slowly, as if the thing will turn to dust if I'm not careful, I lift the little garment into the better light. I can spread it on a single hand.

Then, "Ah!" I snatch it to my chest. Under a smaller leaf of tissue in the parcel, blurred by it, lies another nightgown, like a ghost of the one on my hand. I lift off the tissue-leaf. This gown's not as old, not as yellowed. *Froman*, says the paper pinned to it.

"Froman!"

Wiser now to the old woman, I bend and slide the Froman gown aside: another leaf, another ghost dress, the last.

I rustle the tissue away. Outside, the wind hurls itself about. This third gown is mainland work, finer, softer. Silk-embroidered cornflowers wander out from under the pinned paper.

Hugh. I mouth the name, but no sound comes out. Three babs. Three boys. *No one is to know*.

I'm so astonished, I cannot think. I sit on a box awhile, whispering the names over and over.

I remember asking her, when I started to swell with Penelope, *Should I find me a midwife?*

You have one, she said.

Why, who else's babs have you delivered? Seal-wives'? Are they made the same below?

Not seal-wives'.

Whose, then?

She must have been laughing to herself, the answer right there before me. *People's*, she said. *You've no need to worry.*

Ean, Froman, Hugh. Where do I begin, with the questions I cannot ask her?

I spread the nightgown in my lap, little Ean's. "Perhaps you were too small to live. All of you," I add toward the others in the drawer, "perhaps were small, or sickly. There are plenty of women that's babs don't thrive."

They don't answer, curse it. They lie as they've lain forever, all innocent and silent.

"But *whose*?" I say. "Whose are you? What man of this isle got you on our Miss?"

I will ask about, I vow. When I give the news of her death, I will look in their eyes. I will pry and prod, without telling what I know, until he coughs up the truth himself, this father—or these three, if three different dads there be. I will find out, if only to put my own mind at rest. She shall not have the better of me, the old coot. Who does she think she is, not saying, for all these years? The laughs we might have had at their expense, the fathers', just as we laughed at my girls' dads! When we could tell which was whose, that is, of the old codgers pining for good red loving, or the skinny boys not rich enough yet for a water-wife. Why would old Missk deny me that fun?

I lay the nightgowns back together, wrap them in the tissue, take them out and close the drawer. I gather up what I've found, sidle back to the stair head, down to the door. I pack the shoes, the funeral dress and the parcels into the basket; I manage the coats on and the scarf. One sniff of Miss's collar and there she is, biting the head off my Farthing, scowling out over the sea. I strap on the basket and let myself out into the snow-streaked gale.

And the wind bustles me back down the slippery streets of Potshead town. All the way it wrenches and worries the basket on my back, as if it would love to tear it open, and snatch out the three little secrets Miss wants buried with her. Toss them high, it would, if I only let it, dance them awhile in the storm, in the snow. And then it would drop them far out to sea, maybe, or inland among the crags beyond Windaway Peak—or perhaps nearby, on dune, in field, on cottage roof, in cobbled street, not caring who saw them, not caring a jot who knew.

Acknowledgments

I thank Keith Stevenson for inviting me to write a story for his novellanthology *X6* (coeur de lion, 2009). *Sea-Hearts*, the novella, was the result.

Dani Napton and Jill Grinberg, thank you for initial encouragement to extend the story, and Jodie Webster, Rosalind Price, Bella Pearson, Nancy Siscoe, Simon Mason and Linda Sargent, thank you for advice during the writing, which helped the novel find its final form.

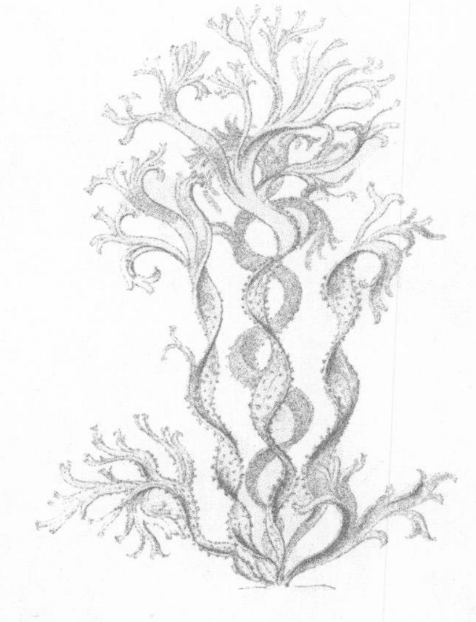